Granby Library

5-9-07
JNF G-
5.99

D1016749

Kat & mouse

① teacher torture

Story by Alex de Campi
Art by Federica Manfredi

GRANBY BRANCH
GRAND COUNTY LIBRARY
P. O. BOX 1049
GRANBY, CO 80446

TOKYOPOP®

HAMBURG // LONDON // LOS ANGELES // TOKYO

Kat & Mouse Vol. 1
Written by Alex de Campi
Illustrated by Federica Manfredi

Tones - Kathy Schilling
Lettering - Erika "Skooter" Terriquez
Production Artist - Erika "Skooter" Terriquez
Cover Design - Anne Marie Horne

Editor - Carol Fox
Digital Imaging Manager - Chris Buford
Managing Editor - Lindsey Johnston
Editorial Director - Jeremy Ross
VP of Production - Ron Klamert
Editor-in-Chief - Rob Tokar
Publisher - Mike Kiley
President and C.O.O. - John Parker
C.E.O. and Chief Creative Officer - Stuart Levy

A  Manga

TOKYOPOP Inc.
5900 Wilshire Blvd. Suite 2000
Los Angeles, CA 90036

E-mail: info@TOKYOPOP.com
Come visit us online at www.TOKYOPOP.com

© 2006 Alex de Campi and TOKYOPOP Inc. All rights reserved. No portion of this book may be reproduced or transmitted in any form or by any means without written permission from the copyright holders. This manga is a work of fiction. Any resemblance to actual events or locales or persons, living or dead, is entirely coincidental.

ISBN: 1-59816-548-8

First TOKYOPOP printing: July 2006
10 9 8 7 6 5 4 3 2 1
Printed in the USA

Kat & Mouse

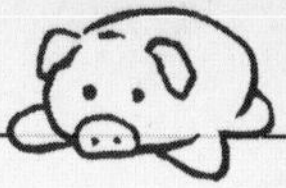

TABLE OF CONTENTS

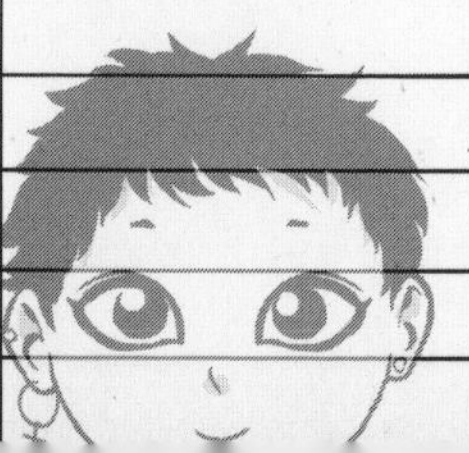

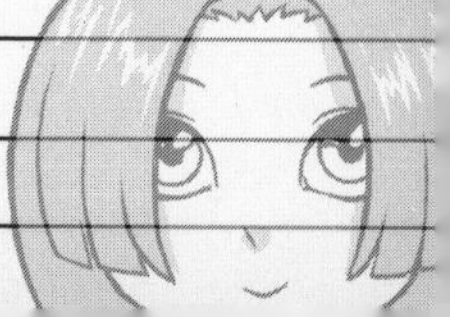

Chapter 1: The Best and Brightest

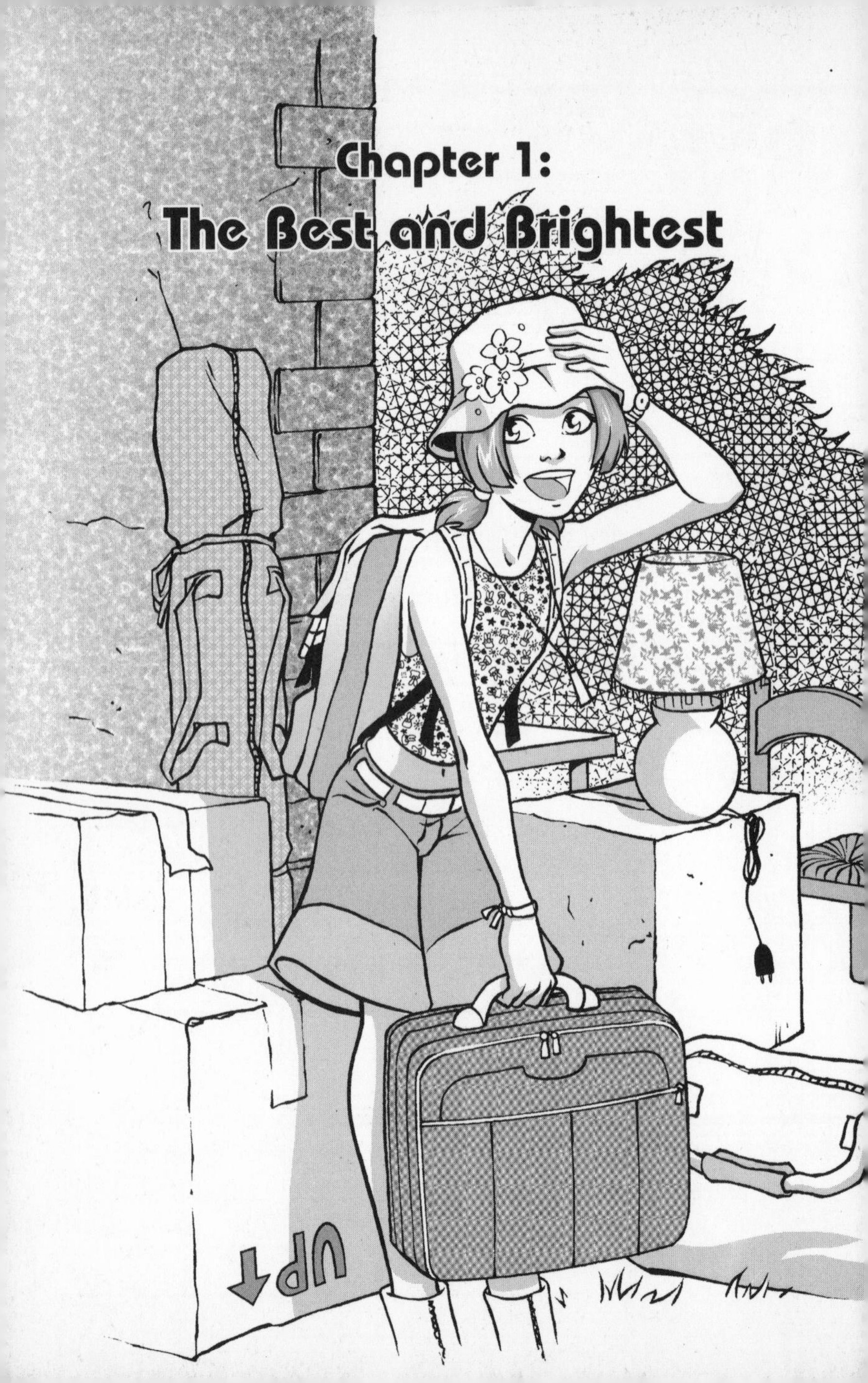
UP

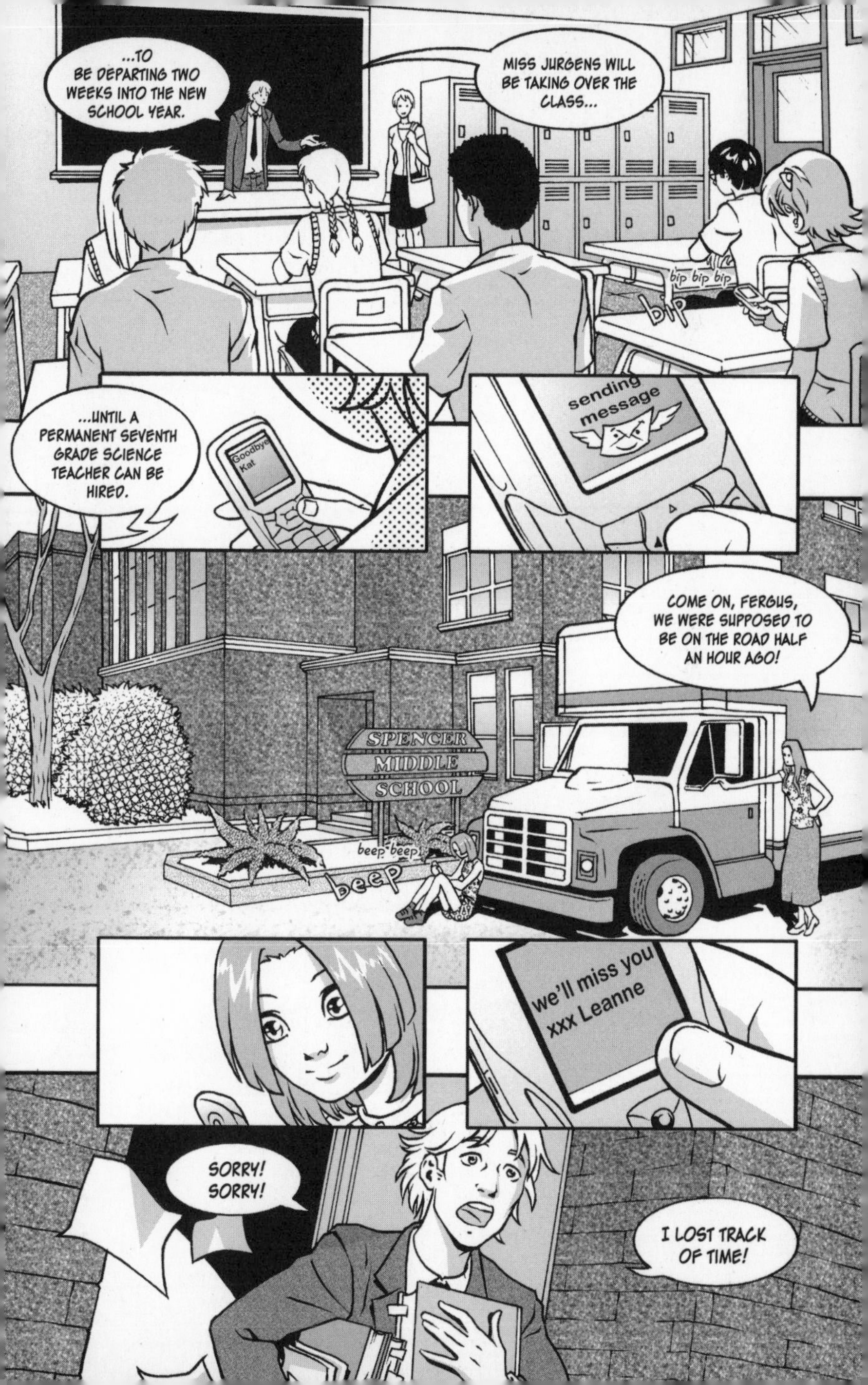
...TO BE DEPARTING TWO WEEKS INTO THE NEW SCHOOL YEAR.
MISS JURGENS WILL BE TAKING OVER THE CLASS...
bip bip bip
bip
...UNTIL A PERMANENT SEVENTH GRADE SCIENCE TEACHER CAN BE HIRED.
Goodbye Kat
sending message
COME ON, FERGUS, WE WERE SUPPOSED TO BE ON THE ROAD HALF AN HOUR AGO!
SPENCER MIDDLE SCHOOL
beep beep
beep
we'll miss you xxx Leanne
SORRY! SORRY!
I LOST TRACK OF TIME!

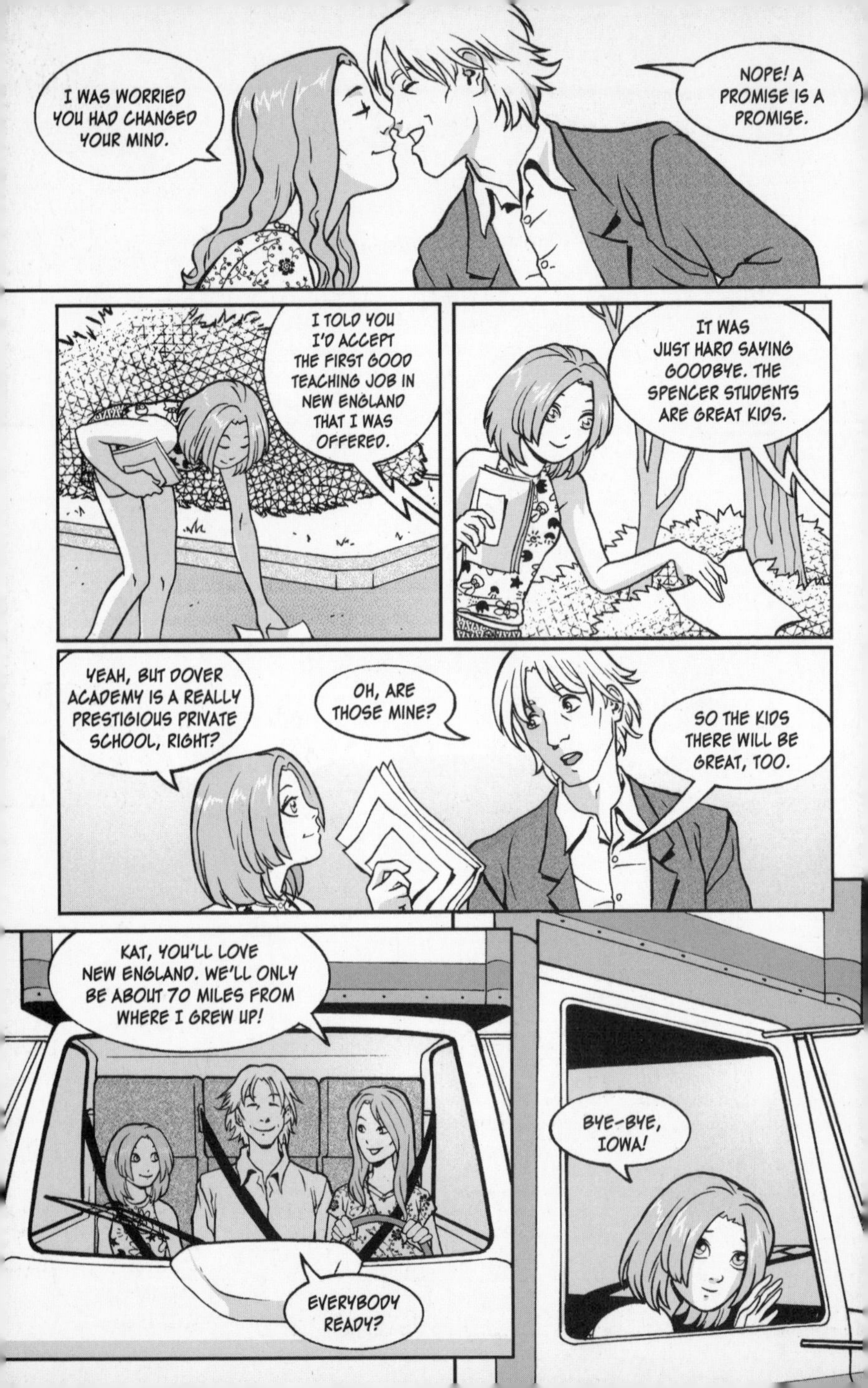
I WAS WORRIED YOU HAD CHANGED YOUR MIND.
NOPE! A PROMISE IS A PROMISE.
I TOLD YOU I'D ACCEPT THE FIRST GOOD TEACHING JOB IN NEW ENGLAND THAT I WAS OFFERED.
IT WAS JUST HARD SAYING GOODBYE. THE SPENCER STUDENTS ARE GREAT KIDS.
YEAH, BUT DOVER ACADEMY IS A REALLY PRESTIGIOUS PRIVATE SCHOOL, RIGHT?
OH, ARE THOSE MINE?
SO THE KIDS THERE WILL BE GREAT, TOO.
KAT, YOU'LL LOVE NEW ENGLAND. WE'LL ONLY BE ABOUT 70 MILES FROM WHERE I GREW UP!
EVERYBODY READY?
BYE-BYE, IOWA!

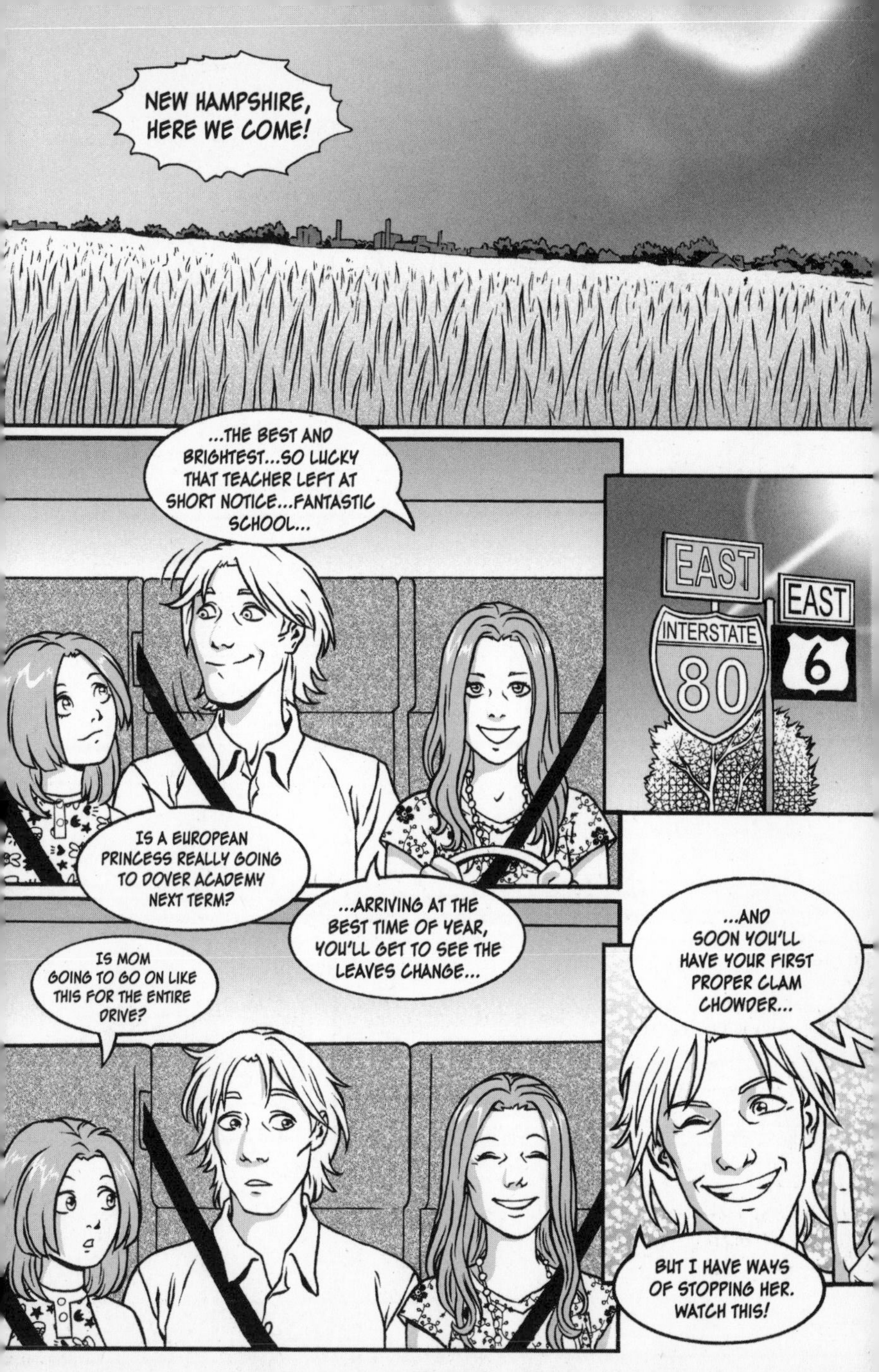
NEW HAMPSHIRE, HERE WE COME!
...THE BEST AND BRIGHTEST...SO LUCKY THAT TEACHER LEFT AT SHORT NOTICE...FANTASTIC SCHOOL...
IS A EUROPEAN PRINCESS REALLY GOING TO DOVER ACADEMY NEXT TERM?
EAST
EAST
INTERSTATE
80
6
...ARRIVING AT THE BEST TIME OF YEAR, YOU'LL GET TO SEE THE LEAVES CHANGE...
IS MOM GOING TO GO ON LIKE THIS FOR THE ENTIRE DRIVE?
...AND SOON YOU'LL HAVE YOUR FIRST PROPER CLAM CHOWDER...
BUT I HAVE WAYS OF STOPPING HER. WATCH THIS!

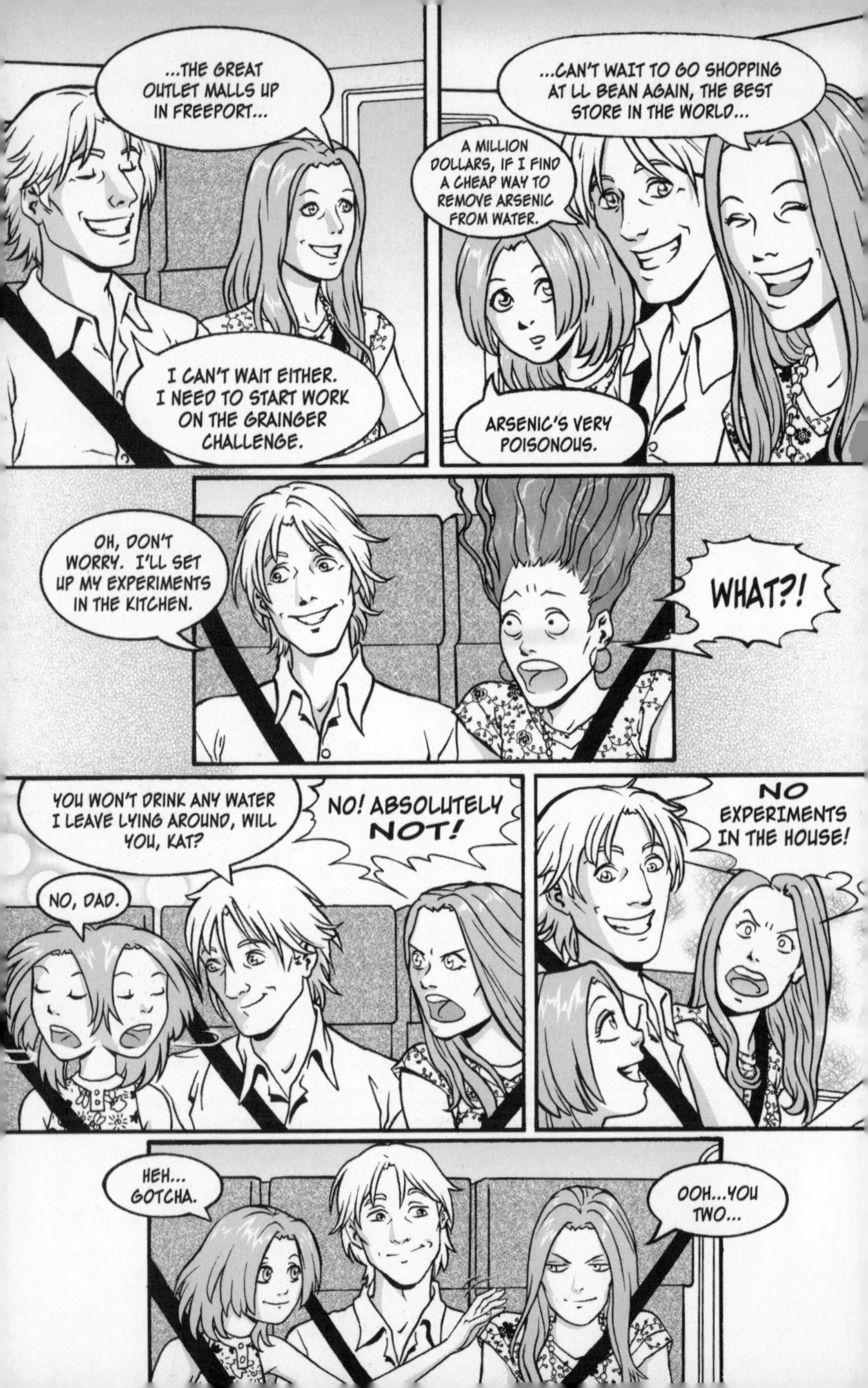
...THE GREAT OUTLET MALLS UP IN FREEPORT...
I CAN'T WAIT EITHER. I NEED TO START WORK ON THE GRAINGER CHALLENGE.
...CAN'T WAIT TO GO SHOPPING AT LL BEAN AGAIN, THE BEST STORE IN THE WORLD...
A MILLION DOLLARS, IF I FIND A CHEAP WAY TO REMOVE ARSENIC FROM WATER.
ARSENIC'S VERY POISONOUS.
OH, DON'T WORRY. I'LL SET UP MY EXPERIMENTS IN THE KITCHEN.
WHAT?!
YOU WON'T DRINK ANY WATER I LEAVE LYING AROUND, WILL YOU, KAT?
NO! ABSOLUTELY NOT!
NO, DAD.
NO EXPERIMENTS IN THE HOUSE!
HEH... GOTCHA.
OOH...YOU TWO...

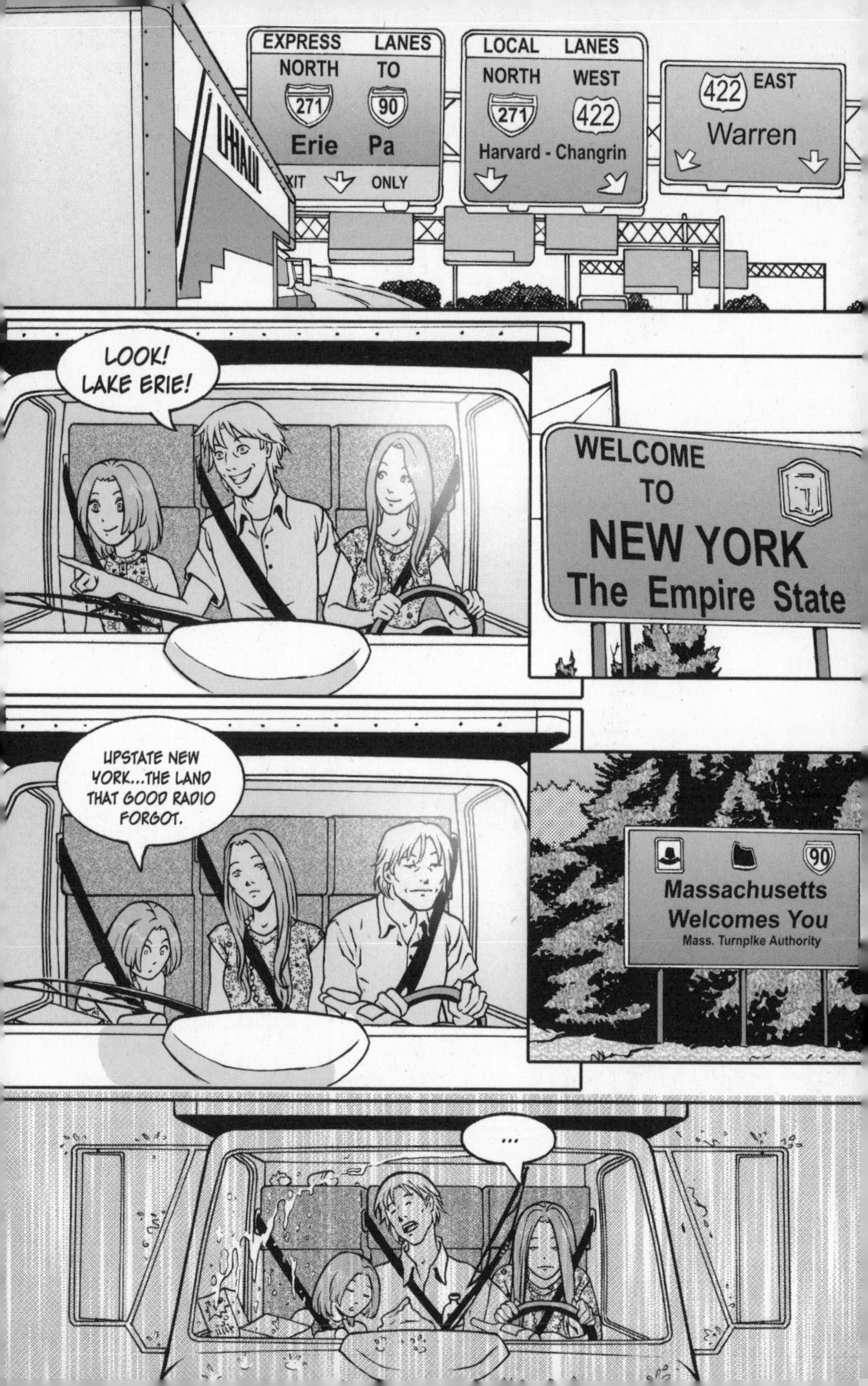
EXPRESS LANES
NORTH TO
271 90
Erie Pa
XIT ONLY
LOCAL LANES
NORTH WEST
271 422
Harvard - Changrin
422 EAST
Warren
LOOK! LAKE ERIE!
WELCOME TO NEW YORK The Empire State
UPSTATE NEW YORK...THE LAND THAT GOOD RADIO FORGOT.
90
Massachusetts Welcomes You
Mass. Turnpike Authority
...

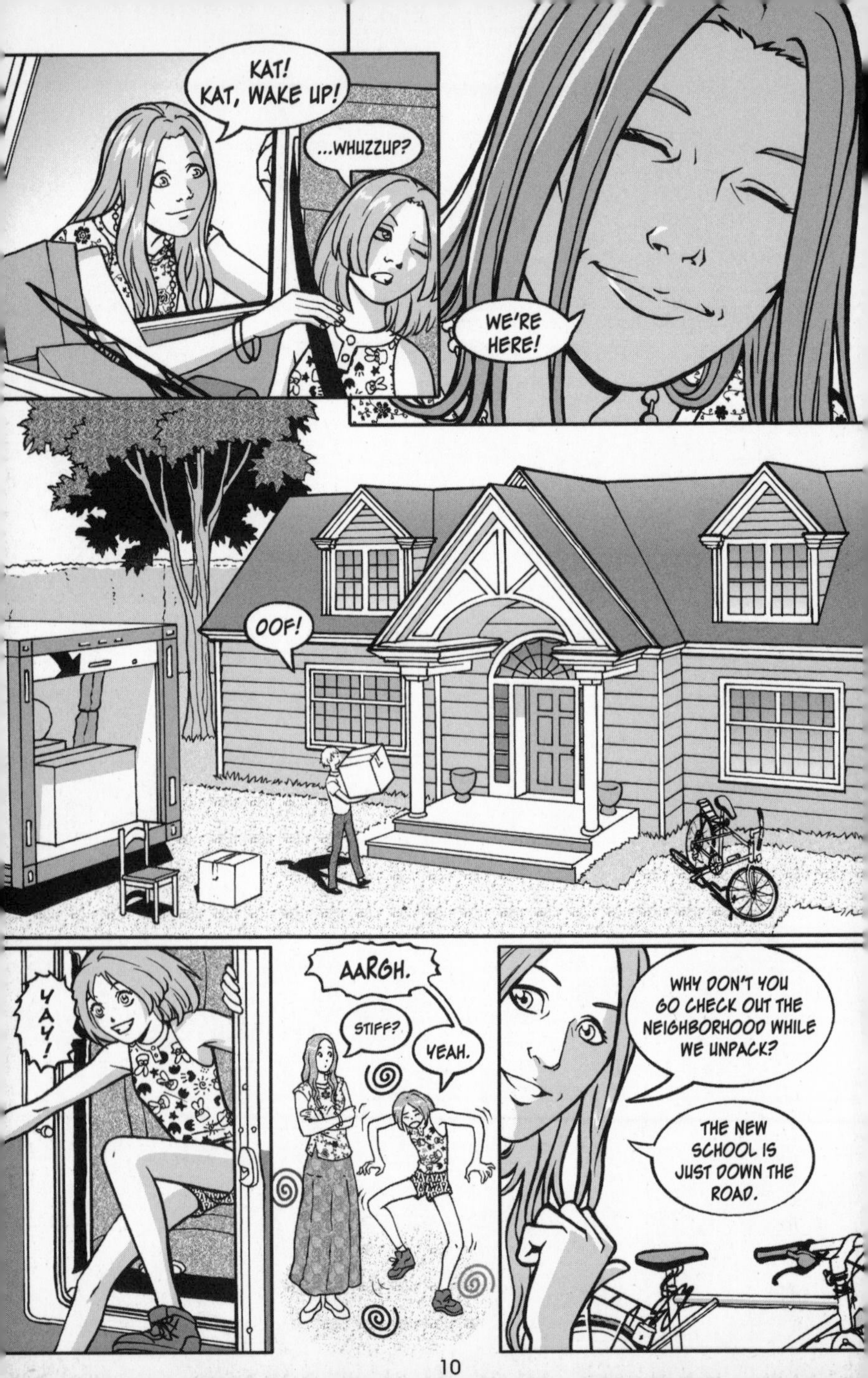
KAT! KAT, WAKE UP!
...WHUZZUP?
WE'RE HERE!
OOF!
YAY!
AARGH.
STIFF?
YEAH.
WHY DON'T YOU GO CHECK OUT THE NEIGHBORHOOD WHILE WE UNPACK?
THE NEW SCHOOL IS JUST DOWN THE ROAD.

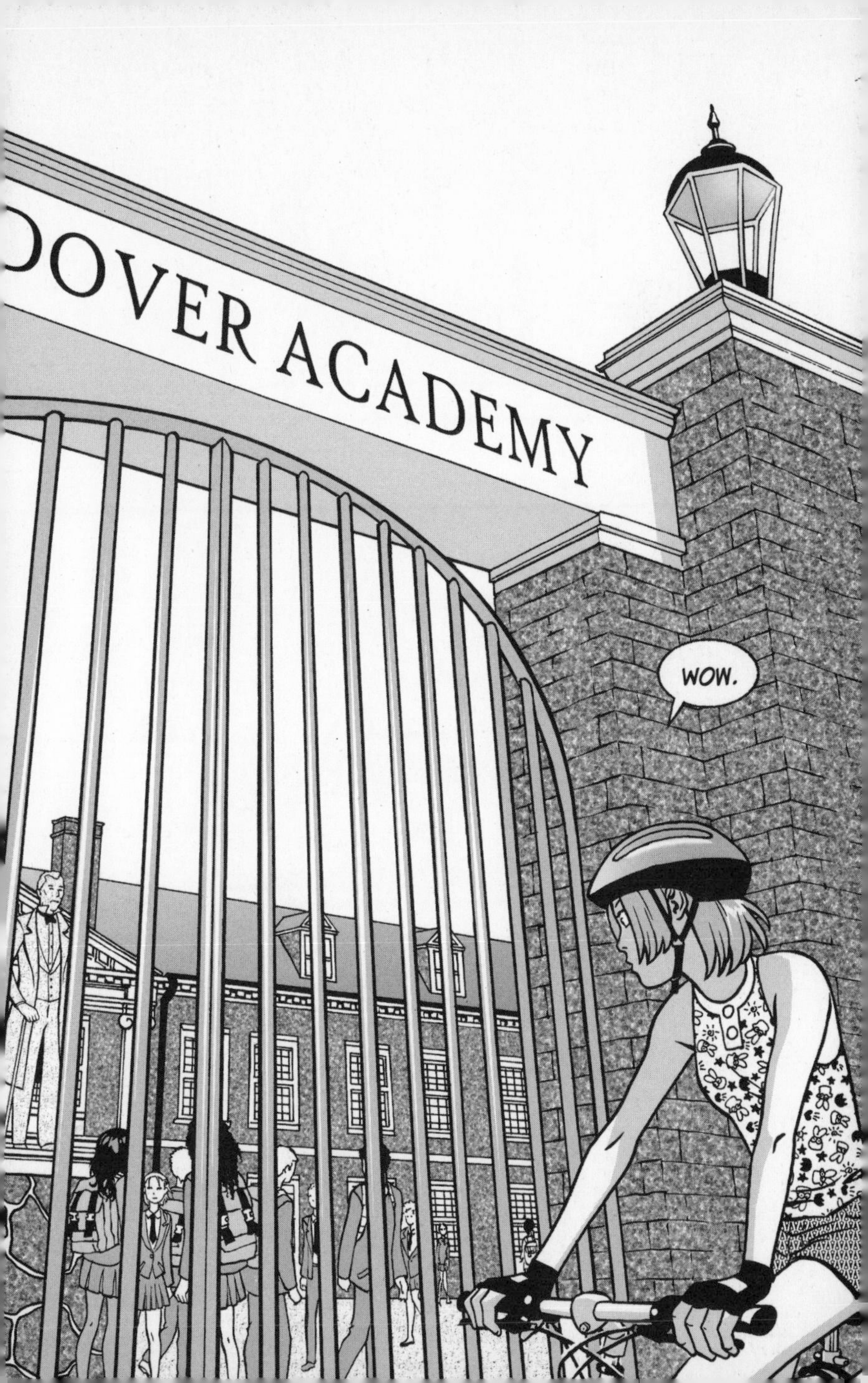
DOVER ACADEMY
WOW.

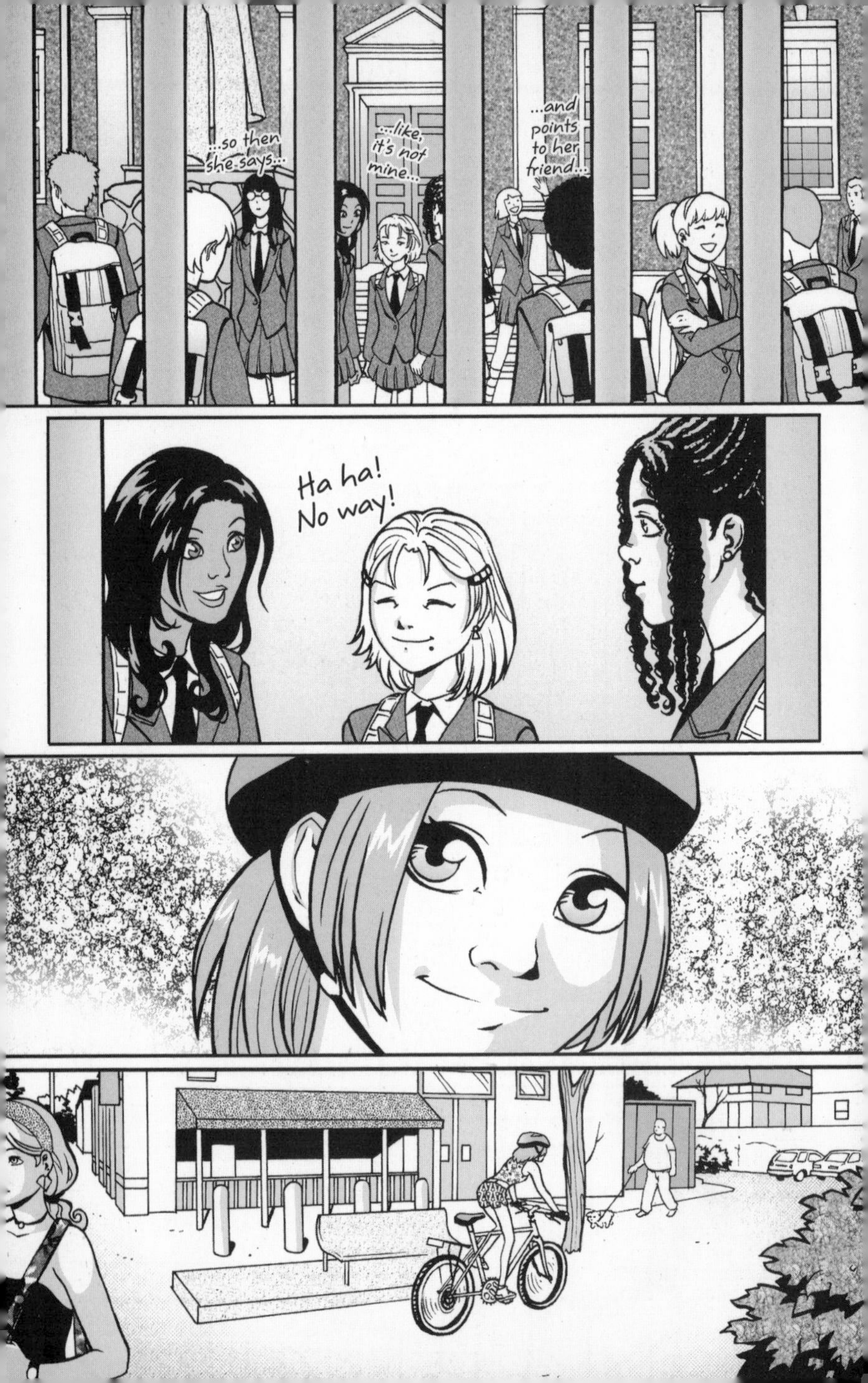
...so then she says...
...like, it's not mine...
...and points to her friend...
Ha ha! No way!

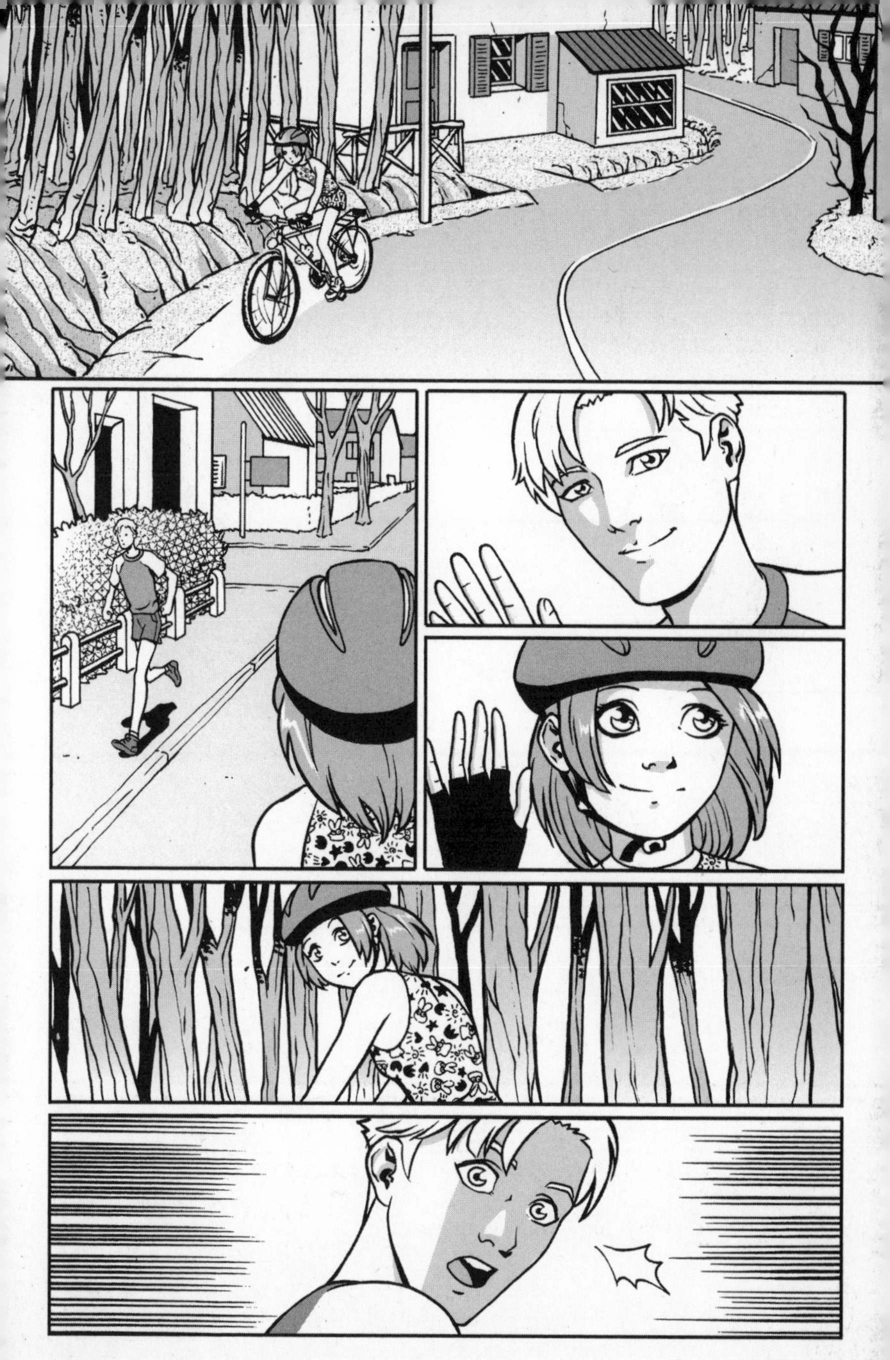

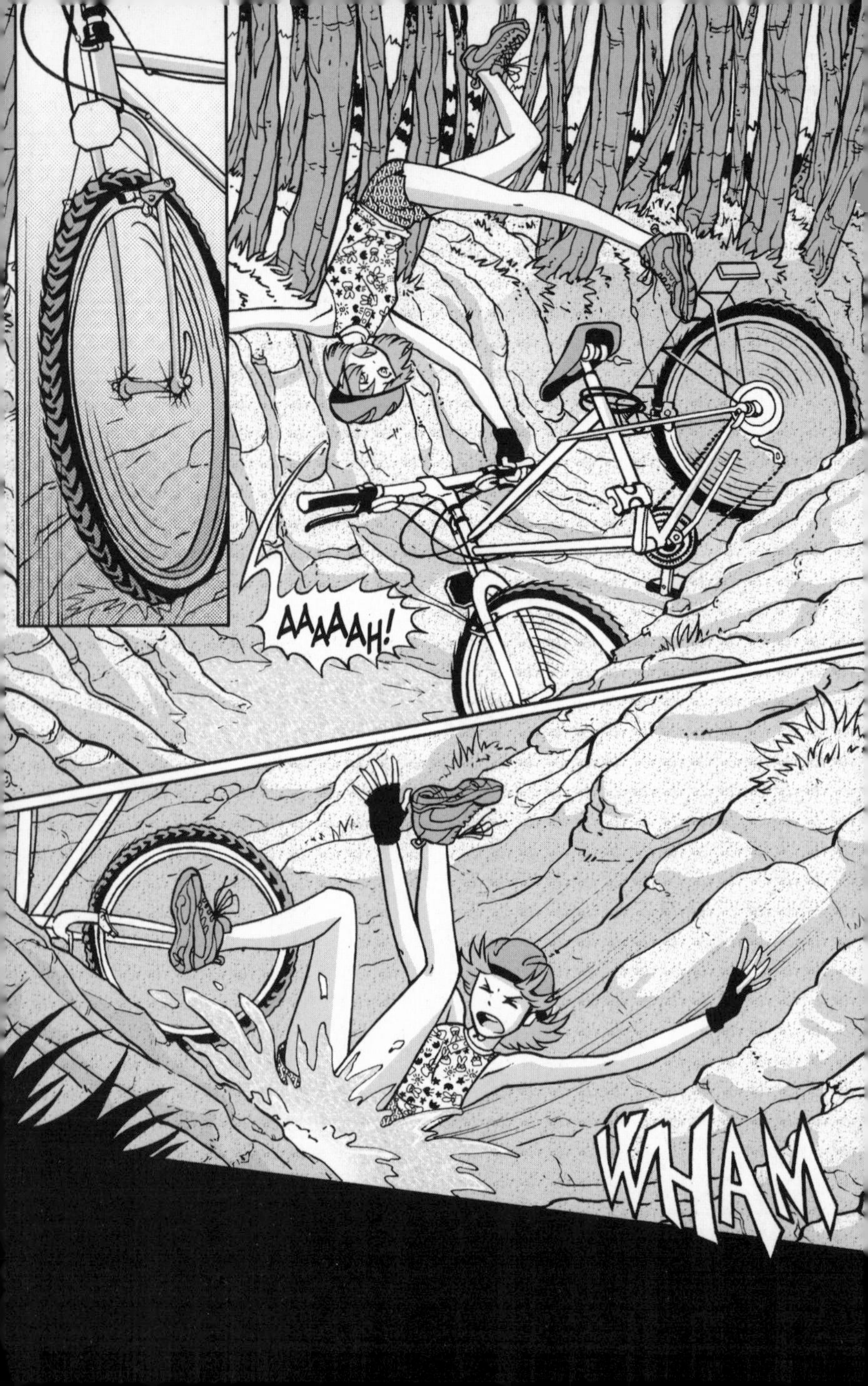
AAAAAH!
WHAM

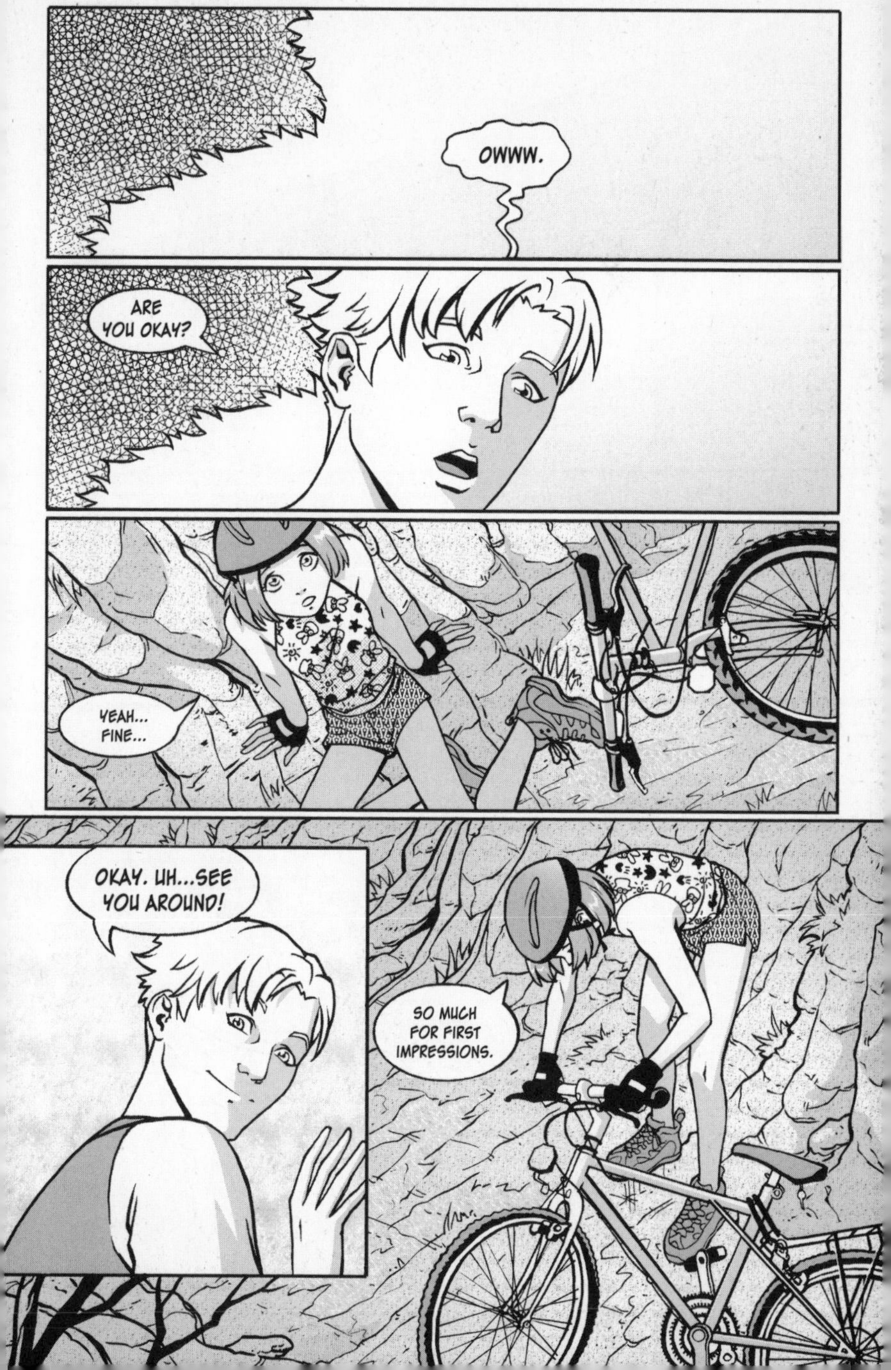
OWWW.
ARE YOU OKAY?
YEAH... FINE...
OKAY. UH...SEE YOU AROUND!
SO MUCH FOR FIRST IMPRESSIONS.

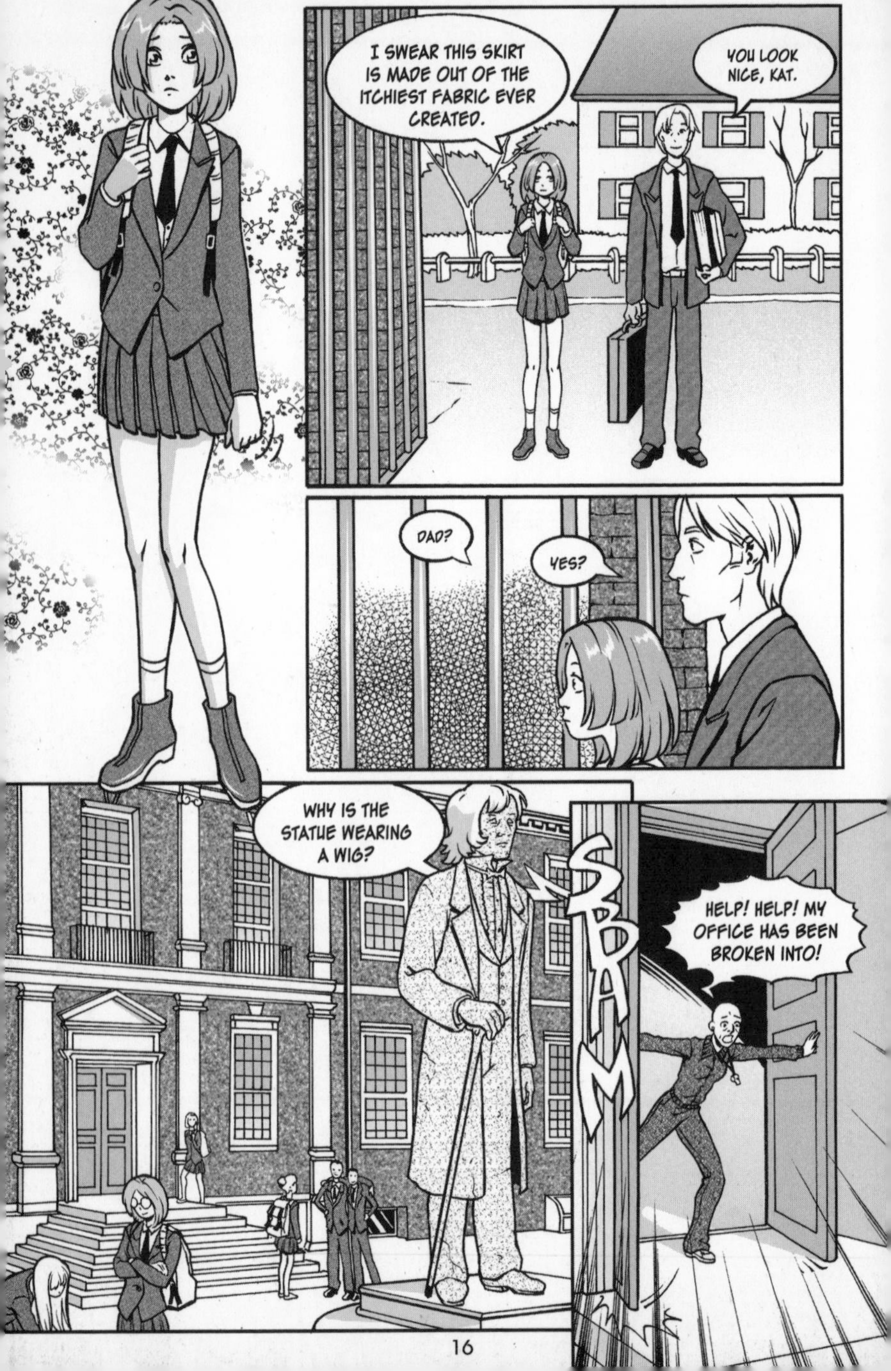
I SWEAR THIS SKIRT IS MADE OUT OF THE ITCHIEST FABRIC EVER CREATED.
YOU LOOK NICE, KAT.
DAD?
YES?
WHY IS THE STATUE WEARING A WIG?
SBAM
HELP! HELP! MY OFFICE HAS BEEN BROKEN INTO!

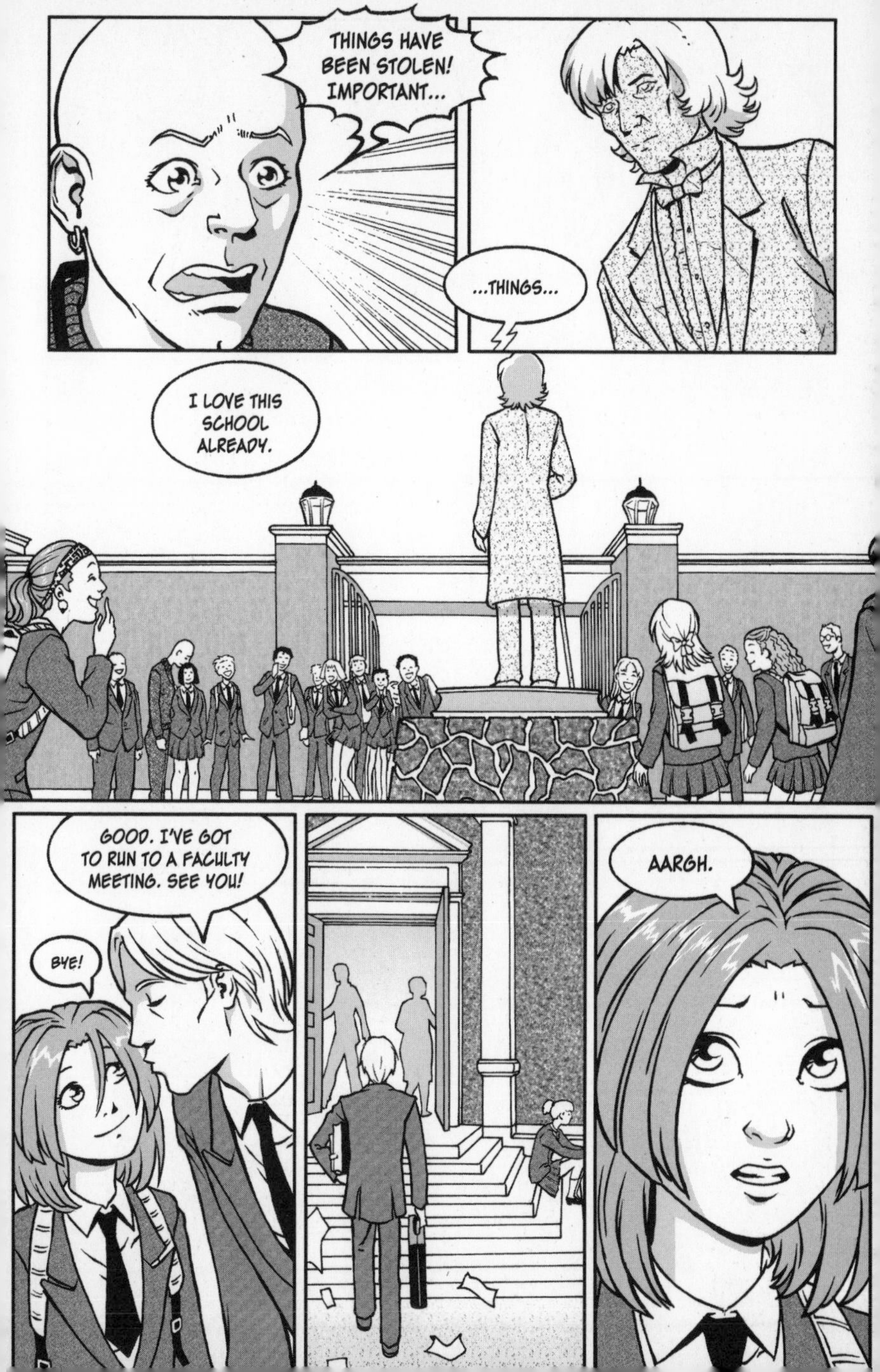
THINGS HAVE BEEN STOLEN! IMPORTANT...
...THINGS...
I LOVE THIS SCHOOL ALREADY.
GOOD. I'VE GOT TO RUN TO A FACULTY MEETING. SEE YOU!
BYE!
AARGH.

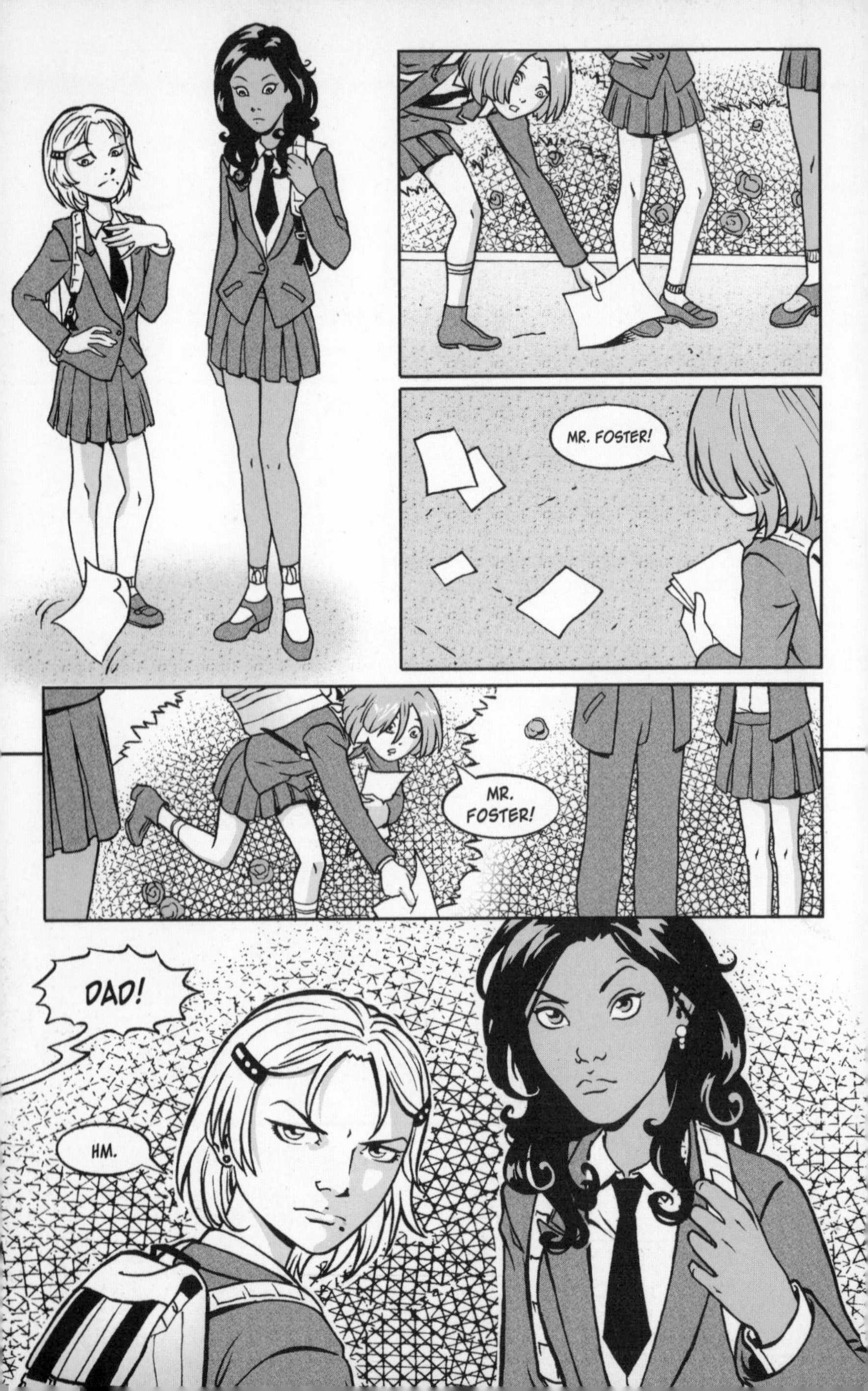
MR. FOSTER!
MR. FOSTER!
DAD!
HM.

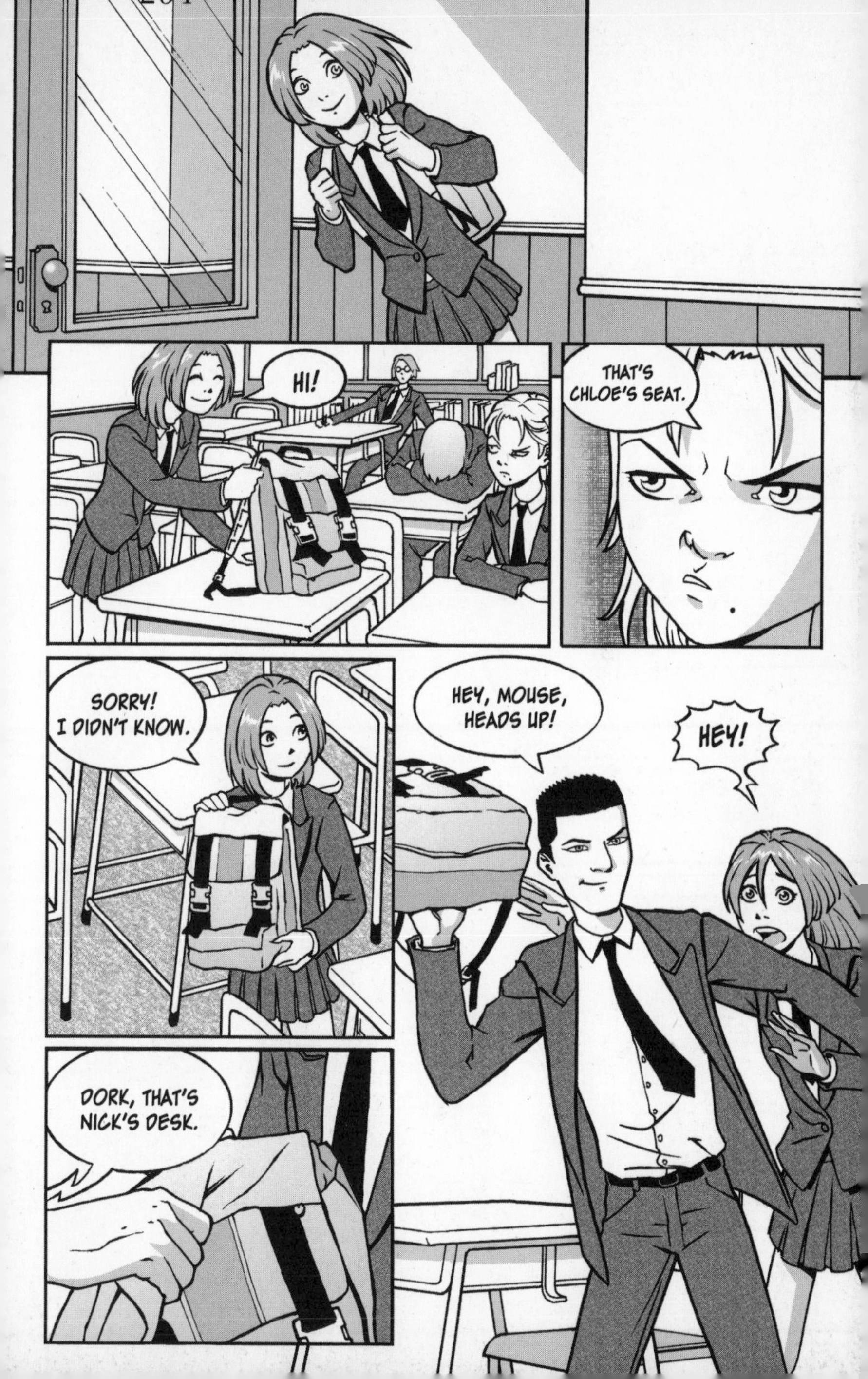
HI!
THAT'S CHLOE'S SEAT.
SORRY! I DIDN'T KNOW.
DORK, THAT'S NICK'S DESK.
HEY, MOUSE, HEADS UP!
HEY!

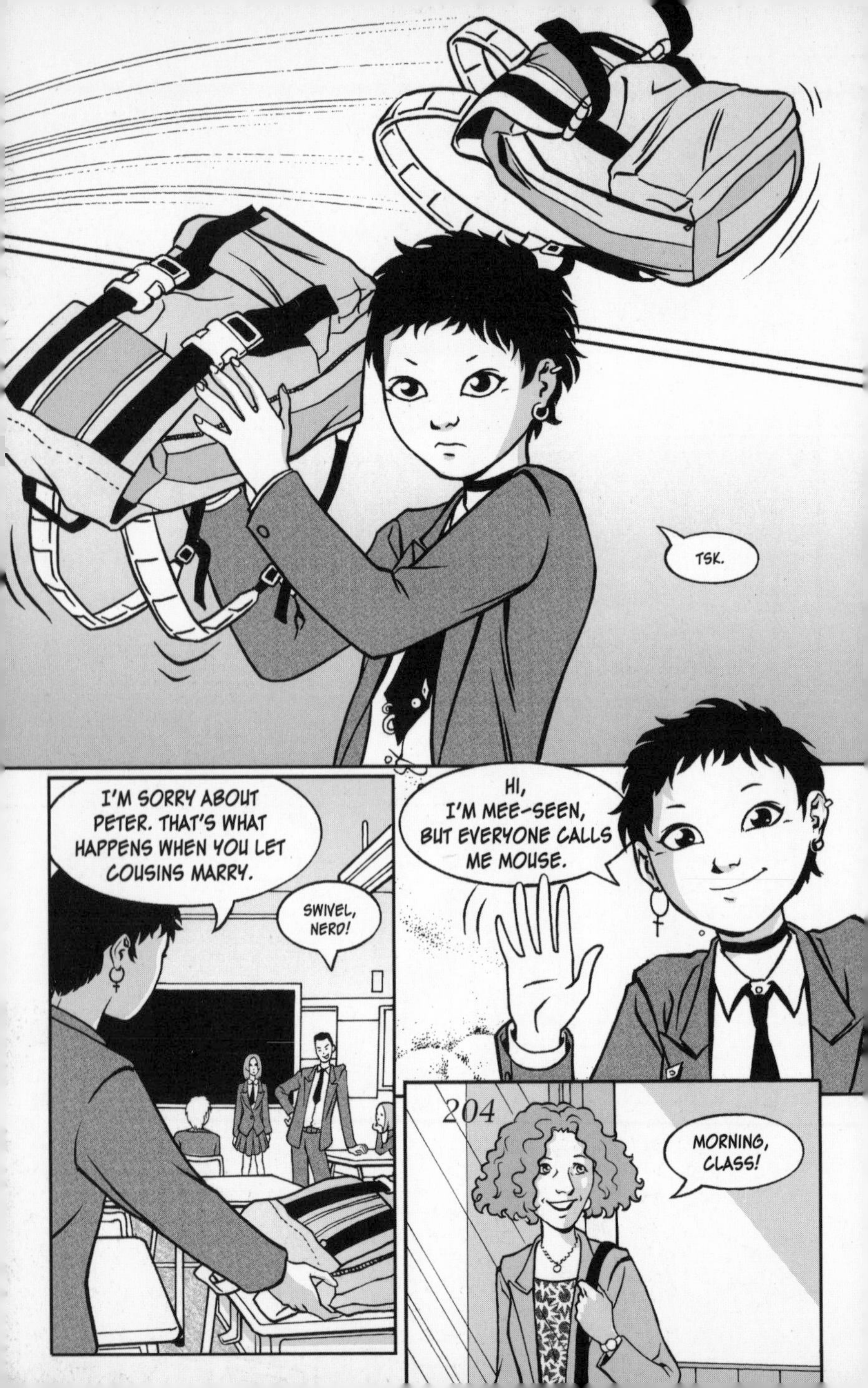
TSK.
I'M SORRY ABOUT PETER. THAT'S WHAT HAPPENS WHEN YOU LET COUSINS MARRY.
SWIVEL, NERD!
HI, I'M MEE-SEEN, BUT EVERYONE CALLS ME MOUSE.
204
MORNING, CLASS!

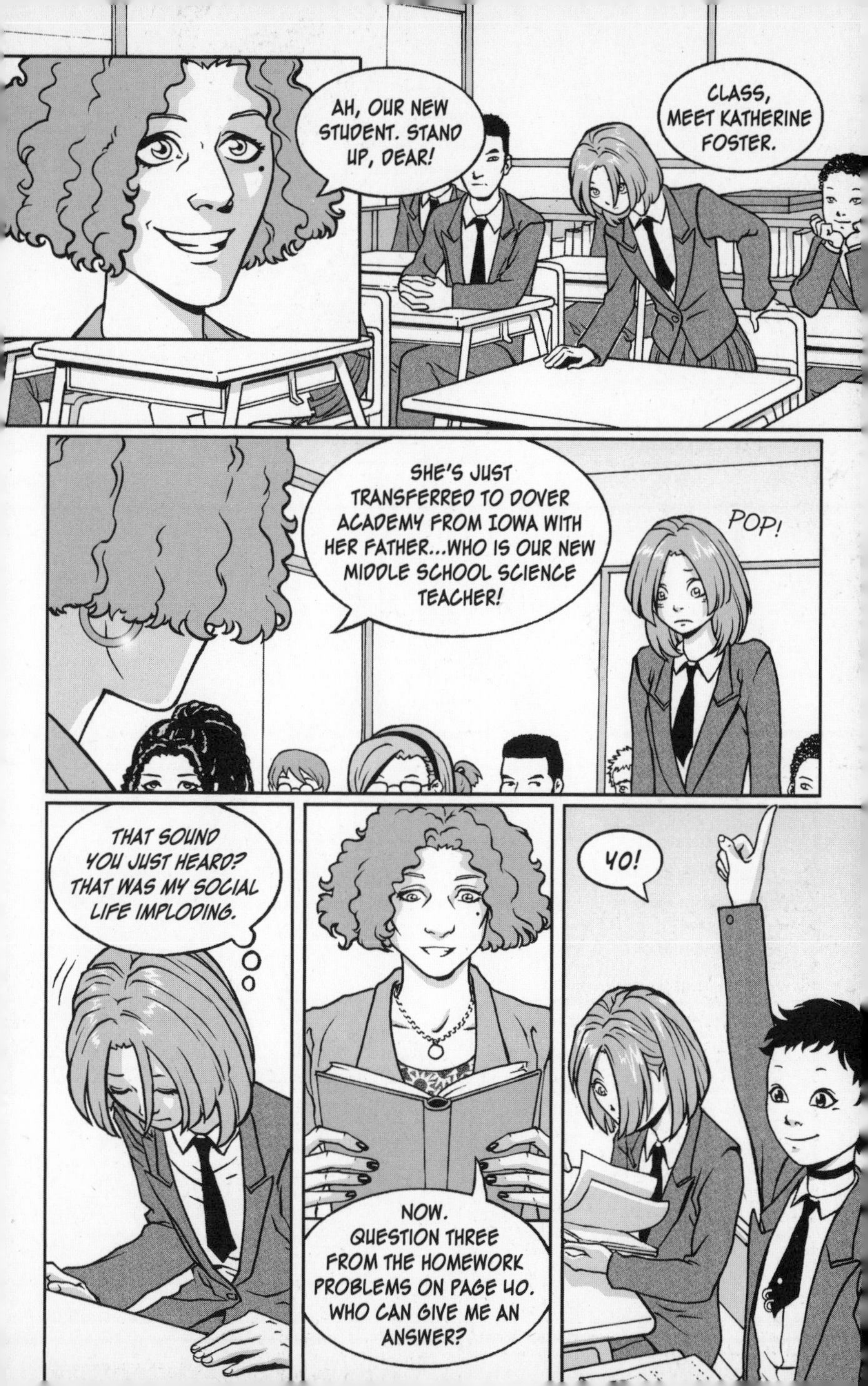
AH, OUR NEW STUDENT. STAND UP, DEAR!
CLASS, MEET KATHERINE FOSTER.
SHE'S JUST TRANSFERRED TO DOVER ACADEMY FROM IOWA WITH HER FATHER...WHO IS OUR NEW MIDDLE SCHOOL SCIENCE TEACHER!
POP!
THAT SOUND YOU JUST HEARD? THAT WAS MY SOCIAL LIFE IMPLODING.
NOW. QUESTION THREE FROM THE HOMEWORK PROBLEMS ON PAGE 40. WHO CAN GIVE ME AN ANSWER?
YO!

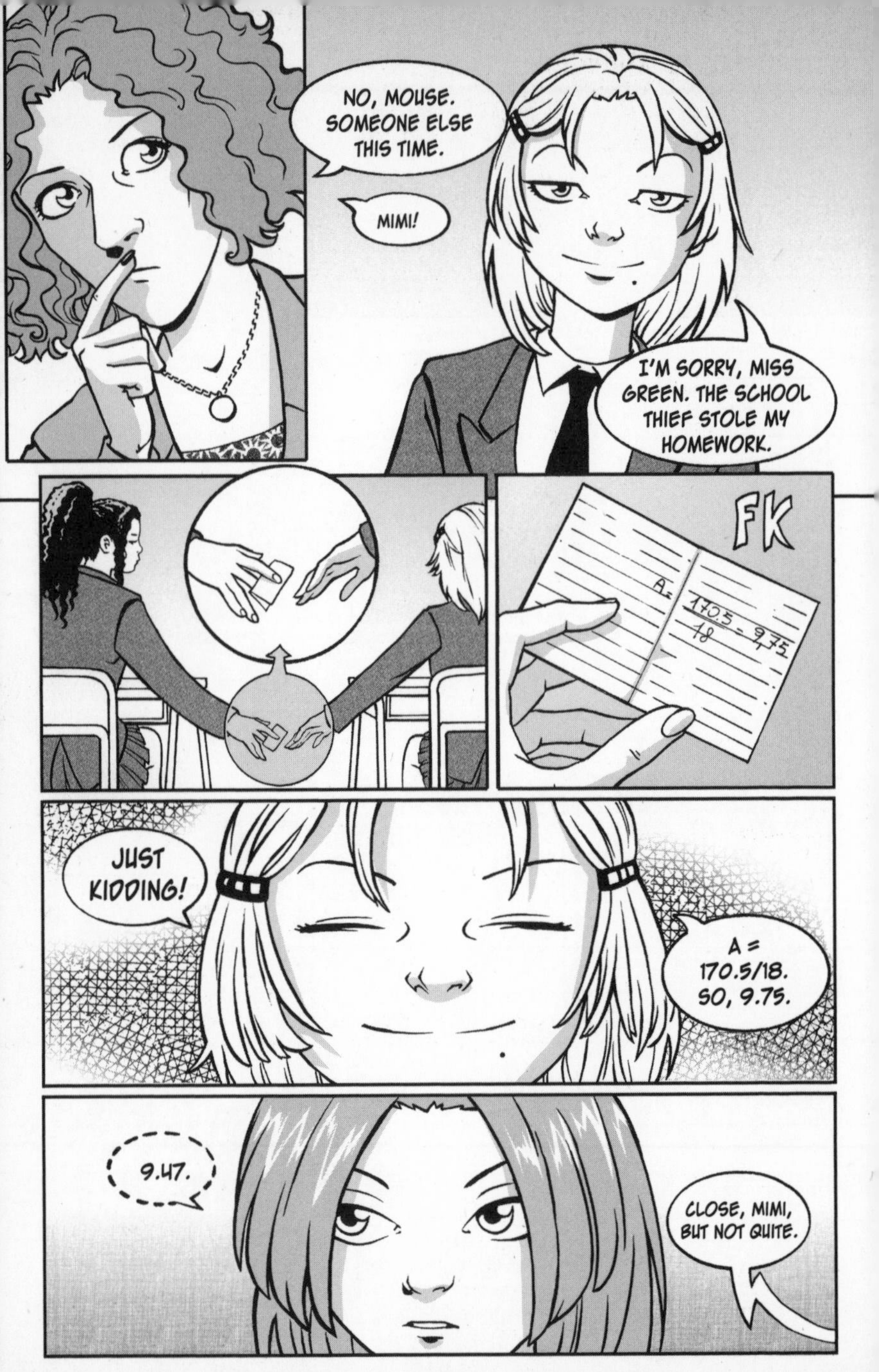
NO, MOUSE. SOMEONE ELSE THIS TIME.
MIMI!
I'M SORRY, MISS GREEN. THE SCHOOL THIEF STOLE MY HOMEWORK.
FK
A = 170.5 / 18 = 9.75
JUST KIDDING!
A = 170.5/18. SO, 9.75.
9.47.
CLOSE, MIMI, BUT NOT QUITE.

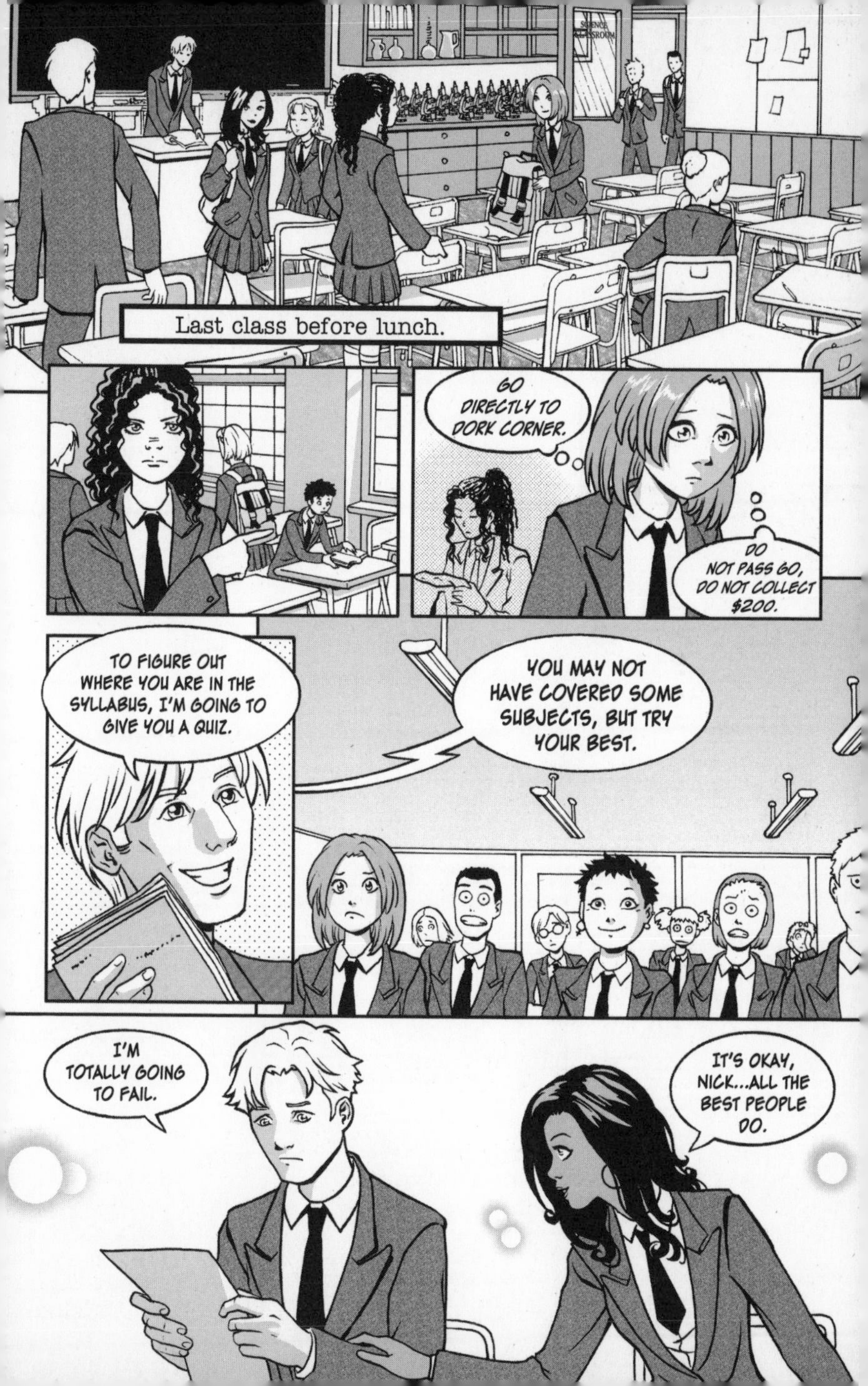
SCIENCE CLASSROOM
Last class before lunch.
GO DIRECTLY TO DORK CORNER.
DO NOT PASS GO, DO NOT COLLECT $200.
TO FIGURE OUT WHERE YOU ARE IN THE SYLLABUS, I'M GOING TO GIVE YOU A QUIZ.
YOU MAY NOT HAVE COVERED SOME SUBJECTS, BUT TRY YOUR BEST.
I'M TOTALLY GOING TO FAIL.
IT'S OKAY, NICK...ALL THE BEST PEOPLE DO.

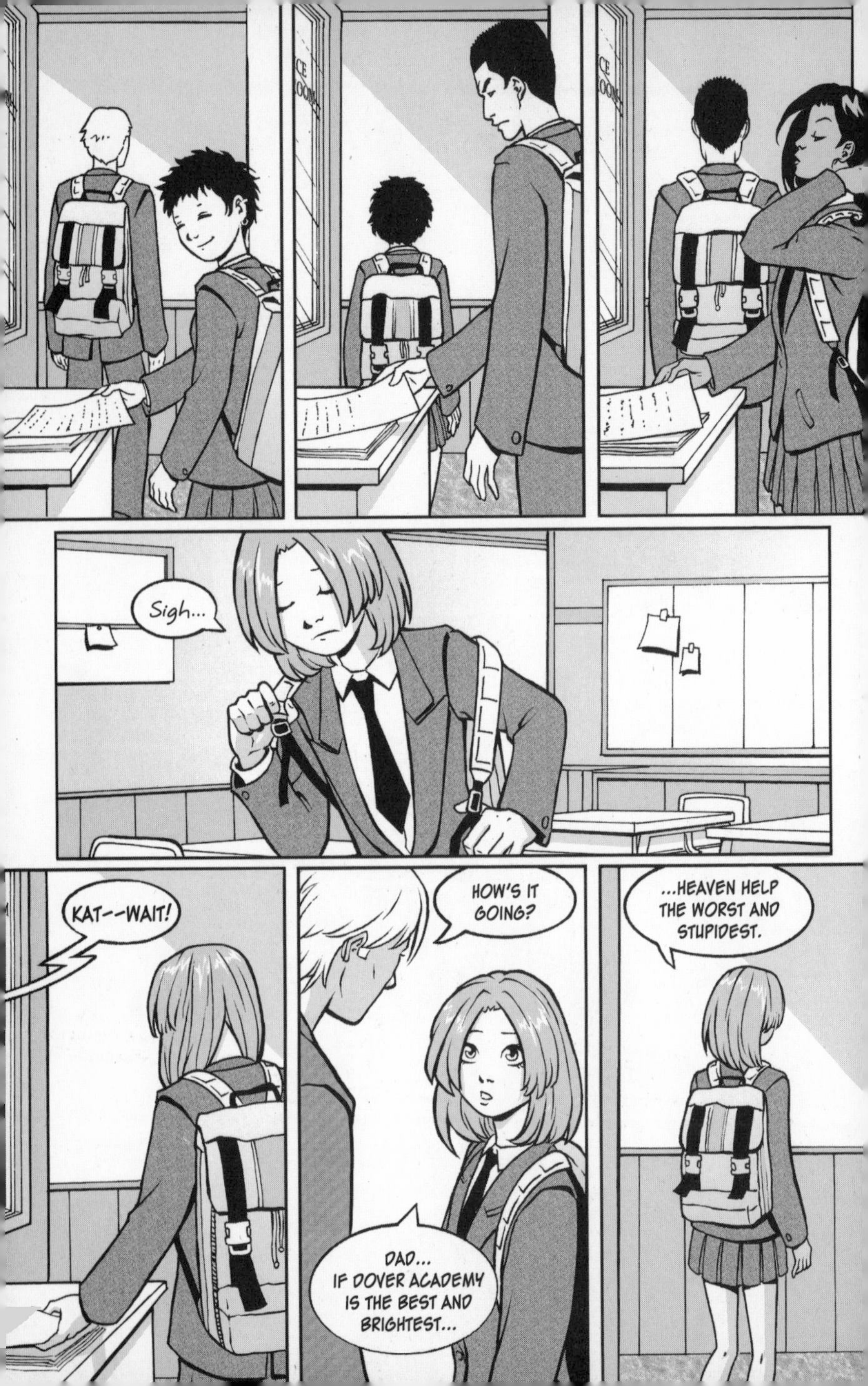
Sigh...
KAT--WAIT!
HOW'S IT GOING?
DAD... IF DOVER ACADEMY IS THE BEST AND BRIGHTEST...
...HEAVEN HELP THE WORST AND STUPIDEST.

Chapter 2:
Student Criminals

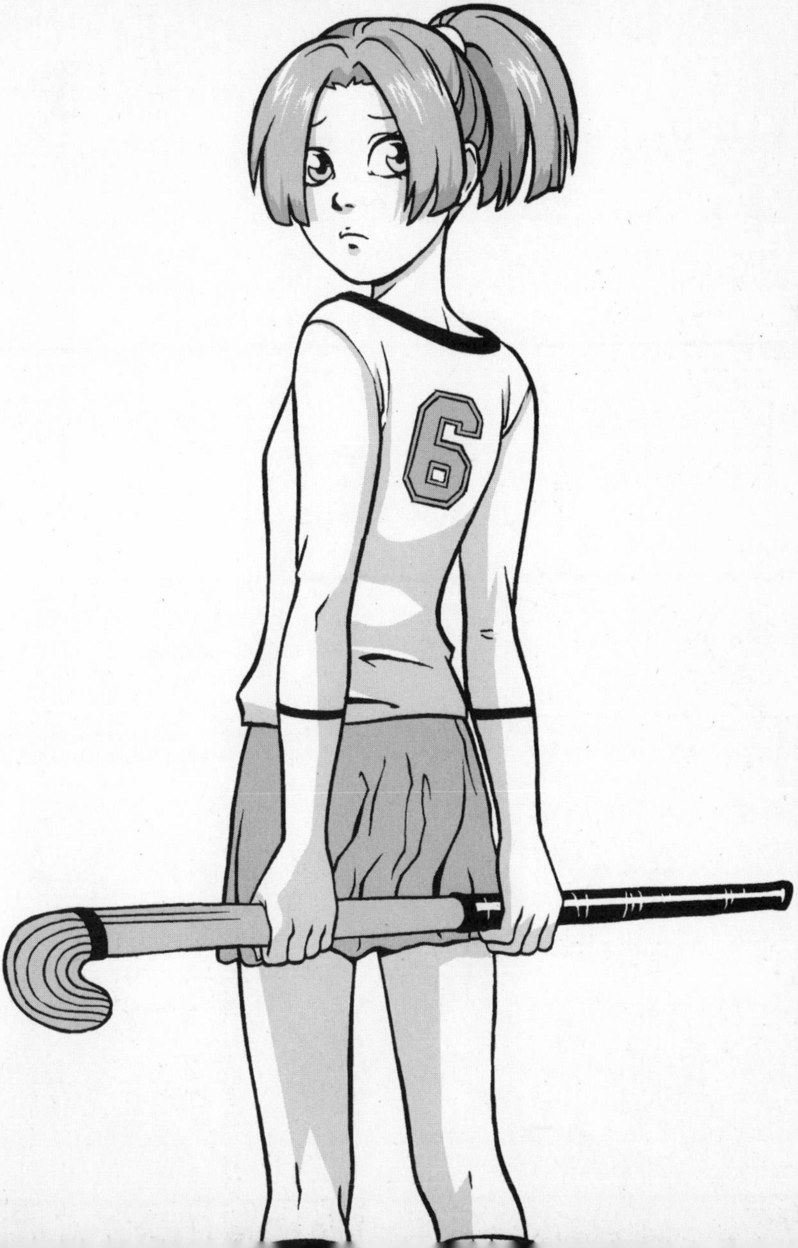
6

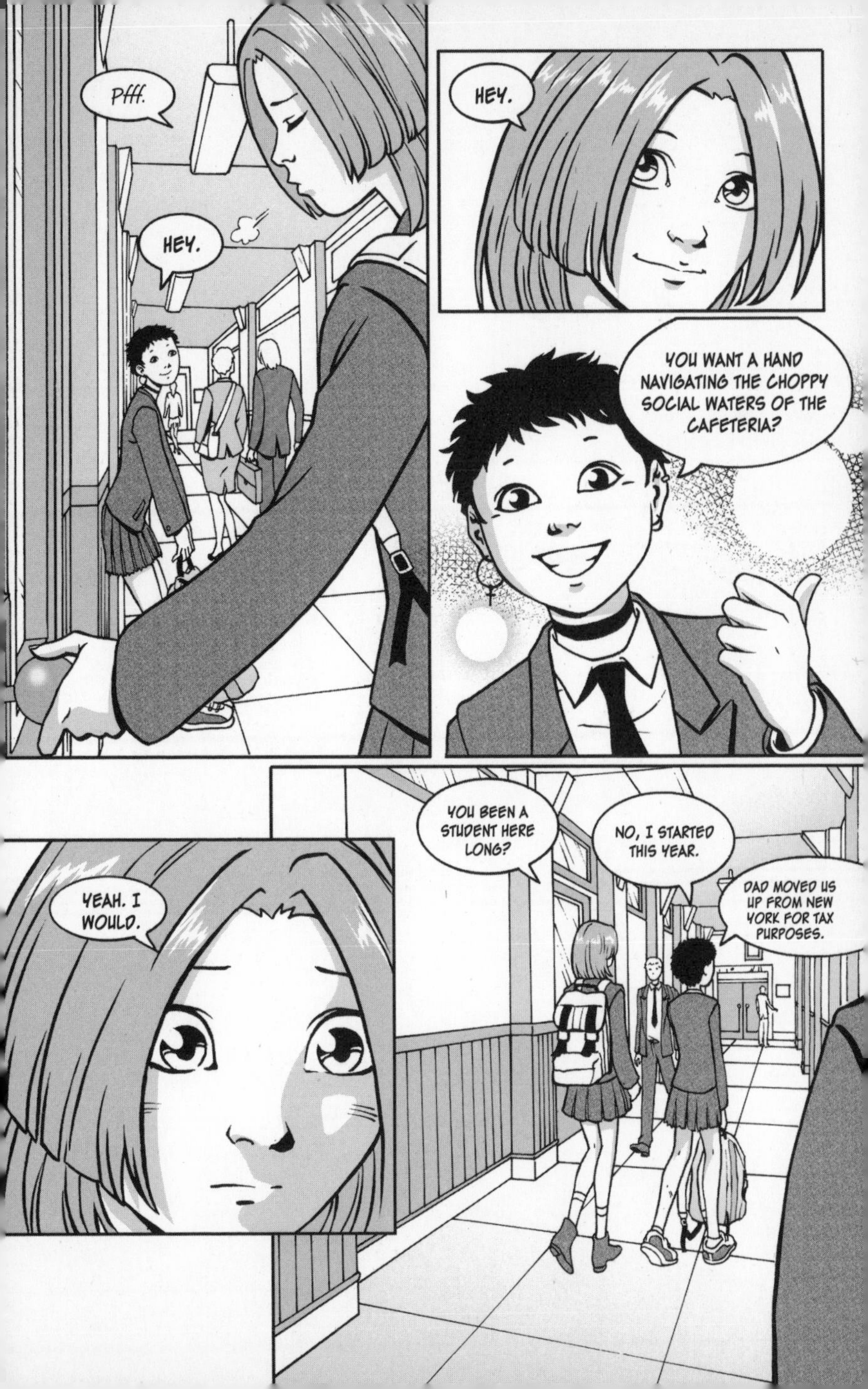
PFFF.
HEY.
HEY.
YOU WANT A HAND NAVIGATING THE CHOPPY SOCIAL WATERS OF THE CAFETERIA?
YEAH. I WOULD.
YOU BEEN A STUDENT HERE LONG?
NO, I STARTED THIS YEAR.
DAD MOVED US UP FROM NEW YORK FOR TAX PURPOSES.

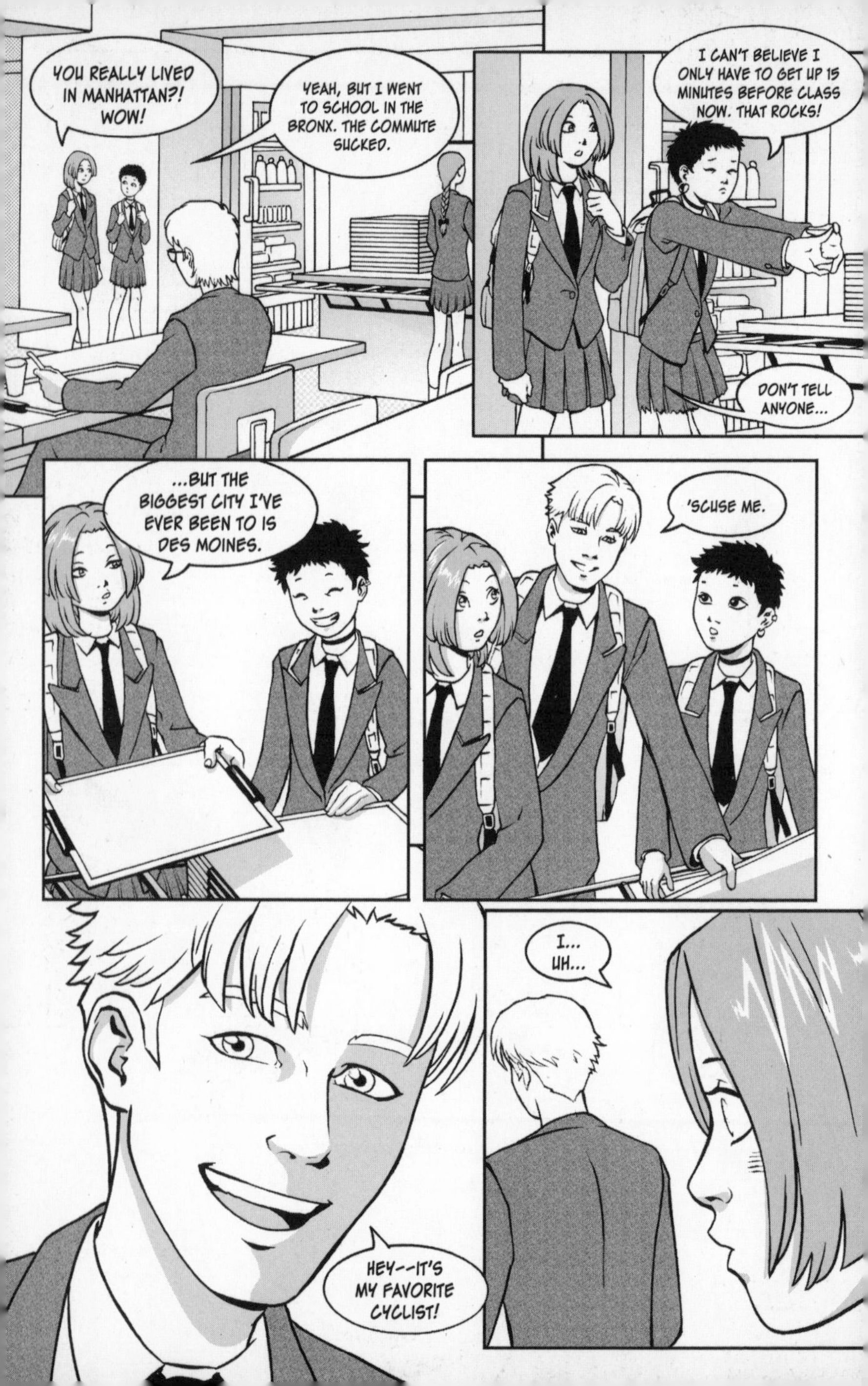
YOU REALLY LIVED IN MANHATTAN?! WOW!
YEAH, BUT I WENT TO SCHOOL IN THE BRONX. THE COMMUTE SUCKED.
I CAN'T BELIEVE I ONLY HAVE TO GET UP 15 MINUTES BEFORE CLASS NOW. THAT ROCKS!
DON'T TELL ANYONE...
...BUT THE BIGGEST CITY I'VE EVER BEEN TO IS DES MOINES.
'SCUSE ME.
HEY--IT'S MY FAVORITE CYCLIST!
I... UH...

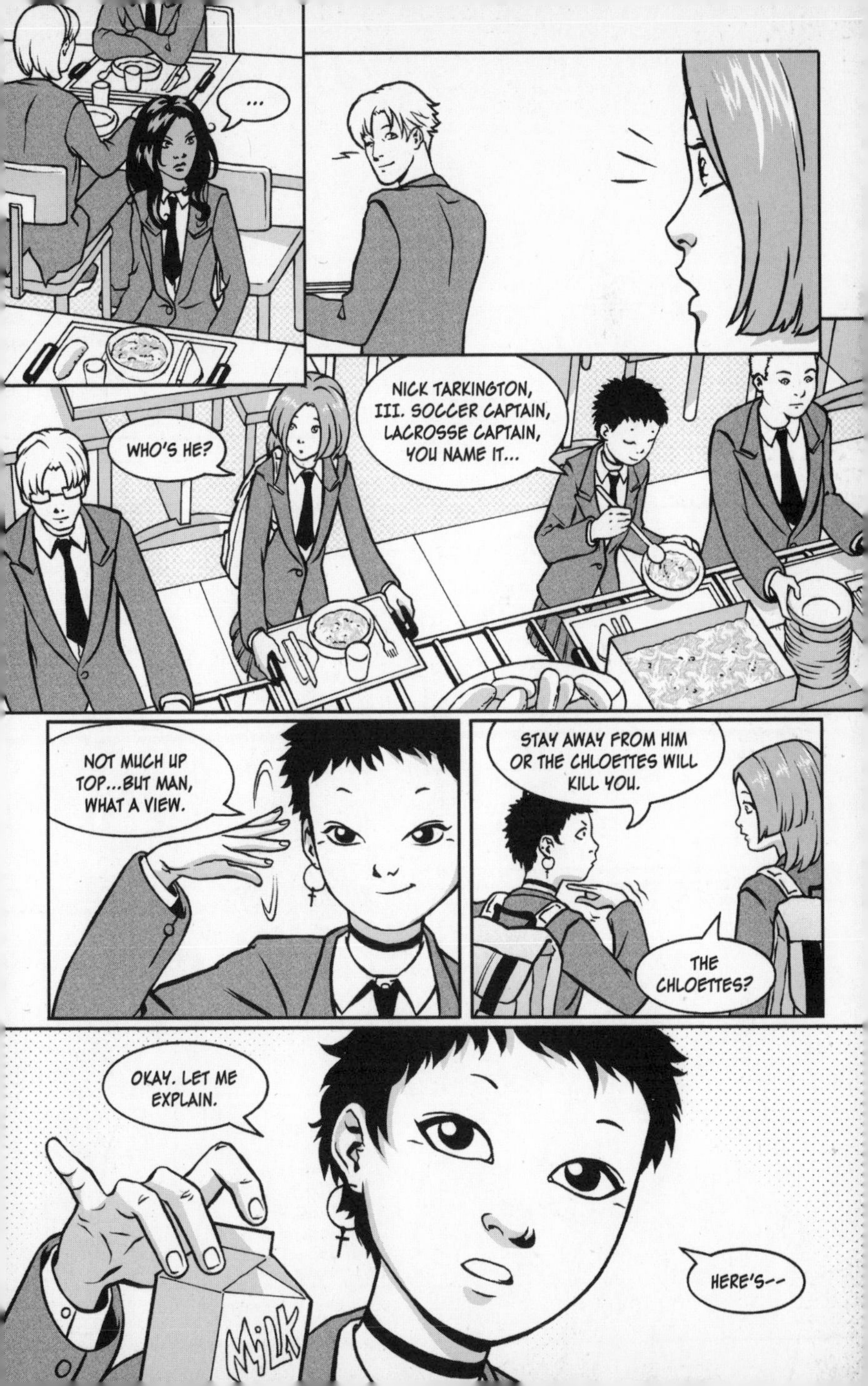
...
WHO'S HE?
NICK TARKINGTON, III. SOCCER CAPTAIN, LACROSSE CAPTAIN, YOU NAME IT...
NOT MUCH UP TOP...BUT MAN, WHAT A VIEW.
STAY AWAY FROM HIM OR THE CHLOETTES WILL KILL YOU.
THE CHLOETTES?
OKAY. LET ME EXPLAIN.
MILK
HERE'S--

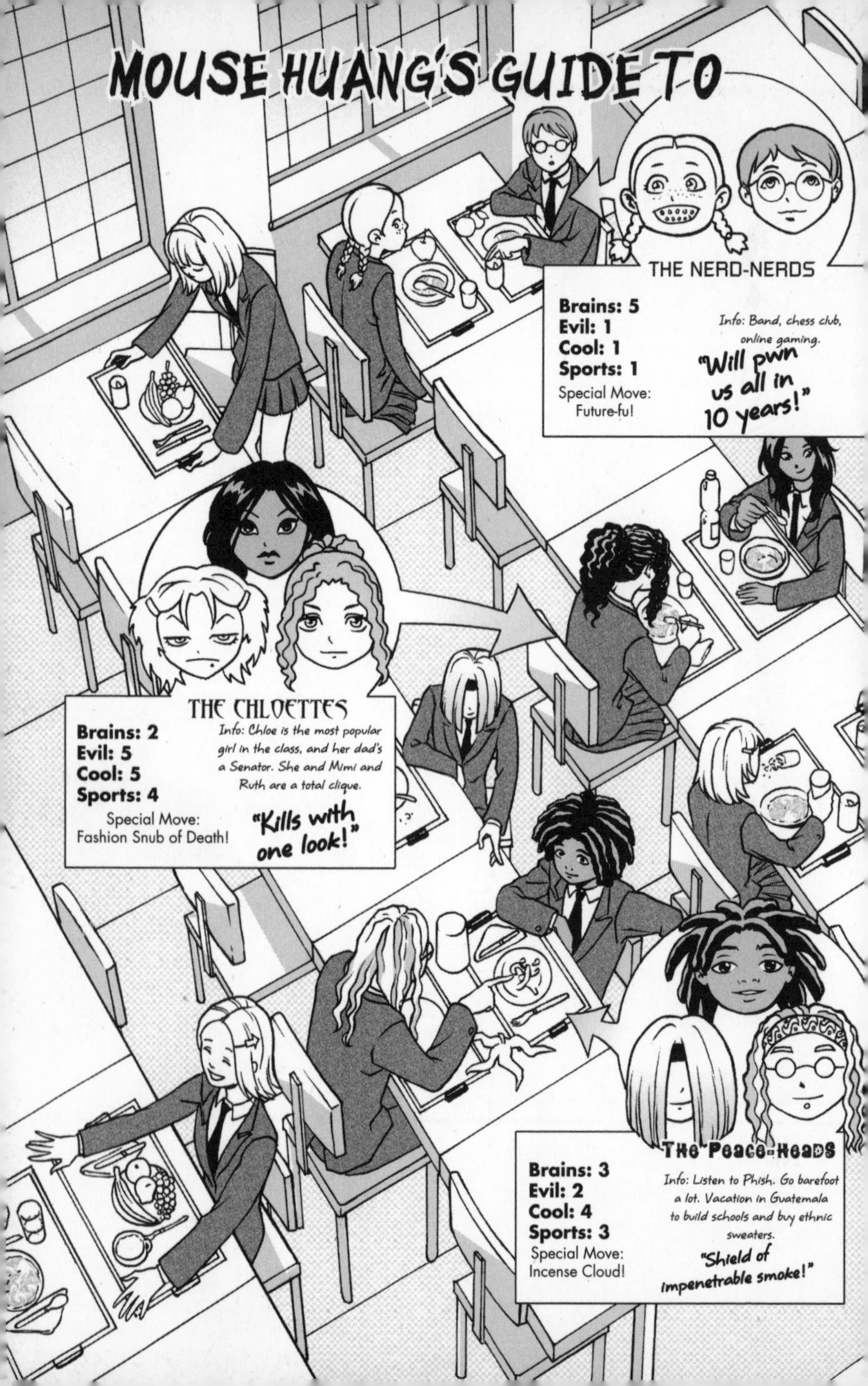
MOUSE HUANG'S GUIDE TO
THE NERD-NERDS
Brains: 5
Evil: 1
Cool: 1
Sports: 1
Special Move: Future-fu!
Info: Band, chess club, online gaming.
"Will pwn us all in 10 years!"
THE CHLOETTES
Brains: 2
Evil: 5
Cool: 5
Sports: 4
Special Move: Fashion Snub of Death!
Info: Chloe is the most popular girl in the class, and her dad's a Senator. She and Mimi and Ruth are a total clique.
"Kills with one look!"
The Peace-Heads
Brains: 3
Evil: 2
Cool: 4
Sports: 3
Special Move: Incense Cloud!
Info: Listen to Phish. Go barefoot a lot. Vacation in Guatemala to build schools and buy ethnic sweaters.
"Shield of impenetrable smoke!"

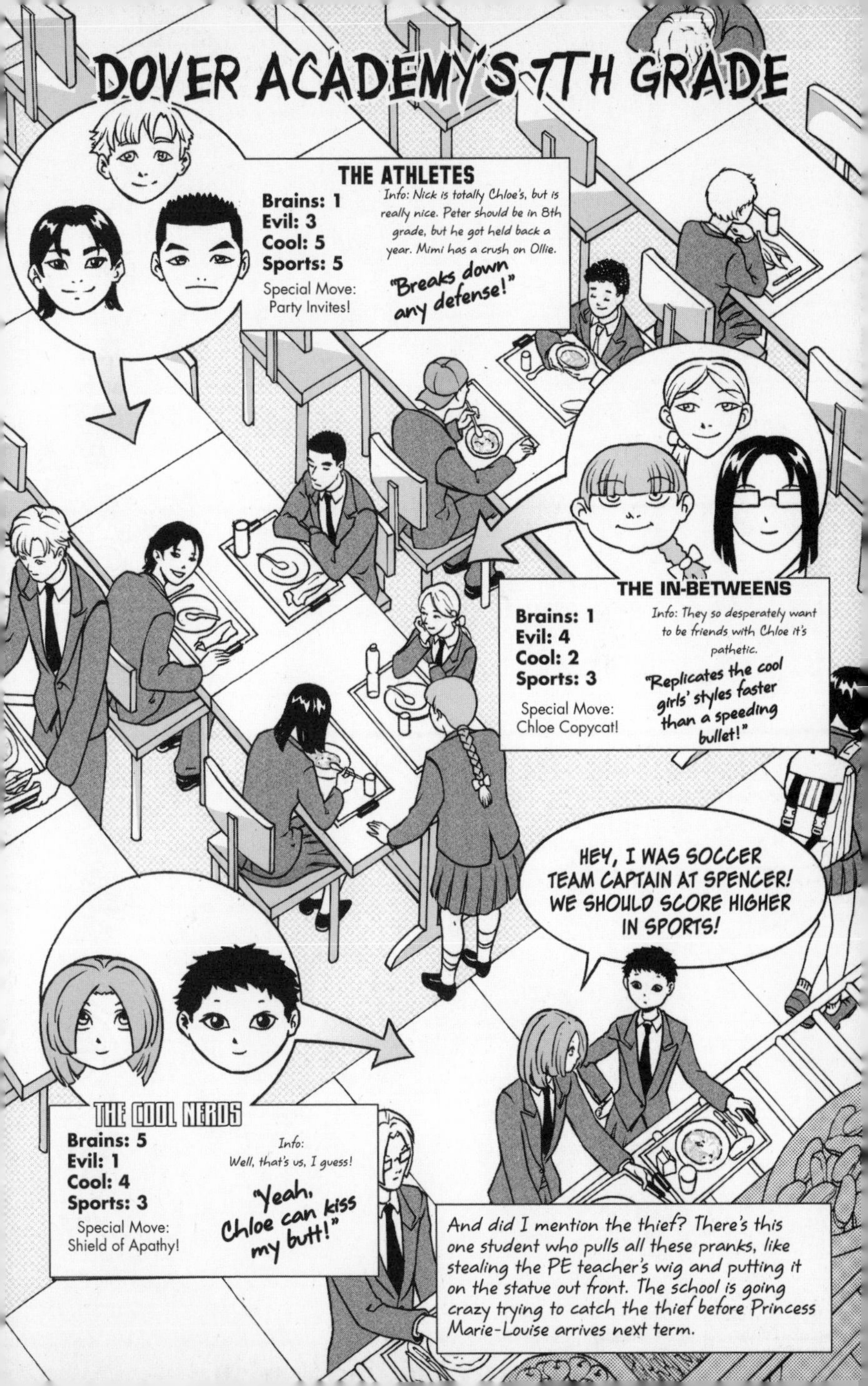
DOVER ACADEMY'S 7TH GRADE
THE ATHLETES
Brains: 1
Evil: 3
Cool: 5
Sports: 5
Special Move: Party Invites!
Info: Nick is totally Chloe's, but is really nice. Peter should be in 8th grade, but he got held back a year. Mimi has a crush on Ollie.
"Breaks down any defense!"
THE IN-BETWEENS
Brains: 1
Evil: 4
Cool: 2
Sports: 3
Special Move: Chloe Copycat!
Info: They so desperately want to be friends with Chloe it's pathetic.
"Replicates the cool girls' styles faster than a speeding bullet!"
HEY, I WAS SOCCER TEAM CAPTAIN AT SPENCER! WE SHOULD SCORE HIGHER IN SPORTS!
THE COOL NERDS
Brains: 5
Evil: 1
Cool: 4
Sports: 3
Special Move: Shield of Apathy!
Info: Well, that's us, I guess!
"Yeah, Chloe can kiss my butt!"
And did I mention the thief? There's this one student who pulls all these pranks, like stealing the PE teacher's wig and putting it on the statue out front. The school is going crazy trying to catch the thief before Princess Marie-Louise arrives next term.

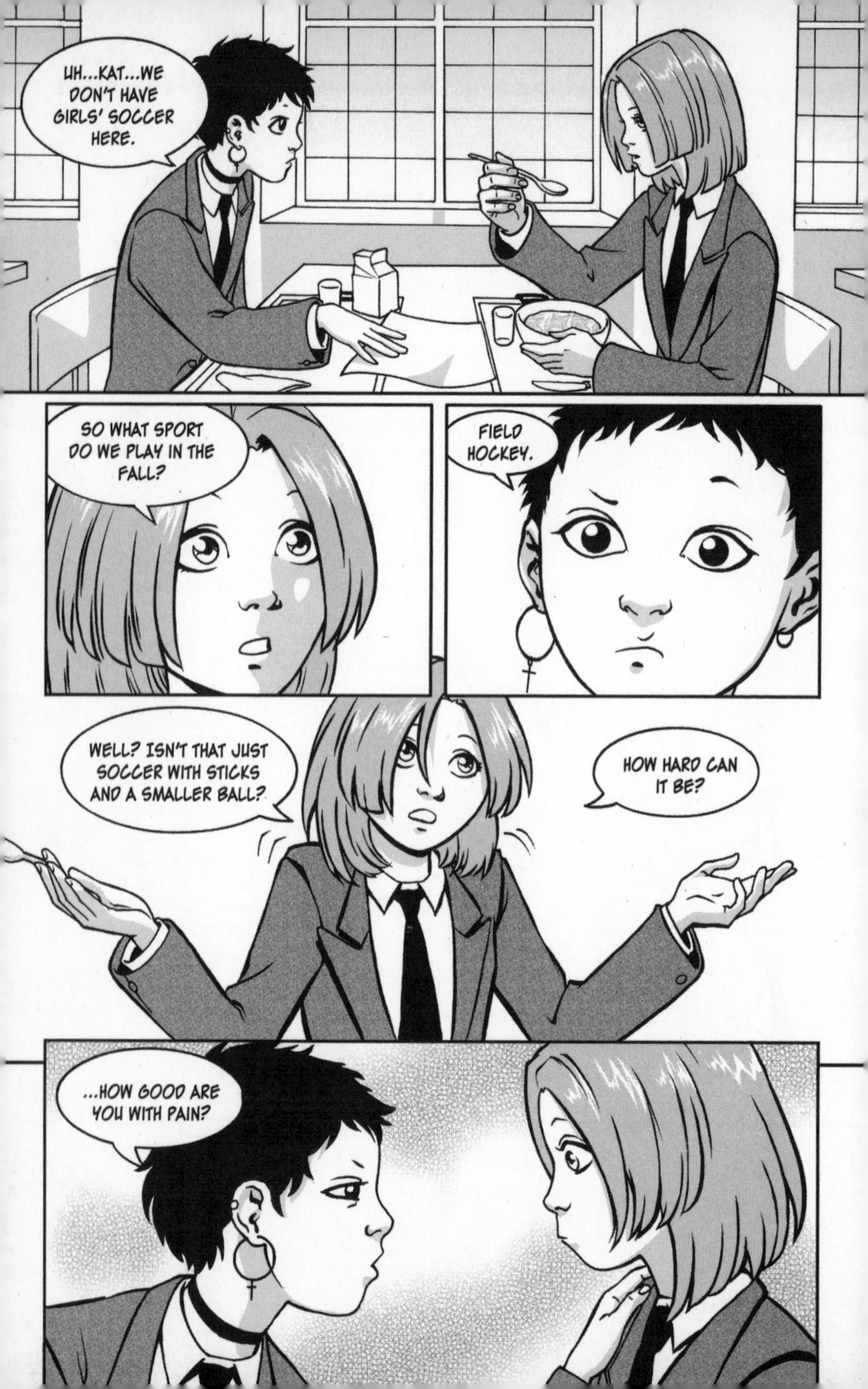
UH...KAT...WE DON'T HAVE GIRLS' SOCCER HERE.
SO WHAT SPORT DO WE PLAY IN THE FALL?
FIELD HOCKEY.
WELL? ISN'T THAT JUST SOCCER WITH STICKS AND A SMALLER BALL?
HOW HARD CAN IT BE?
...HOW GOOD ARE YOU WITH PAIN?

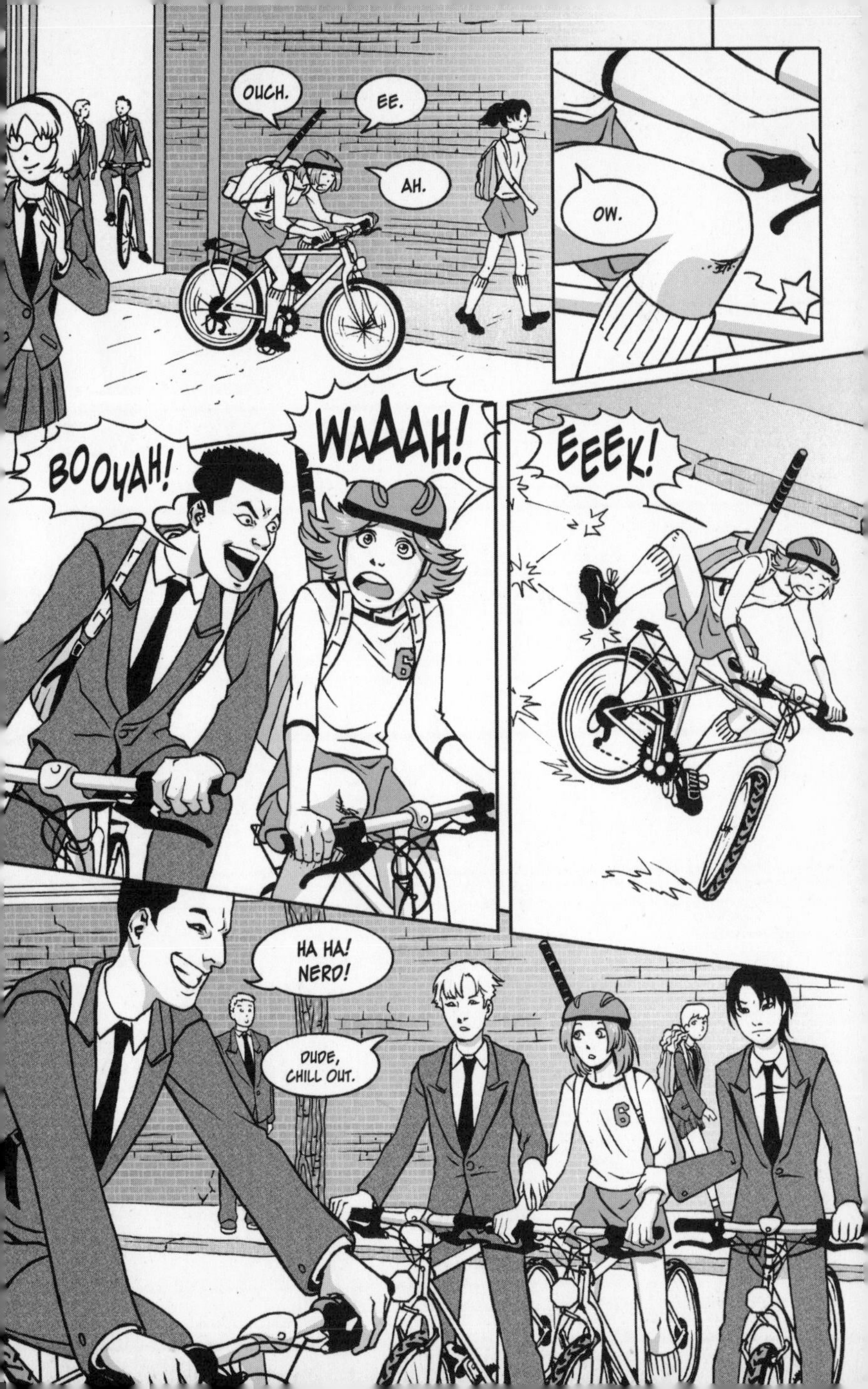
OUCH.
EE.
AH.
OW.
BOOYAH!
WAAAH!
EEEK!
HA HA! NERD!
DUDE, CHILL OUT.

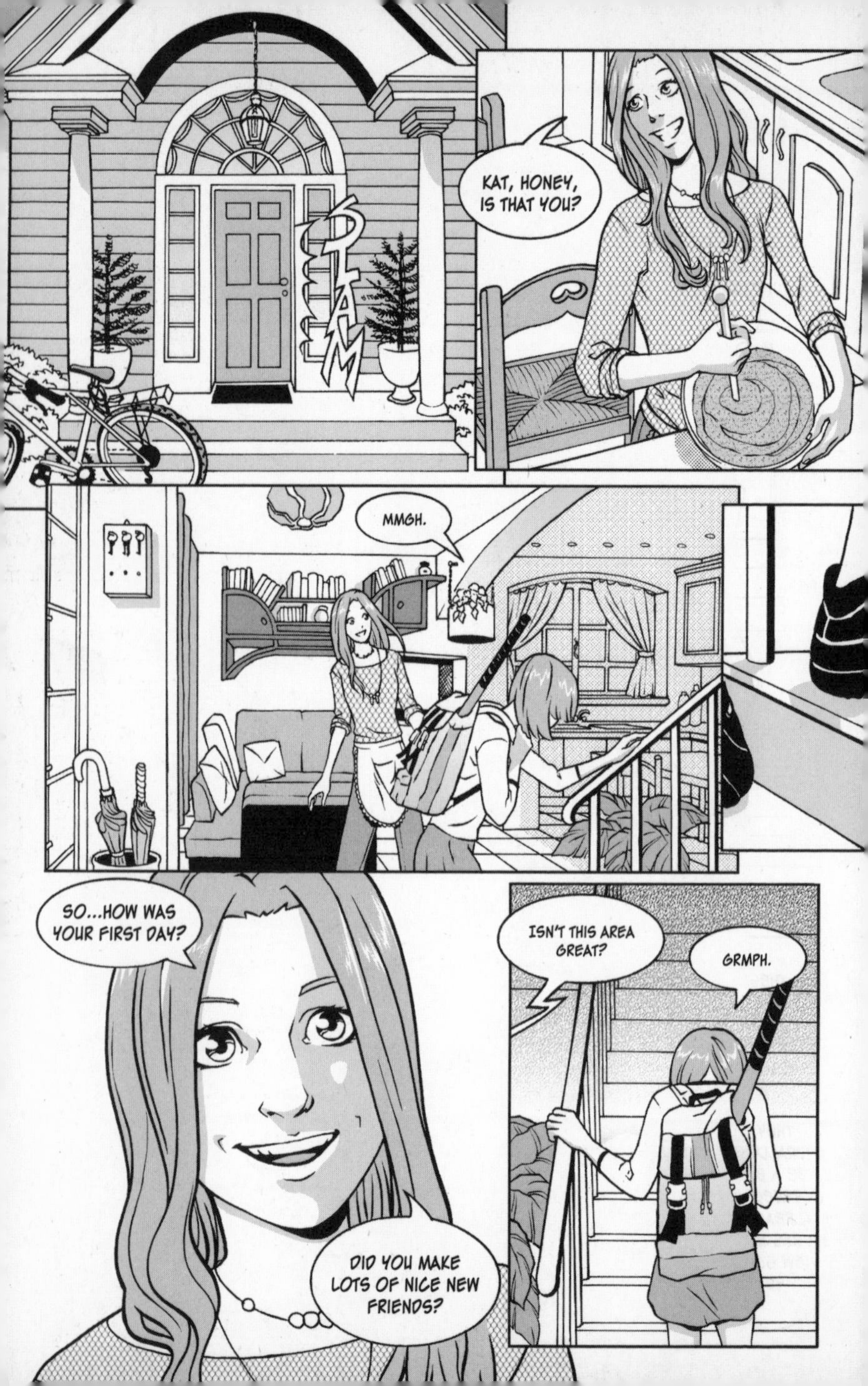
SLAM
KAT, HONEY, IS THAT YOU?
MMGH.
SO...HOW WAS YOUR FIRST DAY?
DID YOU MAKE LOTS OF NICE NEW FRIENDS?
ISN'T THIS AREA GREAT?
GRMPH.

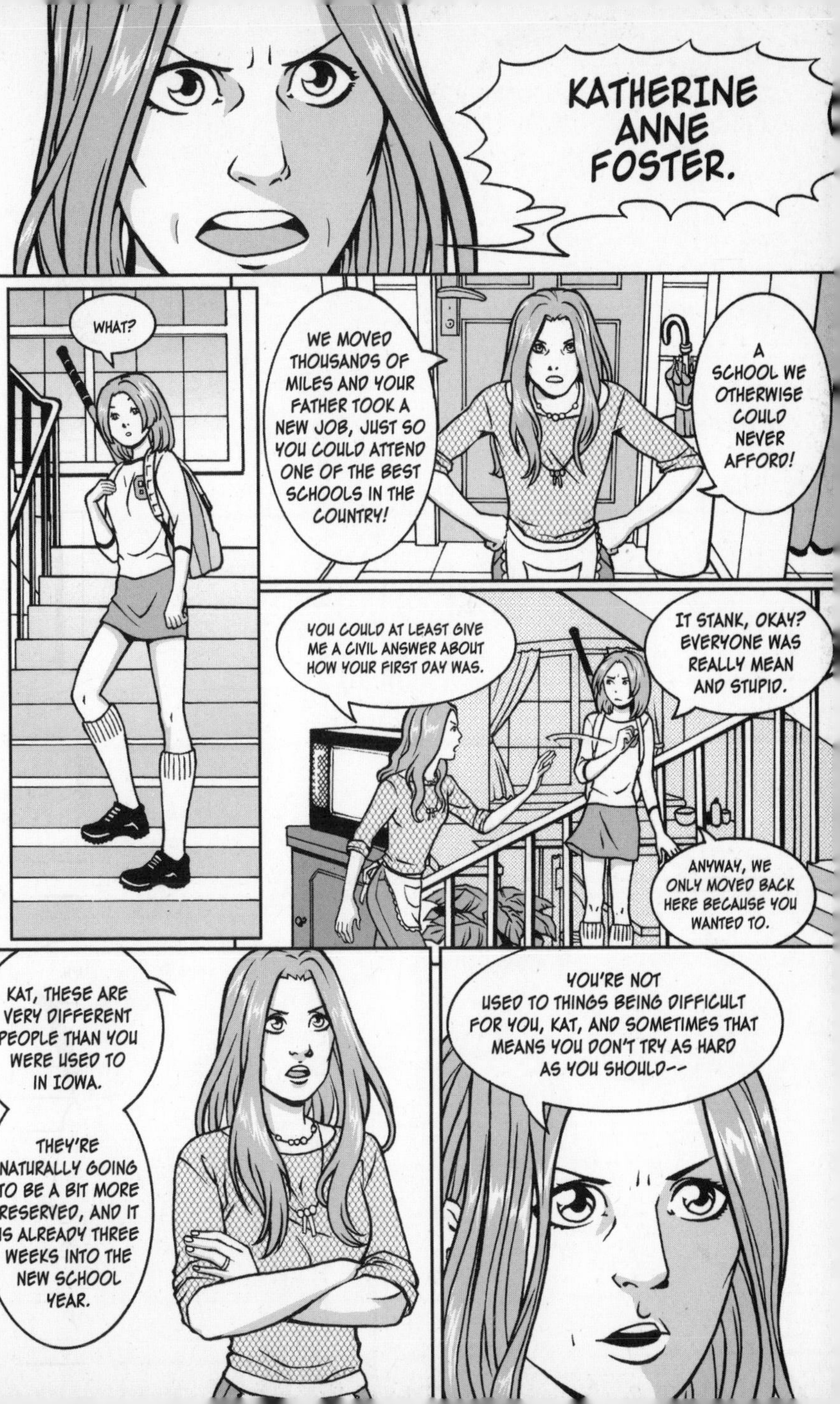
KATHERINE ANNE FOSTER.
WHAT?
WE MOVED THOUSANDS OF MILES AND YOUR FATHER TOOK A NEW JOB, JUST SO YOU COULD ATTEND ONE OF THE BEST SCHOOLS IN THE COUNTRY!
A SCHOOL WE OTHERWISE COULD NEVER AFFORD!
YOU COULD AT LEAST GIVE ME A CIVIL ANSWER ABOUT HOW YOUR FIRST DAY WAS.
IT STANK, OKAY? EVERYONE WAS REALLY MEAN AND STUPID.
ANYWAY, WE ONLY MOVED BACK HERE BECAUSE YOU WANTED TO.
KAT, THESE ARE VERY DIFFERENT PEOPLE THAN YOU WERE USED TO IN IOWA.
THEY'RE NATURALLY GOING TO BE A BIT MORE RESERVED, AND IT IS ALREADY THREE WEEKS INTO THE NEW SCHOOL YEAR.
YOU'RE NOT USED TO THINGS BEING DIFFICULT FOR YOU, KAT, AND SOMETIMES THAT MEANS YOU DON'T TRY AS HARD AS YOU SHOULD--

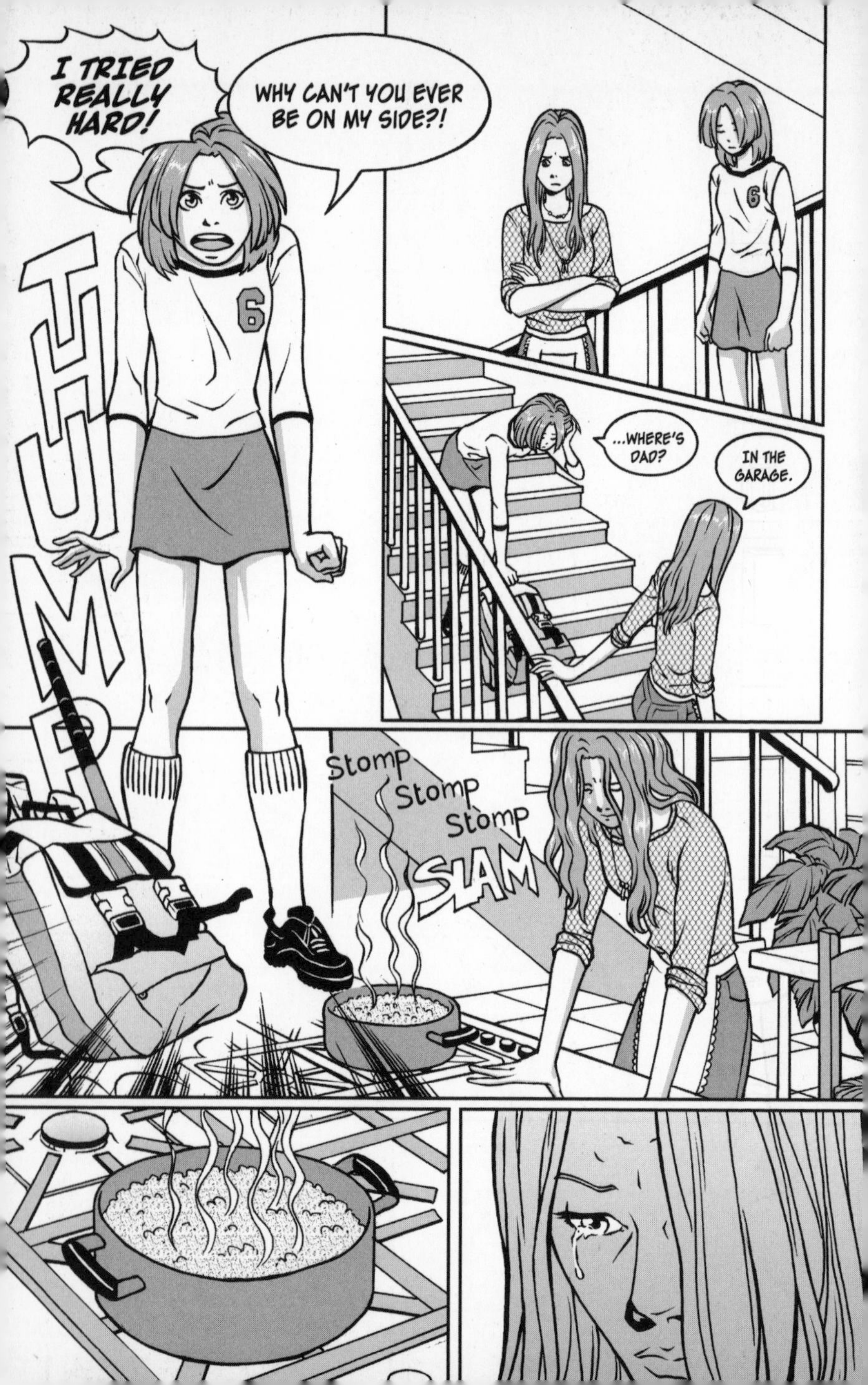
I TRIED REALLY HARD!
WHY CAN'T YOU EVER BE ON MY SIDE?!
THUMP
...WHERE'S DAD?
IN THE GARAGE.
Stomp
Stomp
Stomp
SLAM

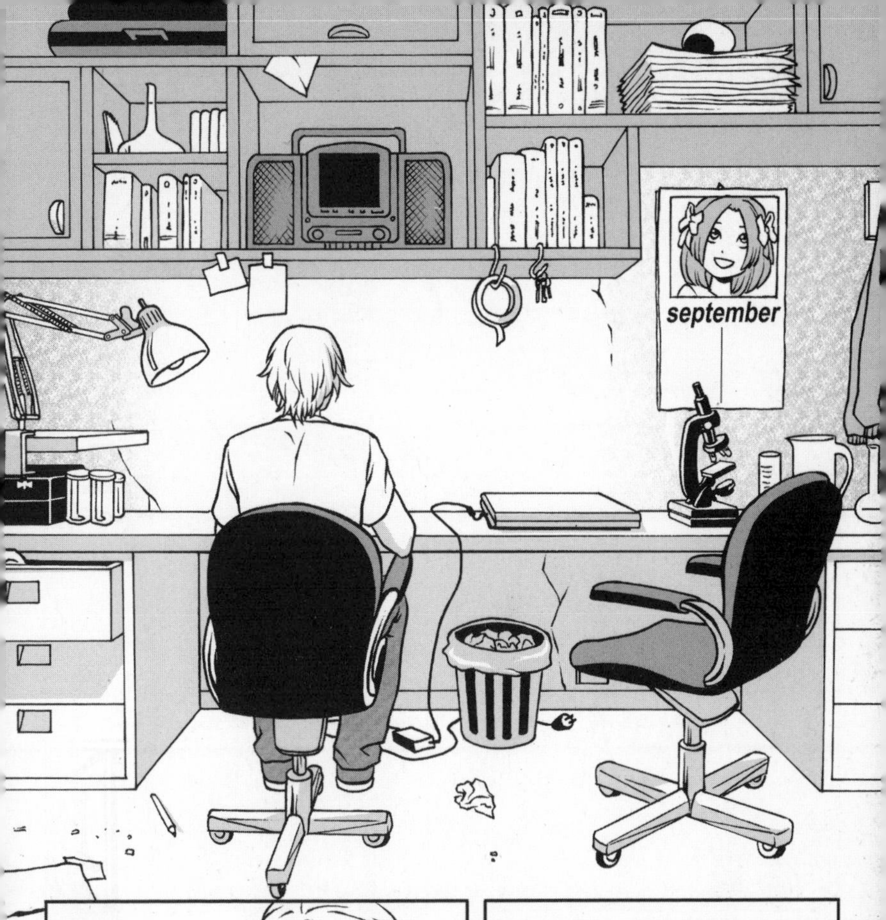
september
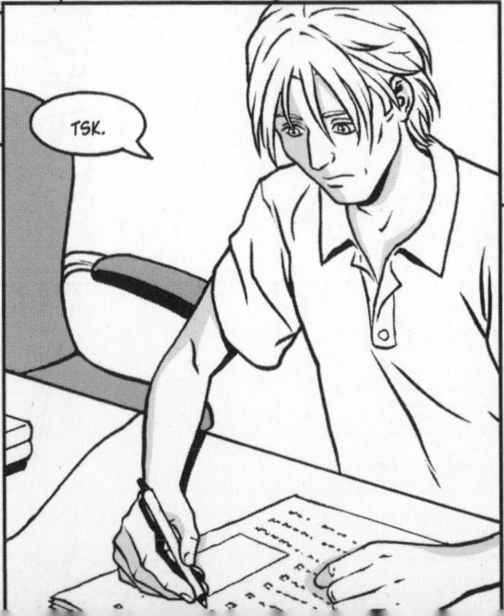
TSK.
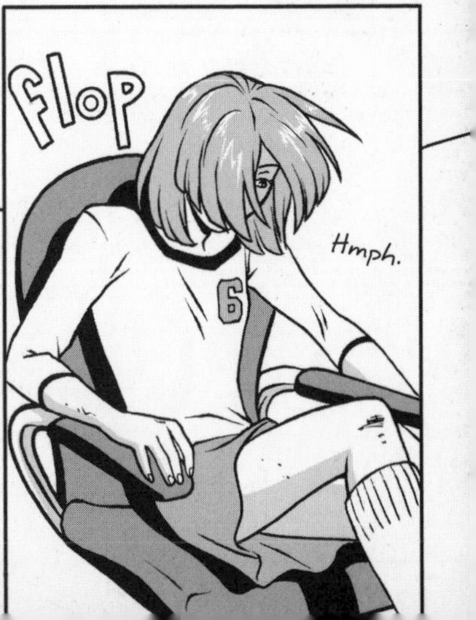
flop
Hmph.

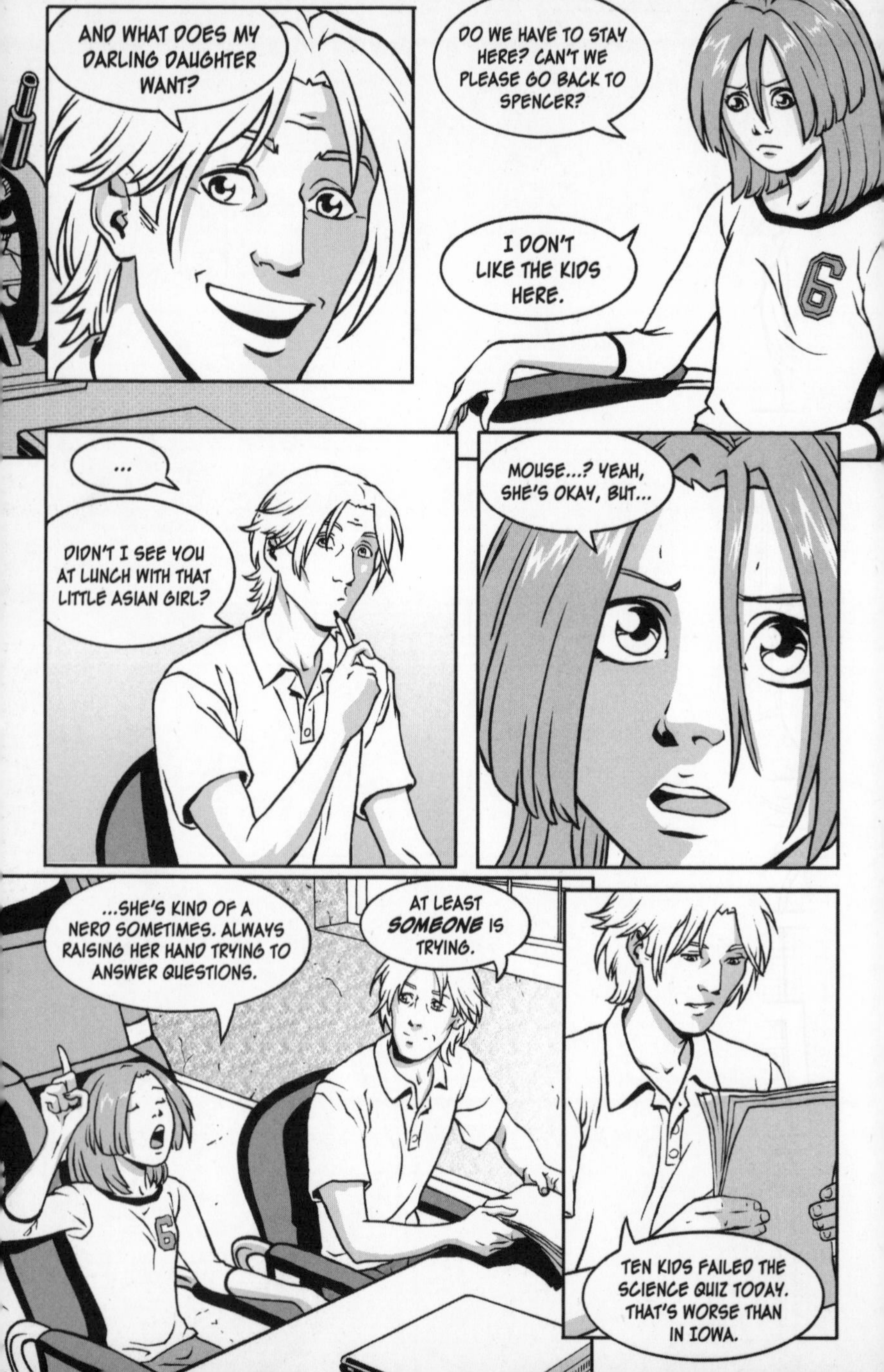
AND WHAT DOES MY DARLING DAUGHTER WANT?
DO WE HAVE TO STAY HERE? CAN'T WE PLEASE GO BACK TO SPENCER?
I DON'T LIKE THE KIDS HERE.
...
DIDN'T I SEE YOU AT LUNCH WITH THAT LITTLE ASIAN GIRL?
MOUSE...? YEAH, SHE'S OKAY, BUT...
...SHE'S KIND OF A NERD SOMETIMES. ALWAYS RAISING HER HAND TRYING TO ANSWER QUESTIONS.
AT LEAST *SOMEONE* IS TRYING.
TEN KIDS FAILED THE SCIENCE QUIZ TODAY. THAT'S WORSE THAN IN IOWA.

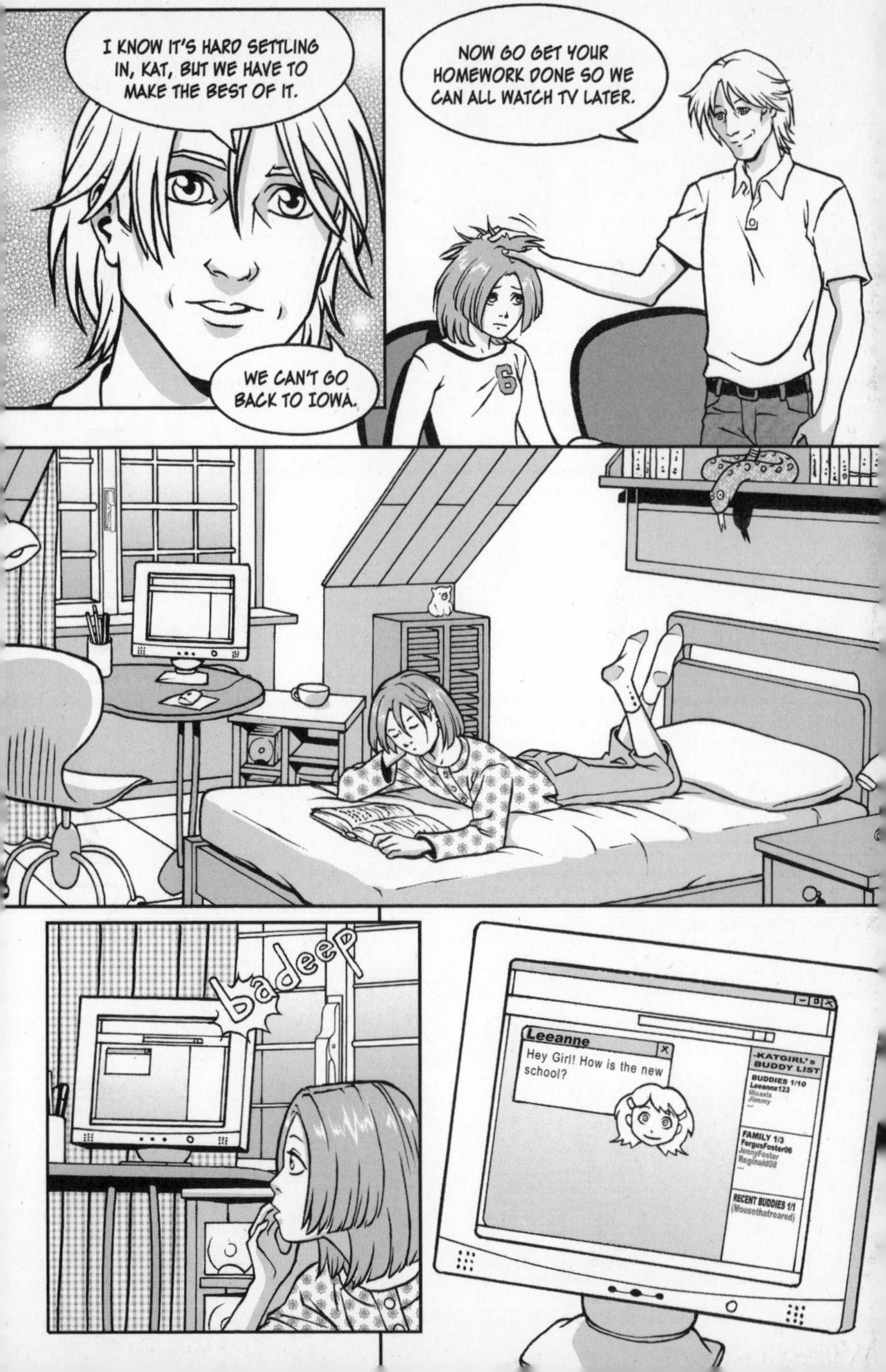
I KNOW IT'S HARD SETTLING IN, KAT, BUT WE HAVE TO MAKE THE BEST OF IT.
WE CAN'T GO BACK TO IOWA.
NOW GO GET YOUR HOMEWORK DONE SO WE CAN ALL WATCH TV LATER.
badeep
Leeanne
Hey Girl! How is the new school?
-KATGIRL's BUDDY LIST
BUDDIES 1/10
Leeanne123
Micaela
Jimmy
FAMILY 1/3
FergusFoster06
JennyFoster
Reginald08
RECENT BUDDIES 1/1
(Mousethatroared)

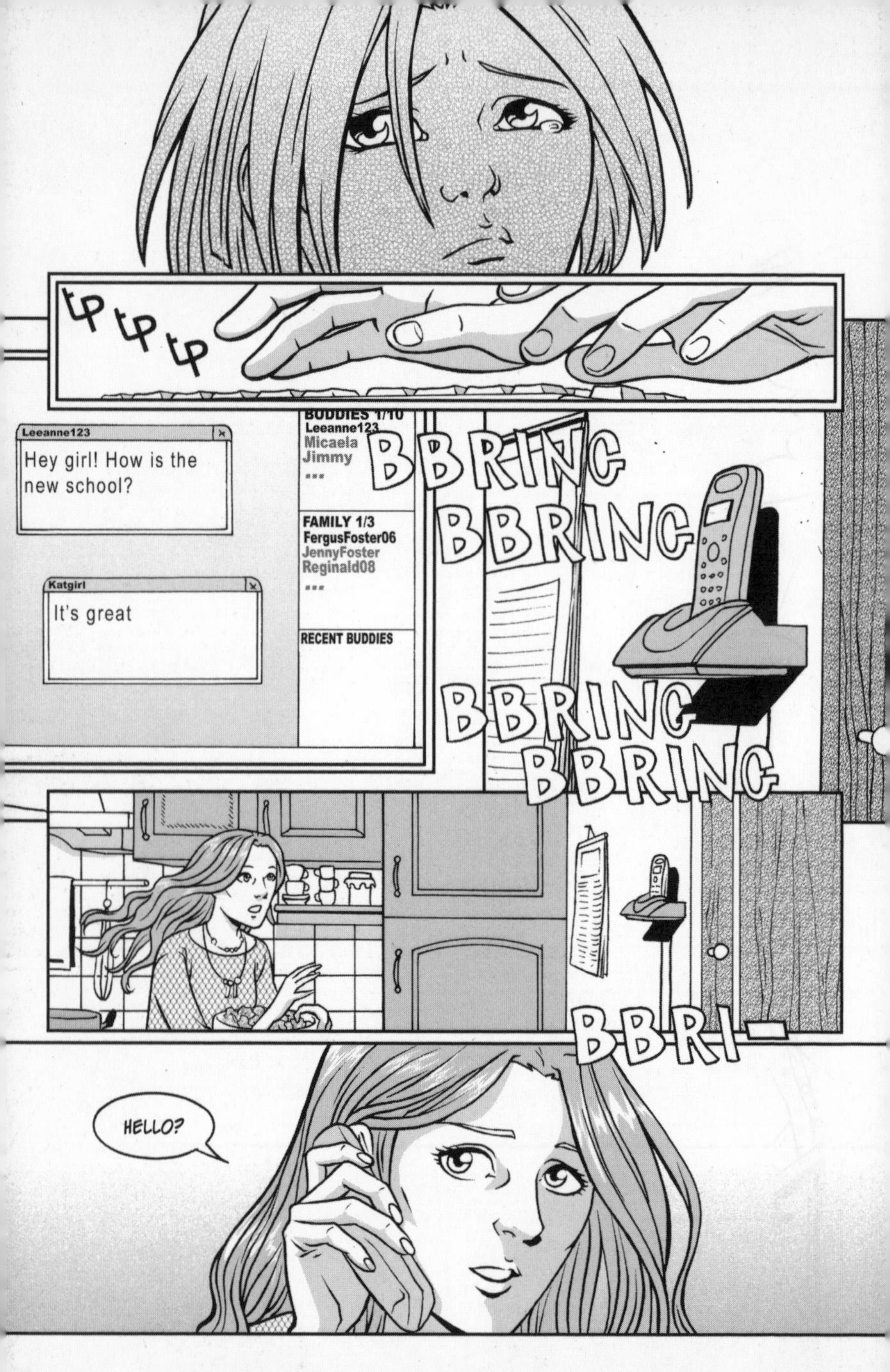

tp tp tp
BUDDIES 1/10
Leeanne123
Micaela
Jimmy
FAMILY 1/3
FergusFoster06
JennyFoster
Reginald08
RECENT BUDDIES
Leeanne123
Hey girl! How is the new school?
Katgirl
It's great
BBRING
BBRING
BBRING
BBRING
BBRI-
HELLO?

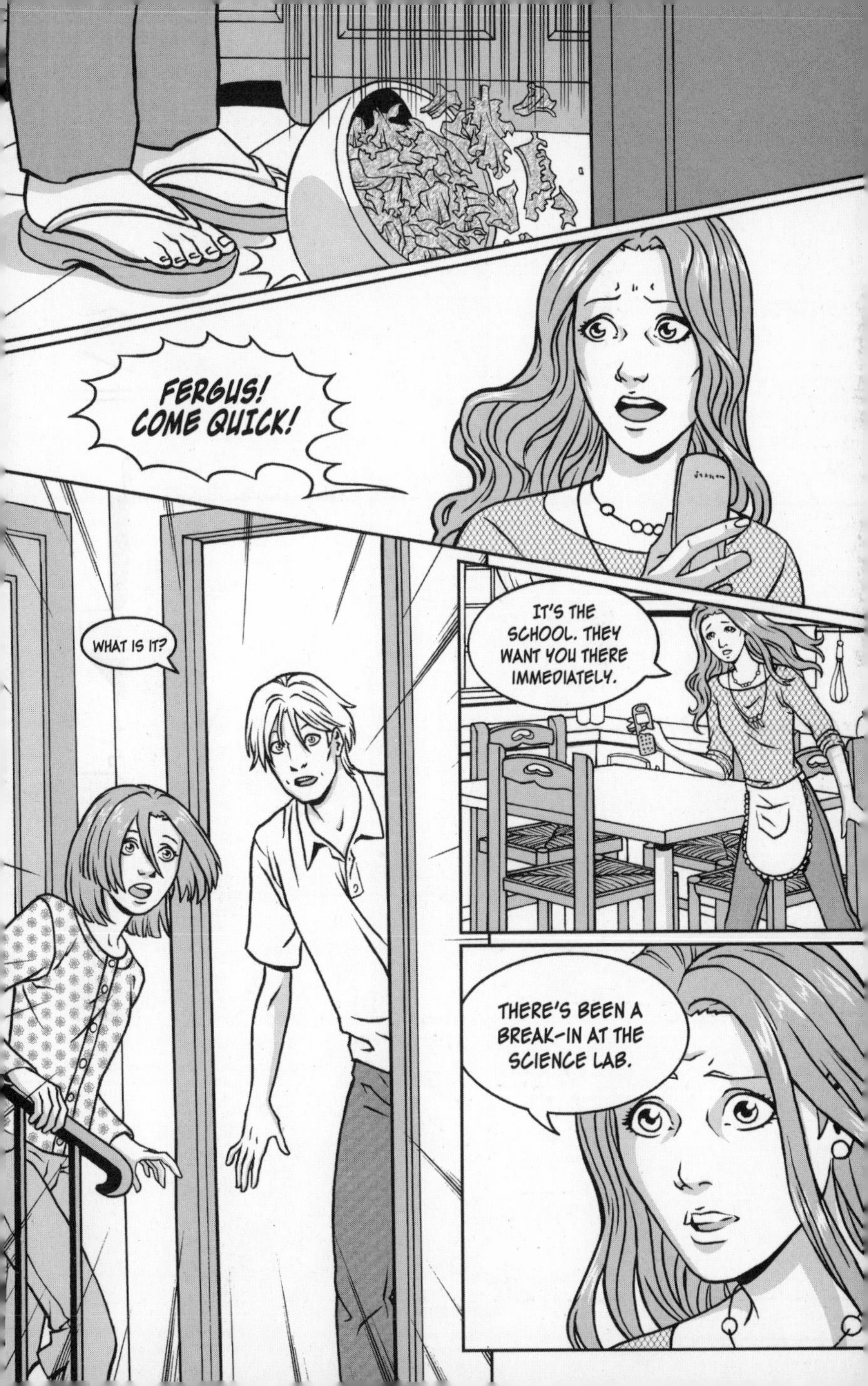
FERGUS! COME QUICK!
WHAT IS IT?
IT'S THE SCHOOL. THEY WANT YOU THERE IMMEDIATELY.
THERE'S BEEN A BREAK-IN AT THE SCIENCE LAB.

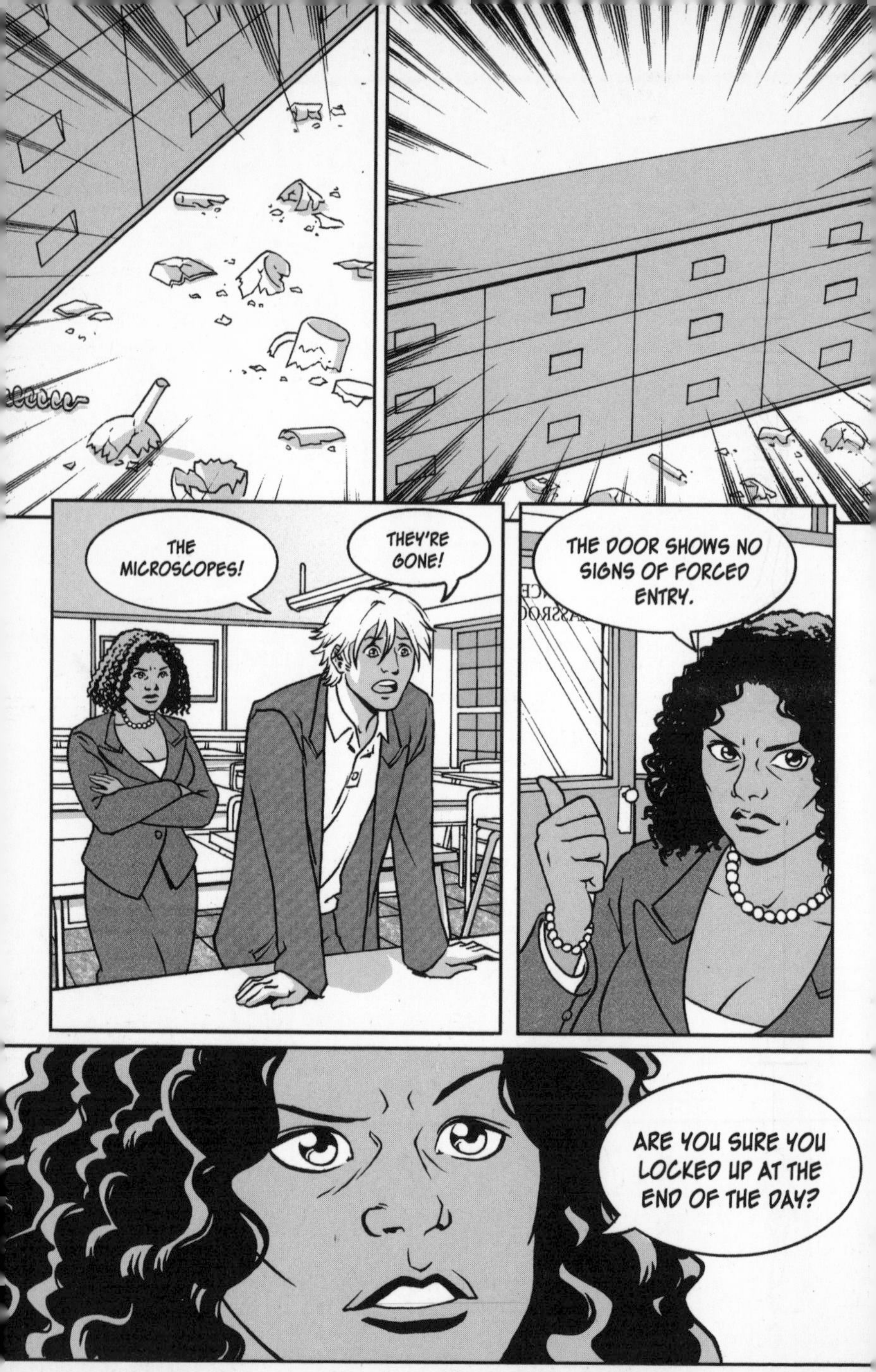
THE MICROSCOPES!
THEY'RE GONE!
THE DOOR SHOWS NO SIGNS OF FORCED ENTRY.
ARE YOU SURE YOU LOCKED UP AT THE END OF THE DAY?

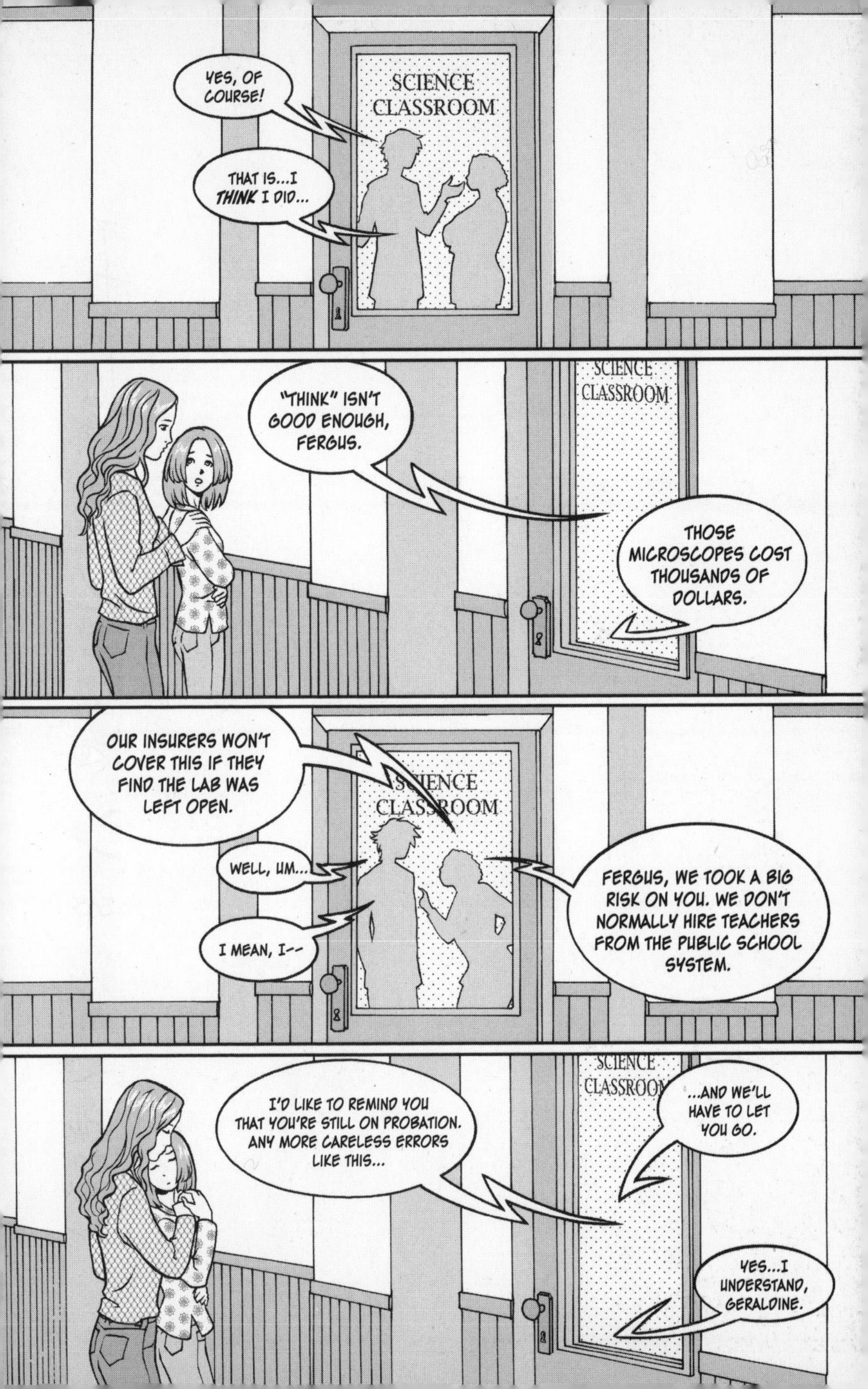
SCIENCE CLASSROOM
YES, OF COURSE!
THAT IS...I *THINK* I DID...
SCIENCE CLASSROOM
"THINK" ISN'T GOOD ENOUGH, FERGUS.
THOSE MICROSCOPES COST THOUSANDS OF DOLLARS.
OUR INSURERS WON'T COVER THIS IF THEY FIND THE LAB WAS LEFT OPEN.
SCIENCE CLASSROOM
WELL, UM...
I MEAN, I--
FERGUS, WE TOOK A BIG RISK ON YOU. WE DON'T NORMALLY HIRE TEACHERS FROM THE PUBLIC SCHOOL SYSTEM.
I'D LIKE TO REMIND YOU THAT YOU'RE STILL ON PROBATION. ANY MORE CARELESS ERRORS LIKE THIS...
SCIENCE CLASSROOM
...AND WE'LL HAVE TO LET YOU GO.
YES...I UNDERSTAND, GERALDINE.

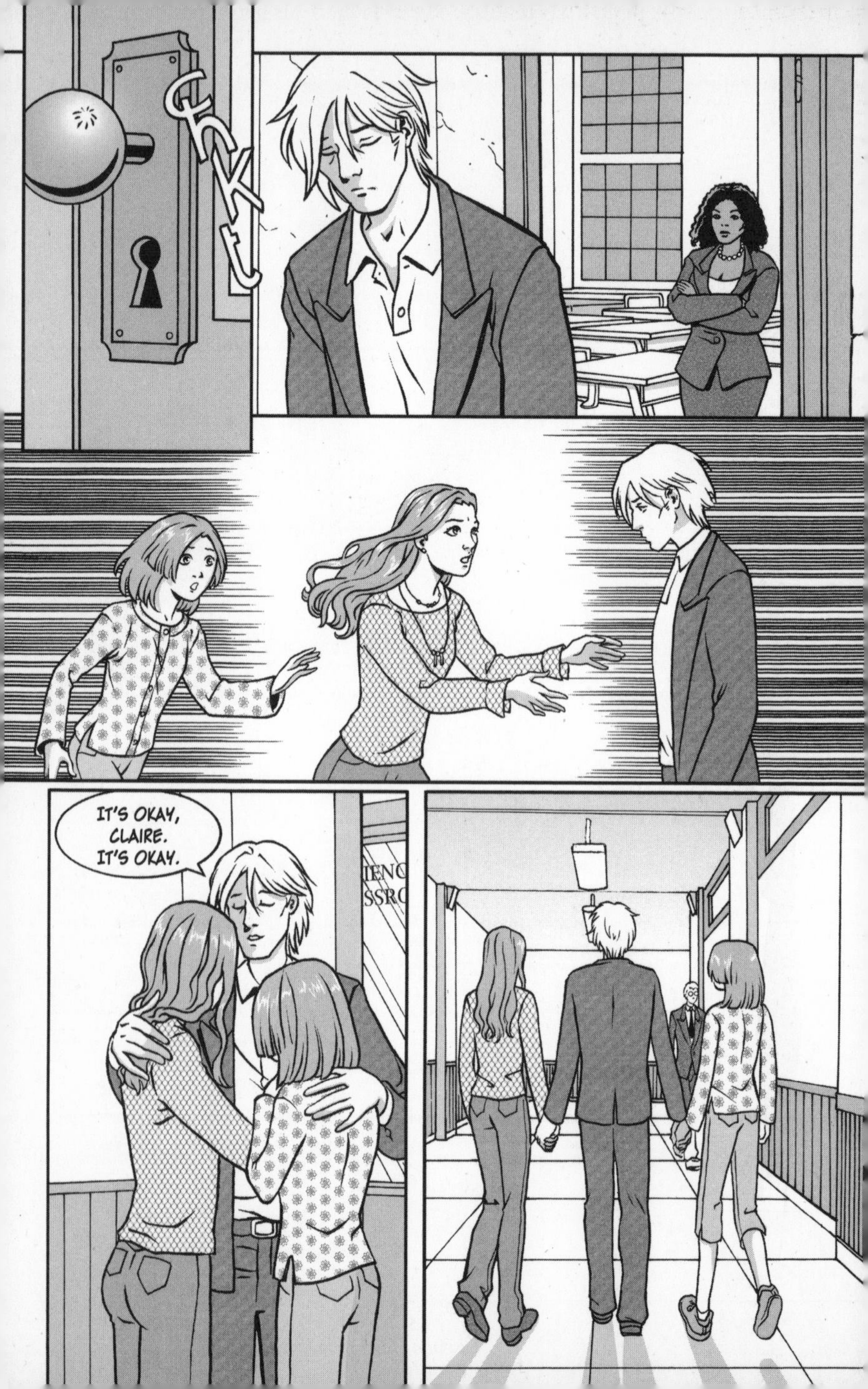
chkt
IT'S OKAY, CLAIRE. IT'S OKAY.

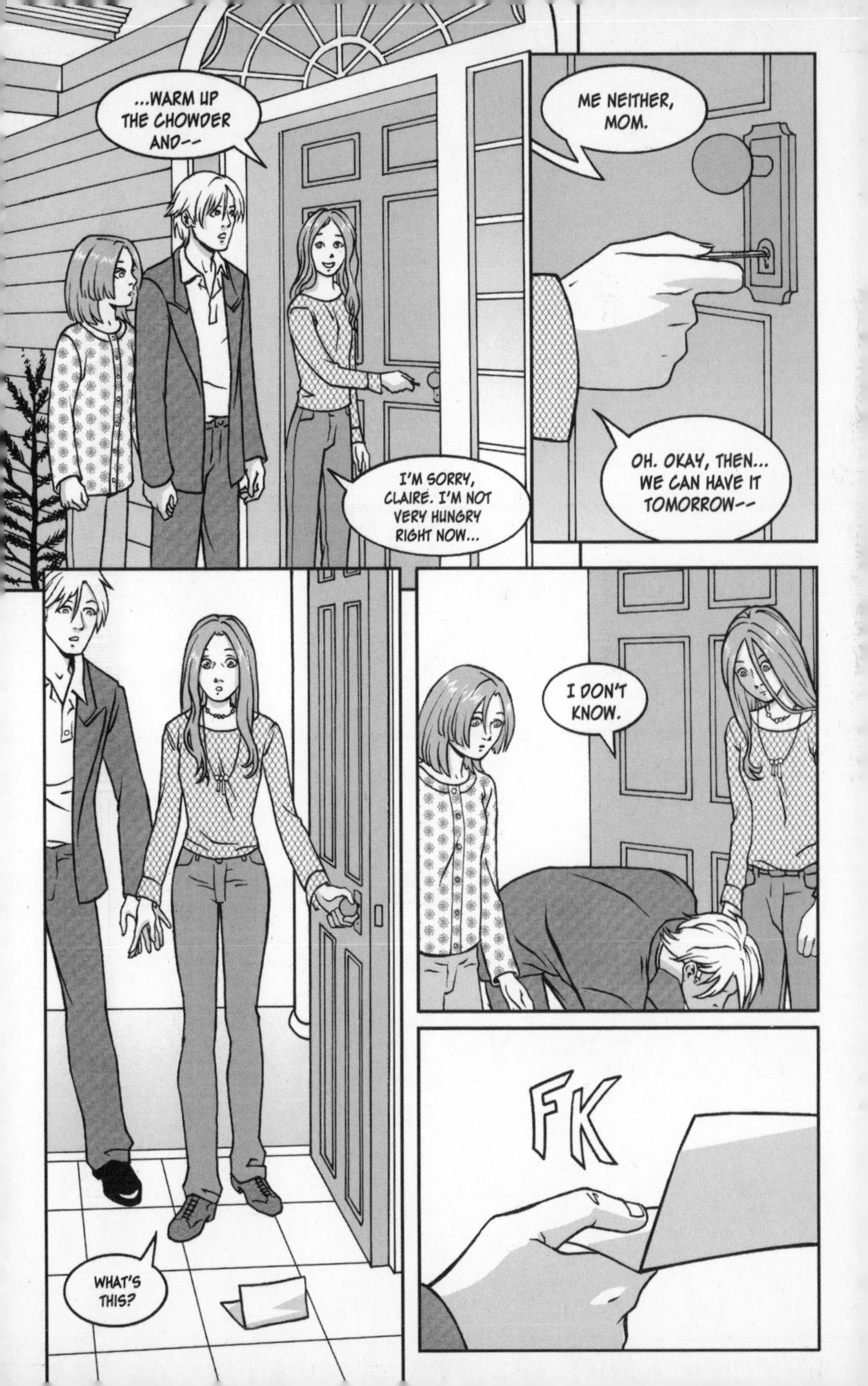
...WARM UP THE CHOWDER AND--
I'M SORRY, CLAIRE. I'M NOT VERY HUNGRY RIGHT NOW...
ME NEITHER, MOM.
OH. OKAY, THEN... WE CAN HAVE IT TOMORROW--
WHAT'S THIS?
I DON'T KNOW.
FK

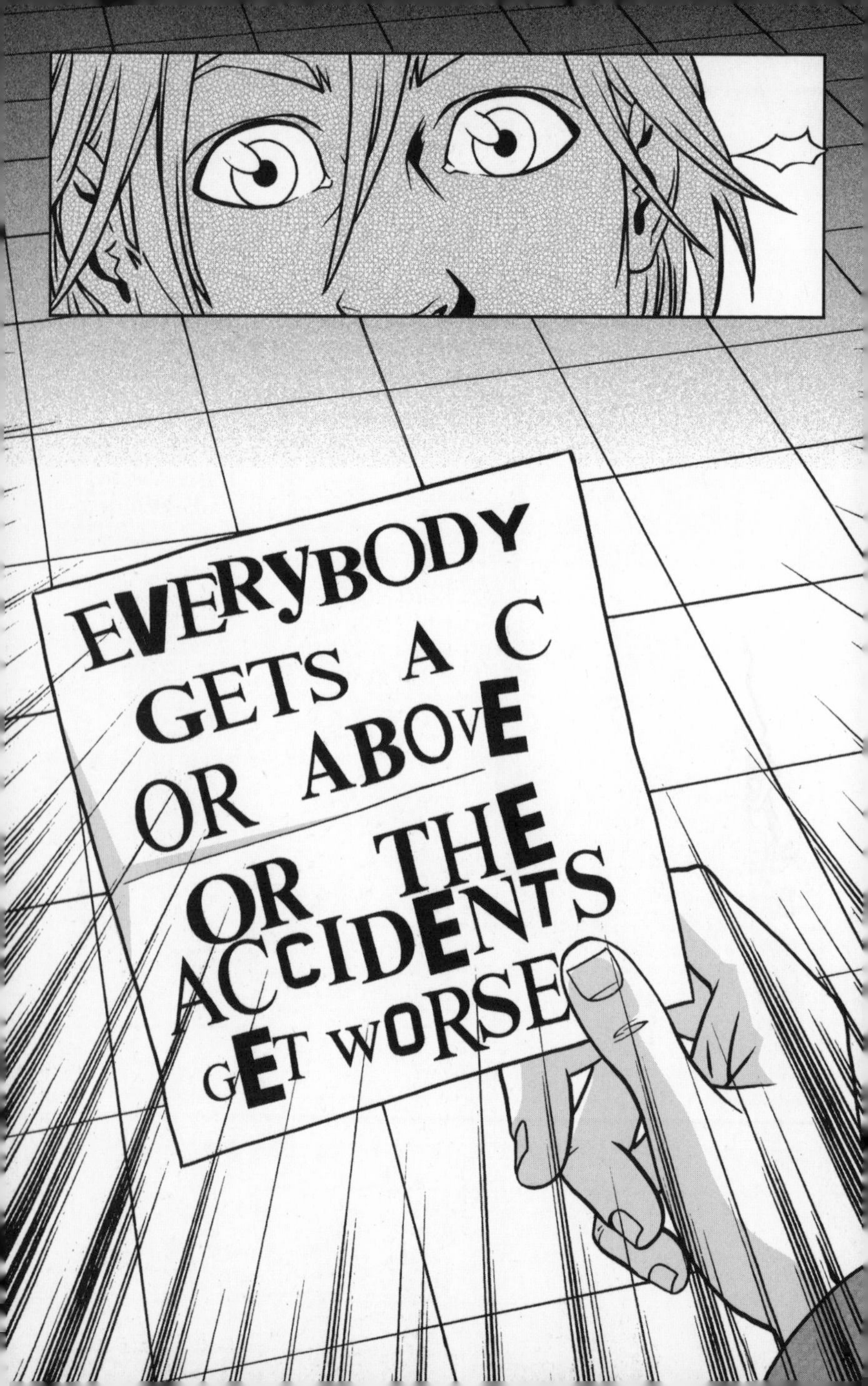
EVERYBODY GETS A C OR ABOVE OR THE ACCIDENTS GET WORSE

Chapter 3:
Blackmail

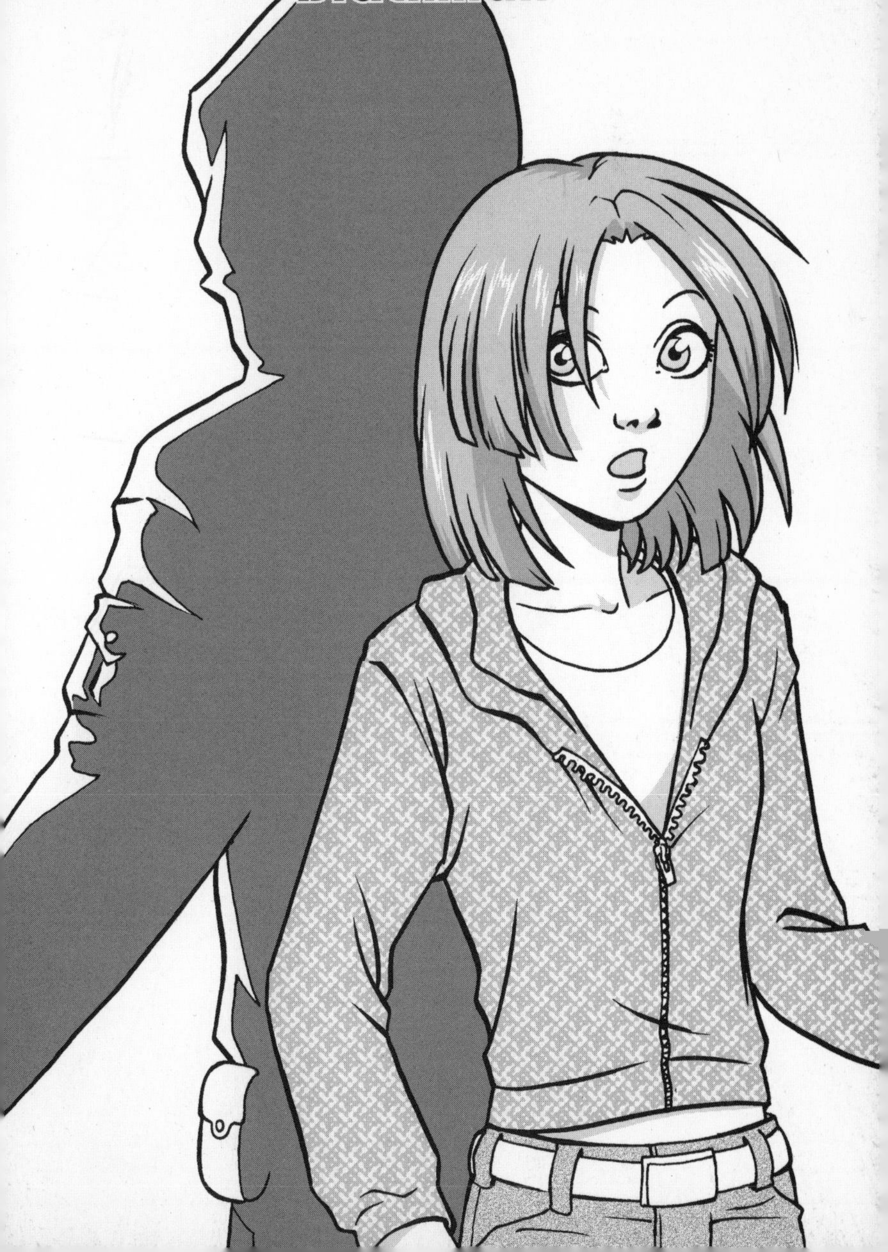

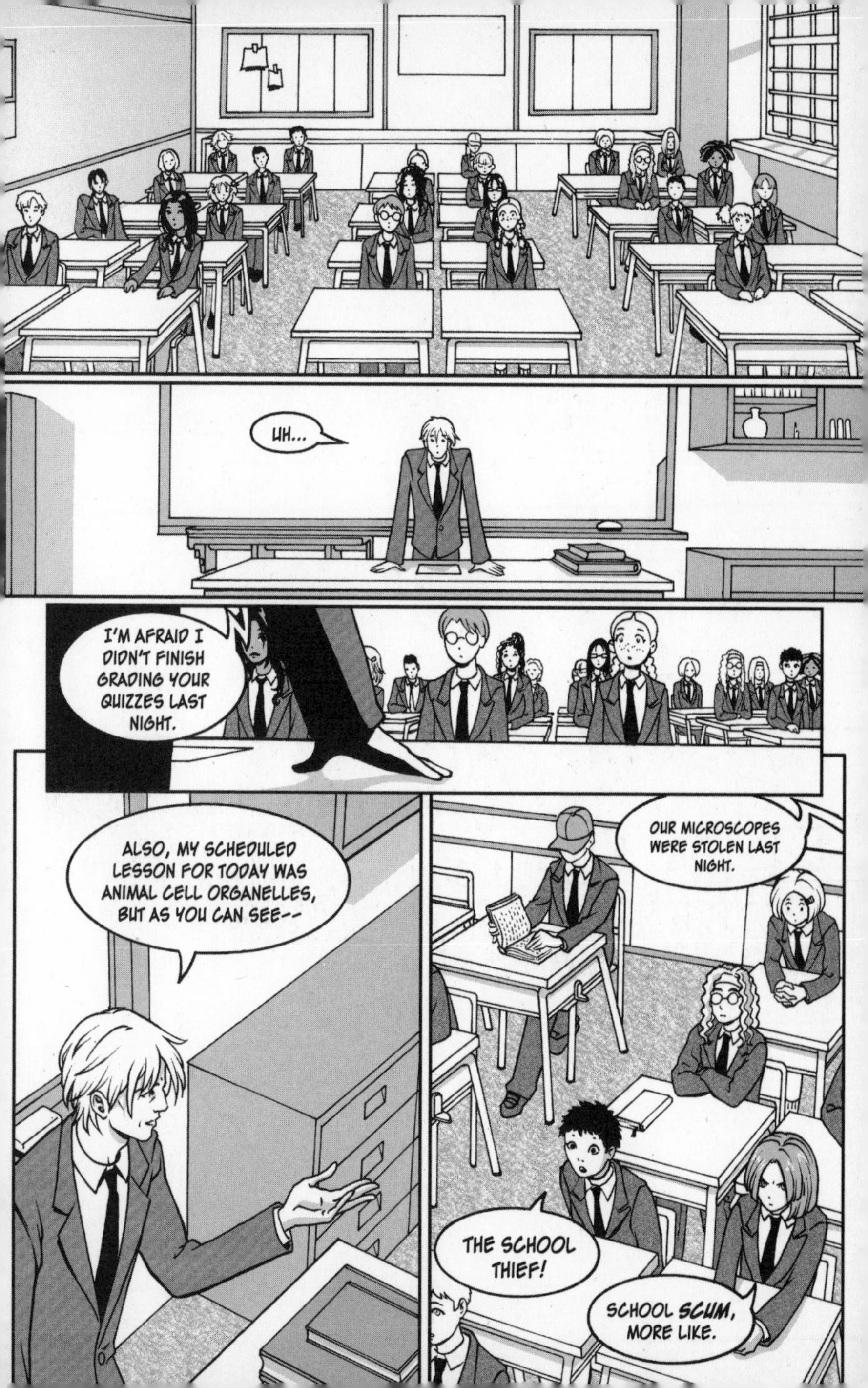
UH...
I'M AFRAID I DIDN'T FINISH GRADING YOUR QUIZZES LAST NIGHT.
ALSO, MY SCHEDULED LESSON FOR TODAY WAS ANIMAL CELL ORGANELLES, BUT AS YOU CAN SEE--
OUR MICROSCOPES WERE STOLEN LAST NIGHT.
THE SCHOOL THIEF!
SCHOOL **SCUM**, MORE LIKE.

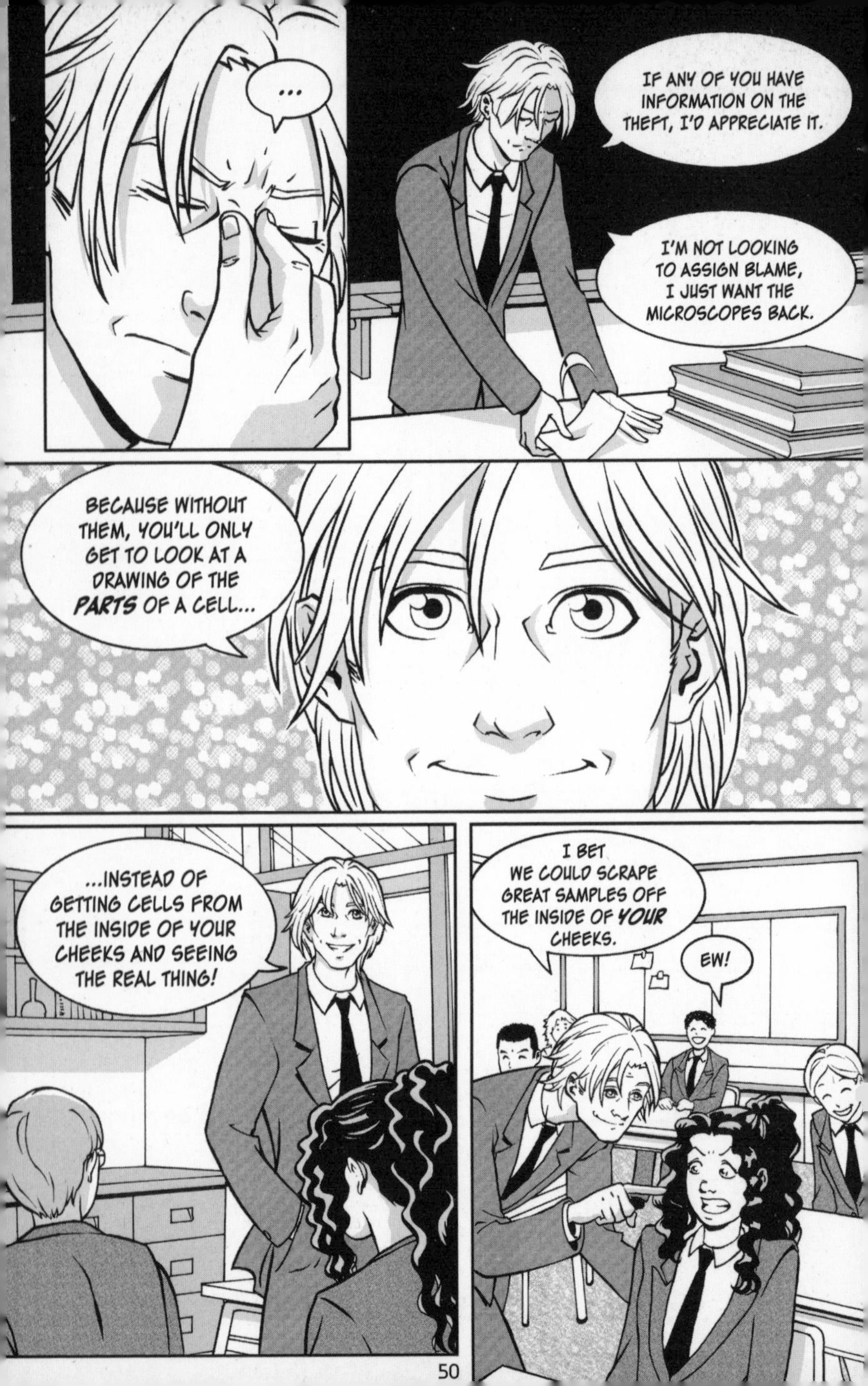
...
IF ANY OF YOU HAVE INFORMATION ON THE THEFT, I'D APPRECIATE IT.
I'M NOT LOOKING TO ASSIGN BLAME, I JUST WANT THE MICROSCOPES BACK.
BECAUSE WITHOUT THEM, YOU'LL ONLY GET TO LOOK AT A DRAWING OF THE *PARTS* OF A CELL...
...INSTEAD OF GETTING CELLS FROM THE INSIDE OF YOUR CHEEKS AND SEEING THE REAL THING!
I BET WE COULD SCRAPE GREAT SAMPLES OFF THE INSIDE OF *YOUR* CHEEKS.
EW!

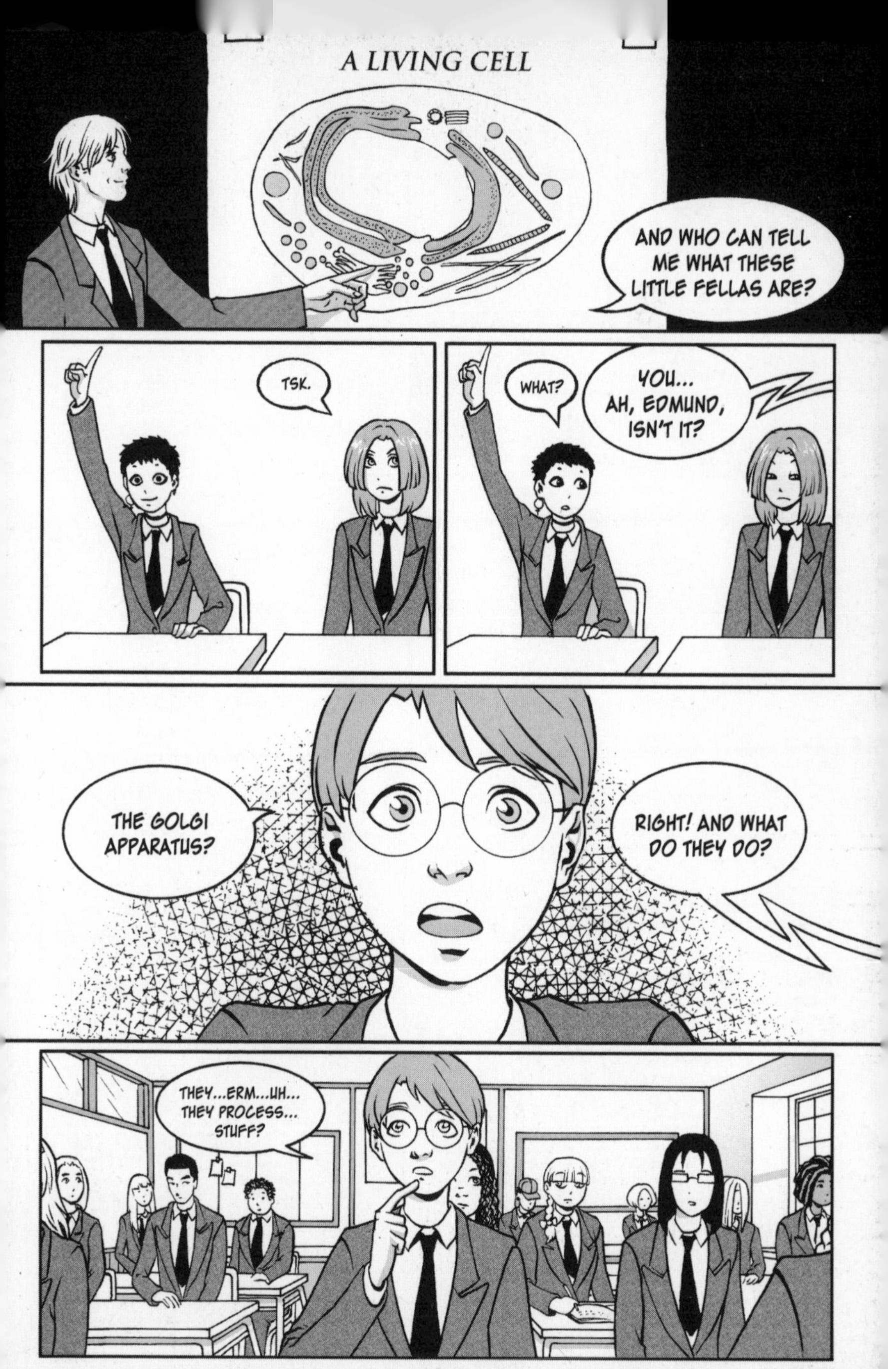
A LIVING CELL
AND WHO CAN TELL ME WHAT THESE LITTLE FELLAS ARE?
TSK.
WHAT?
YOU... AH, EDMUND, ISN'T IT?
THE GOLGI APPARATUS?
RIGHT! AND WHAT DO THEY DO?
THEY...ERM...UH... THEY PROCESS... STUFF?

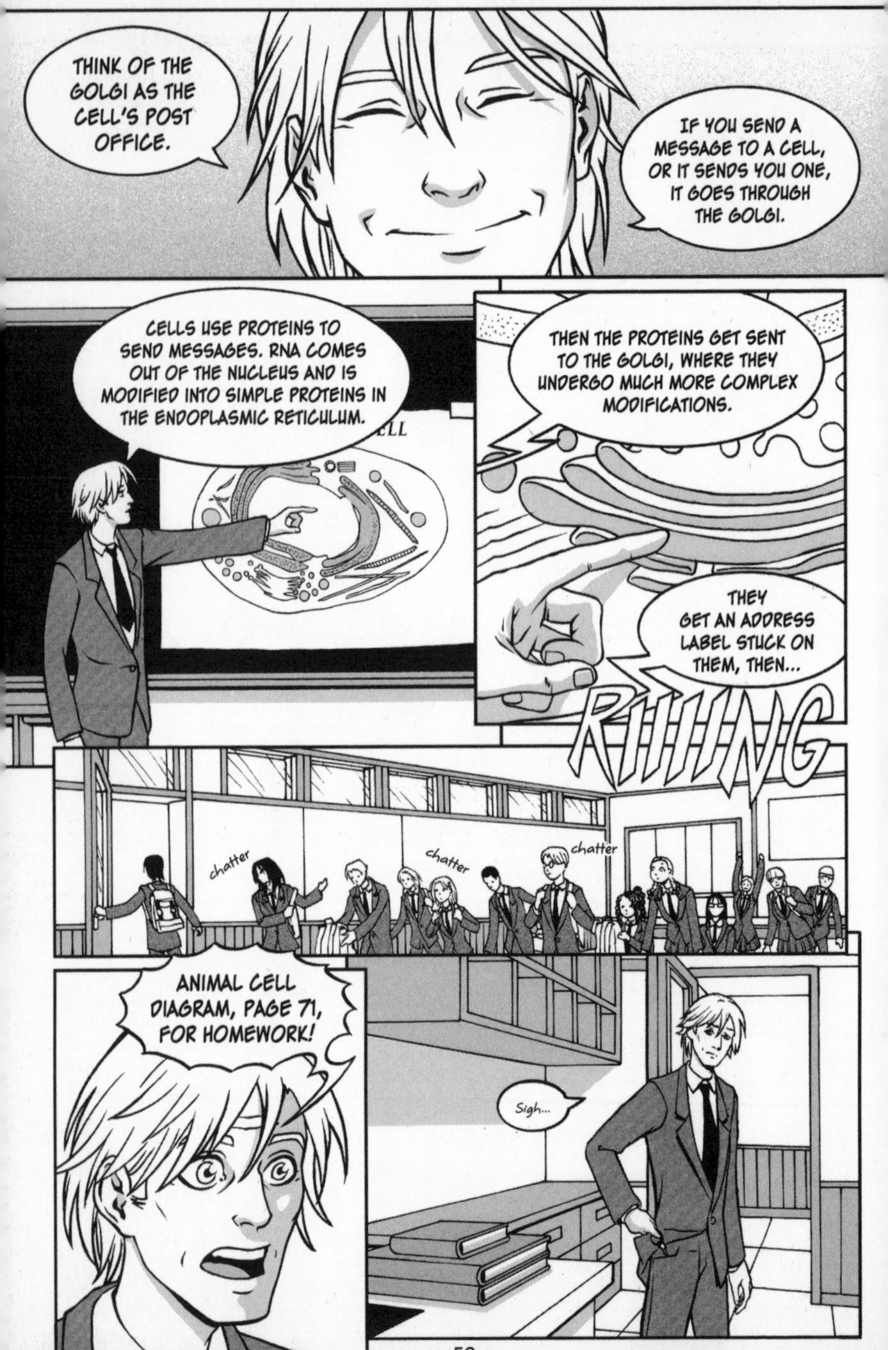
THINK OF THE GOLGI AS THE CELL'S POST OFFICE.
IF YOU SEND A MESSAGE TO A CELL, OR IT SENDS YOU ONE, IT GOES THROUGH THE GOLGI.
CELLS USE PROTEINS TO SEND MESSAGES. RNA COMES OUT OF THE NUCLEUS AND IS MODIFIED INTO SIMPLE PROTEINS IN THE ENDOPLASMIC RETICULUM.
THEN THE PROTEINS GET SENT TO THE GOLGI, WHERE THEY UNDERGO MUCH MORE COMPLEX MODIFICATIONS.
THEY GET AN ADDRESS LABEL STUCK ON THEM, THEN...
RIIING
chatter
chatter
chatter
ANIMAL CELL DIAGRAM, PAGE 71, FOR HOMEWORK!
Sigh...

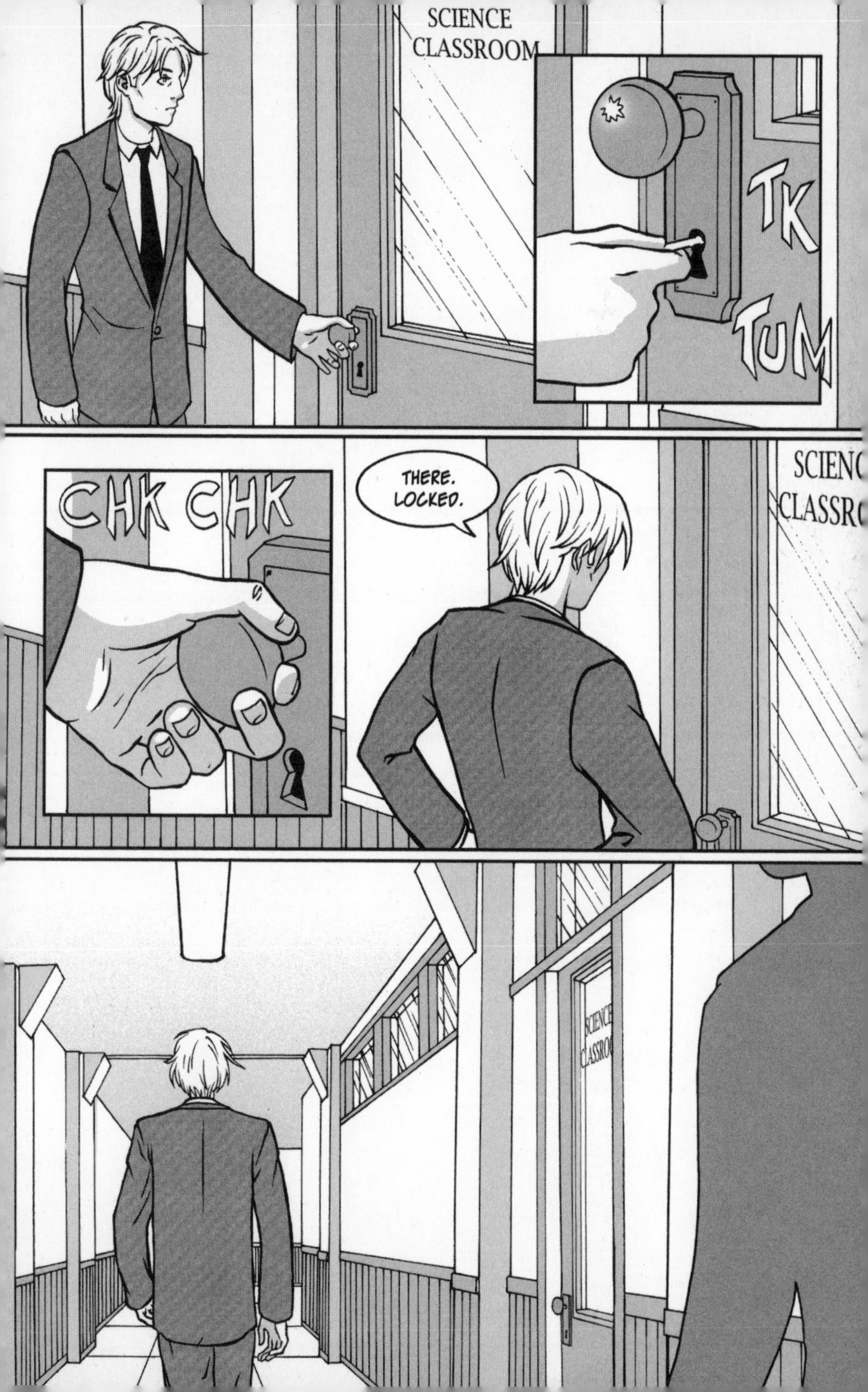
SCIENCE CLASSROOM
TK
TUM
CHK CHK
THERE. LOCKED.
SCIENC CLASSRO
SCIENCE CLASSROO

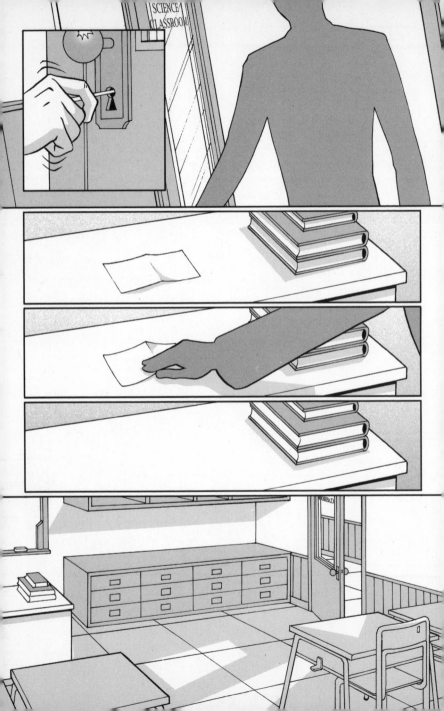

SCIENCE CLASSROOM

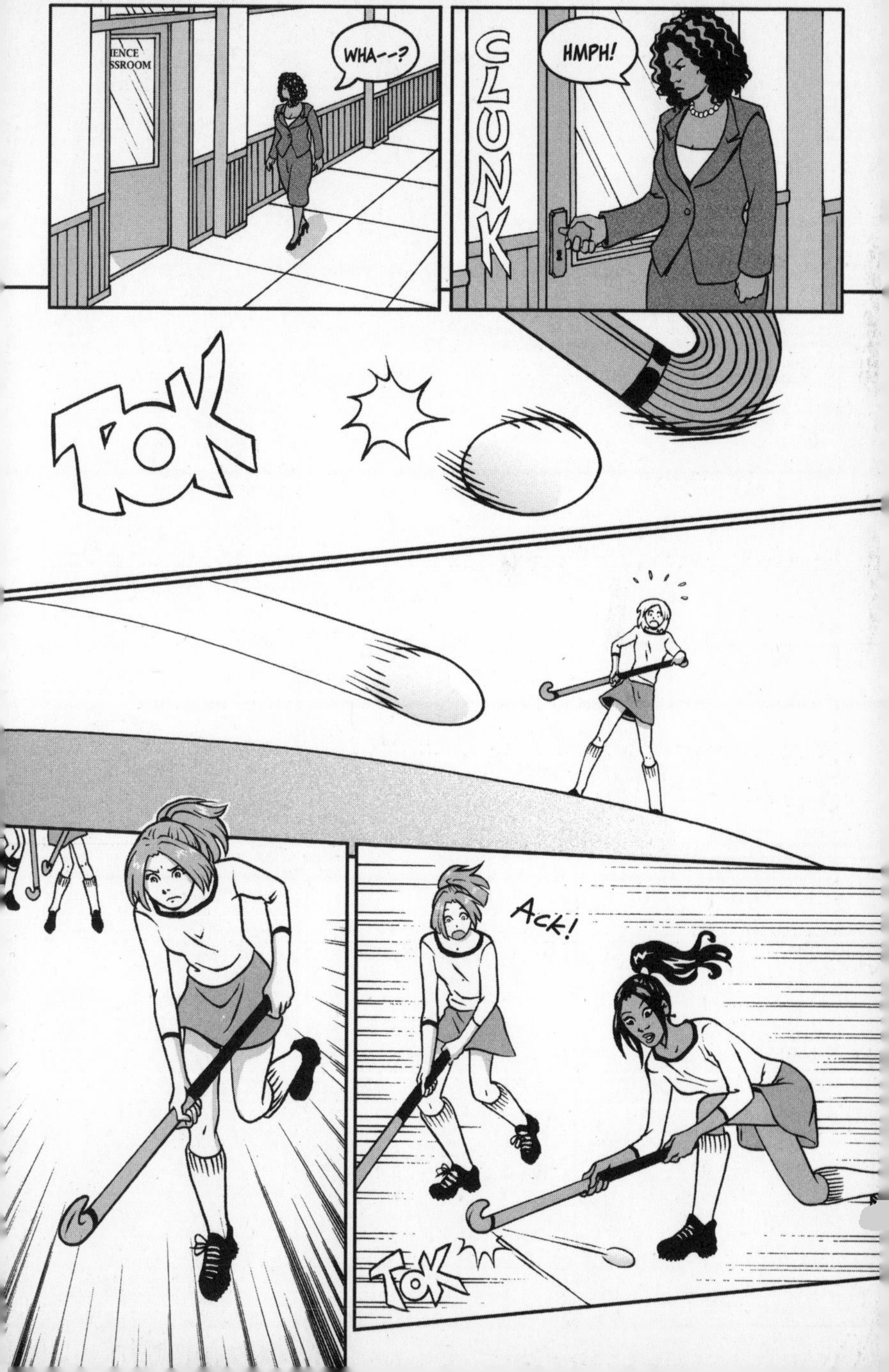
IENCE
SSROOM
WHA--?
CLUNK
HMPH!
TOK
Ack!
TOK

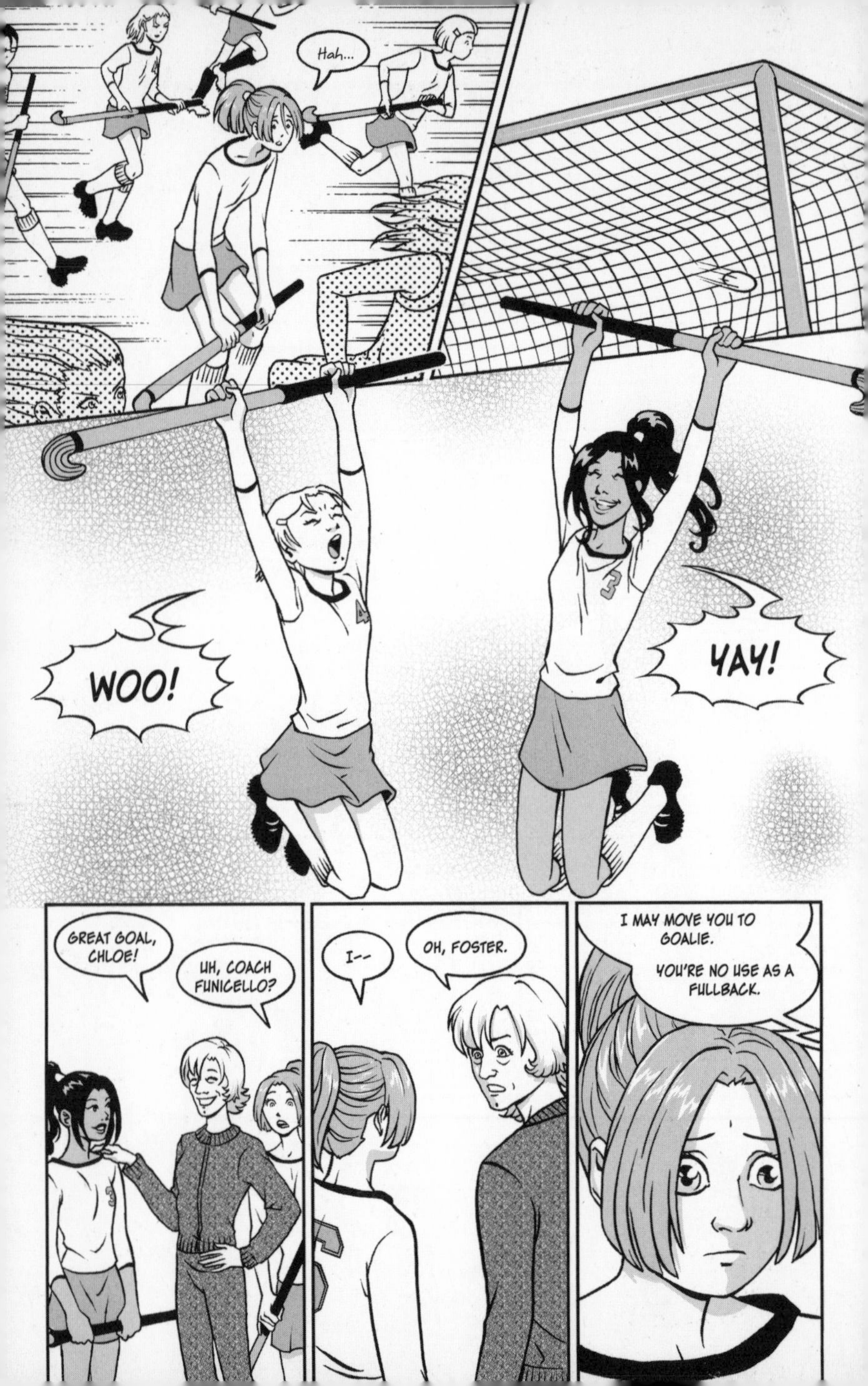
Hah...
WOO!
YAY!
GREAT GOAL, CHLOE!
UH, COACH FUNICELLO?
I--
OH, FOSTER.
I MAY MOVE YOU TO GOALIE.
YOU'RE NO USE AS A FULLBACK.

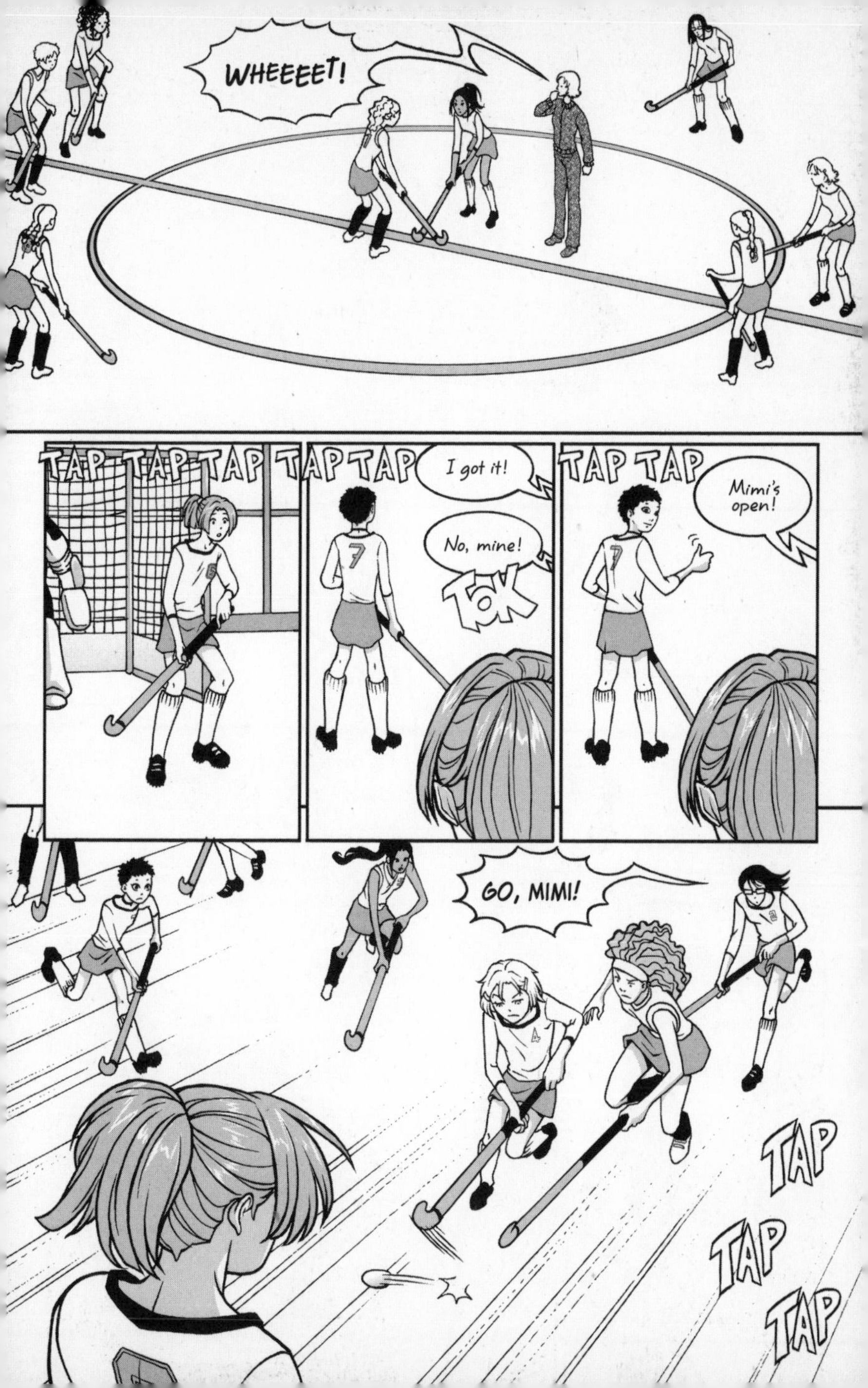
WHEEEET!
TAP TAP TAP TAP TAP
I got it!
No, mine!
TOK
TAP TAP
Mimi's open!
GO, MIMI!
TAP
TAP
TAP

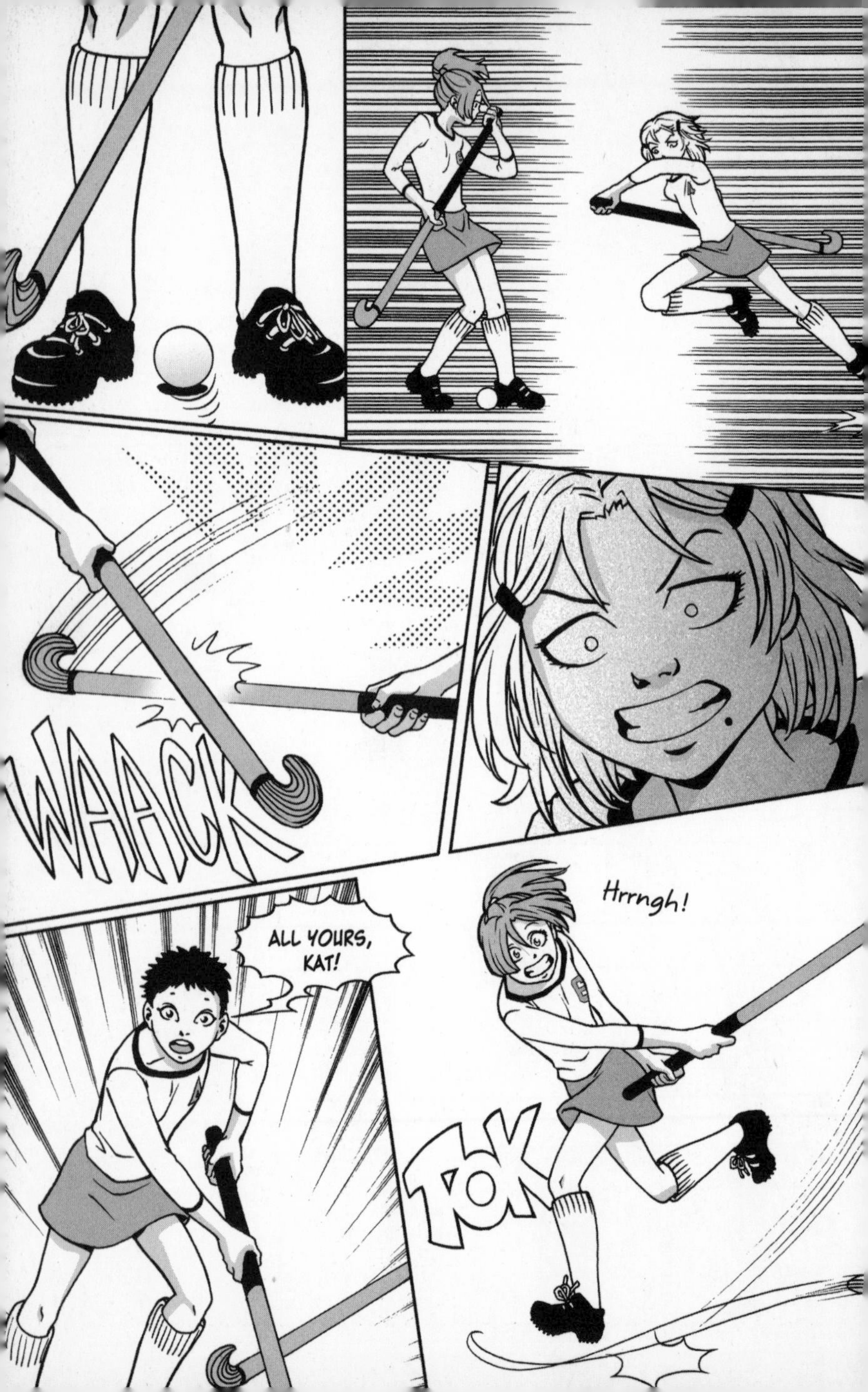
WAACK
ALL YOURS, KAT!
Hrrngh!
TOK

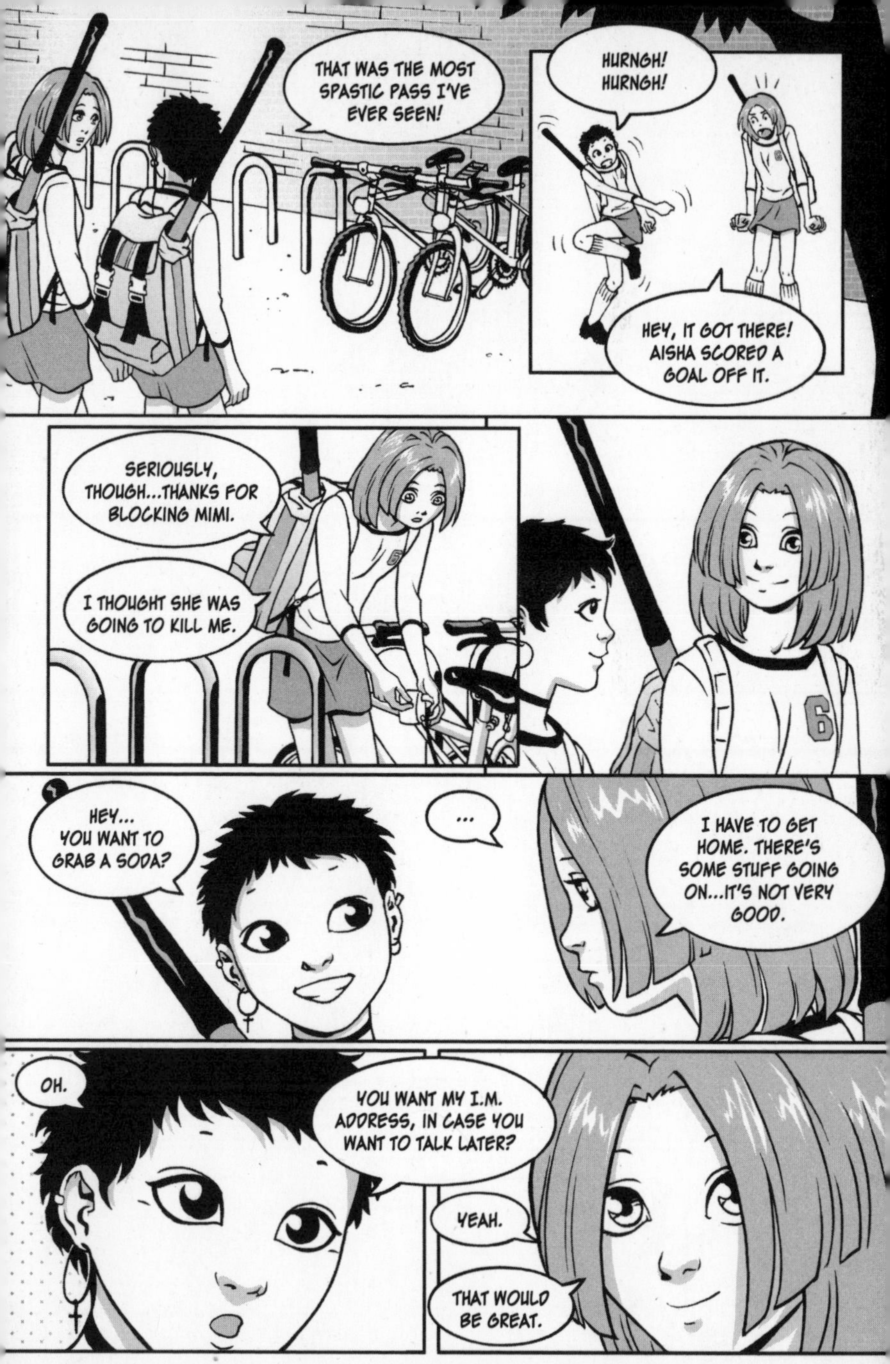
THAT WAS THE MOST SPASTIC PASS I'VE EVER SEEN!
HURNGH! HURNGH!
HEY, IT GOT THERE! AISHA SCORED A GOAL OFF IT.
SERIOUSLY, THOUGH...THANKS FOR BLOCKING MIMI.
I THOUGHT SHE WAS GOING TO KILL ME.
HEY... YOU WANT TO GRAB A SODA?
...
I HAVE TO GET HOME. THERE'S SOME STUFF GOING ON...IT'S NOT VERY GOOD.
OH.
YOU WANT MY I.M. ADDRESS, IN CASE YOU WANT TO TALK LATER?
YEAH.
THAT WOULD BE GREAT.

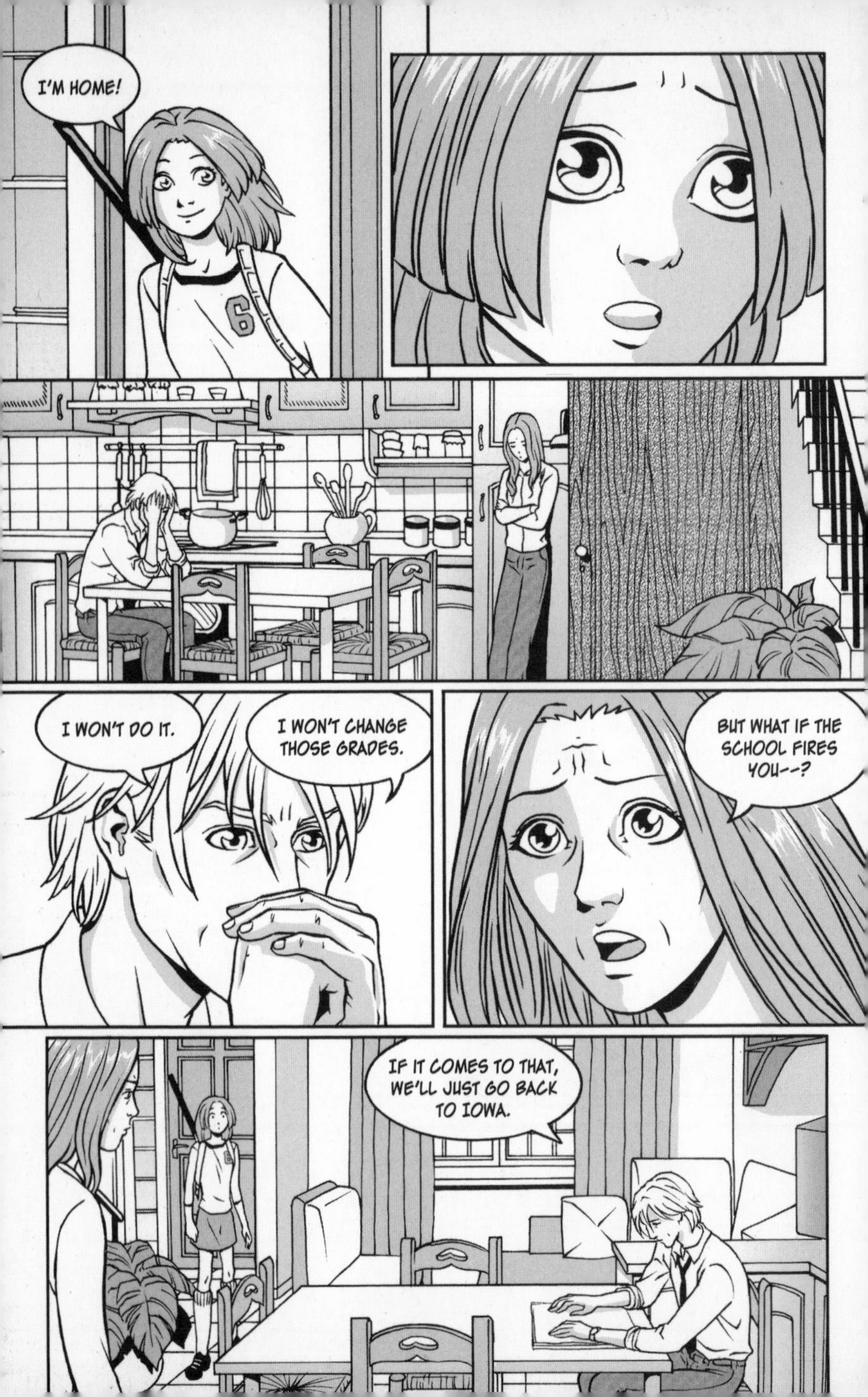
I'M HOME!
I WON'T DO IT.
I WON'T CHANGE THOSE GRADES.
BUT WHAT IF THE SCHOOL FIRES YOU--?
IF IT COMES TO THAT, WE'LL JUST GO BACK TO IOWA.

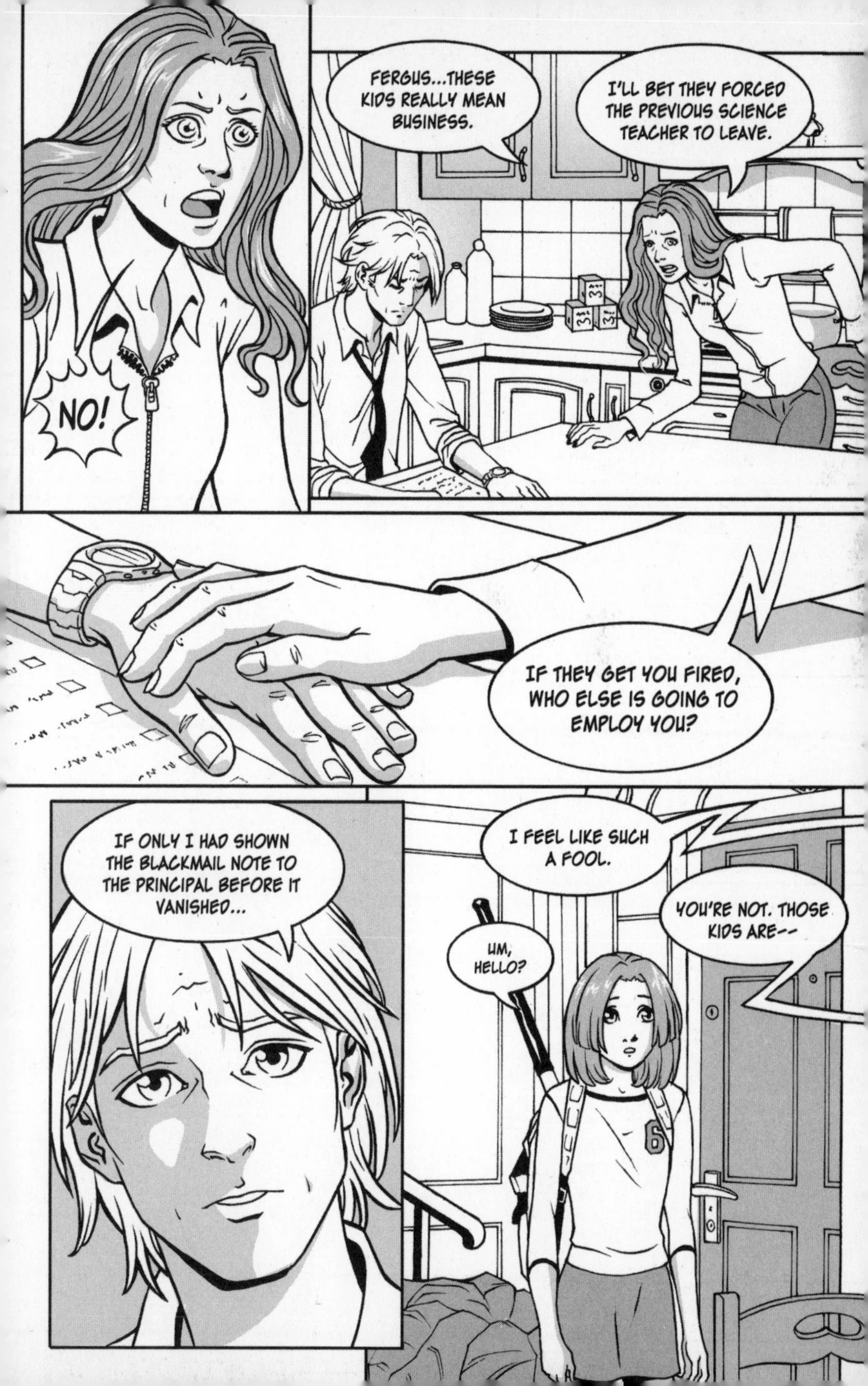
NO!
FERGUS...THESE KIDS REALLY MEAN BUSINESS.
I'LL BET THEY FORCED THE PREVIOUS SCIENCE TEACHER TO LEAVE.
IF THEY GET YOU FIRED, WHO ELSE IS GOING TO EMPLOY YOU?
IF ONLY I HAD SHOWN THE BLACKMAIL NOTE TO THE PRINCIPAL BEFORE IT VANISHED...
I FEEL LIKE SUCH A FOOL.
YOU'RE NOT. THOSE KIDS ARE--
UM, HELLO?

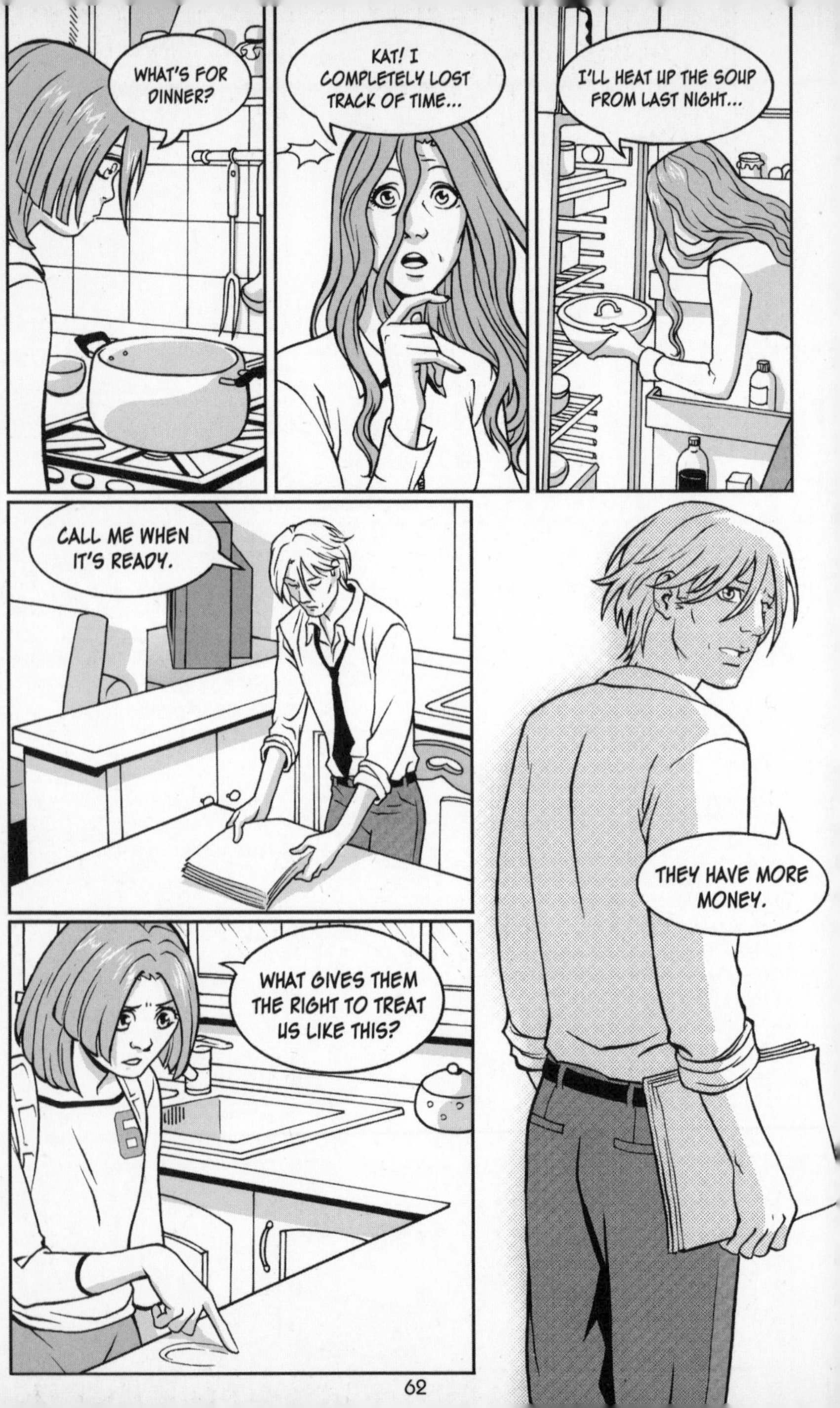
WHAT'S FOR DINNER?
KAT! I COMPLETELY LOST TRACK OF TIME...
I'LL HEAT UP THE SOUP FROM LAST NIGHT...
CALL ME WHEN IT'S READY.
THEY HAVE MORE MONEY.
WHAT GIVES THEM THE RIGHT TO TREAT US LIKE THIS?

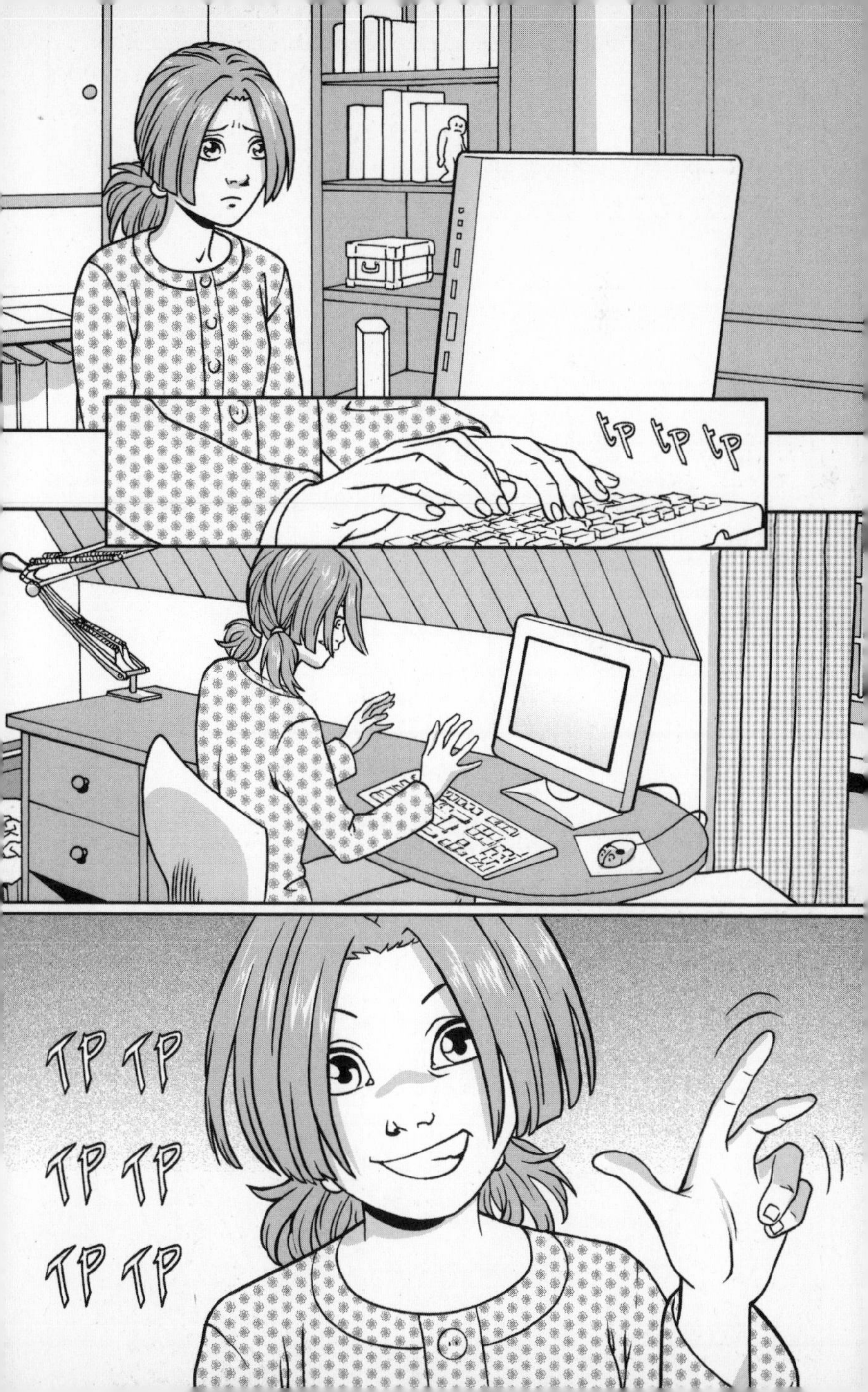
tp tp tp
TP TP
TP TP
TP TP

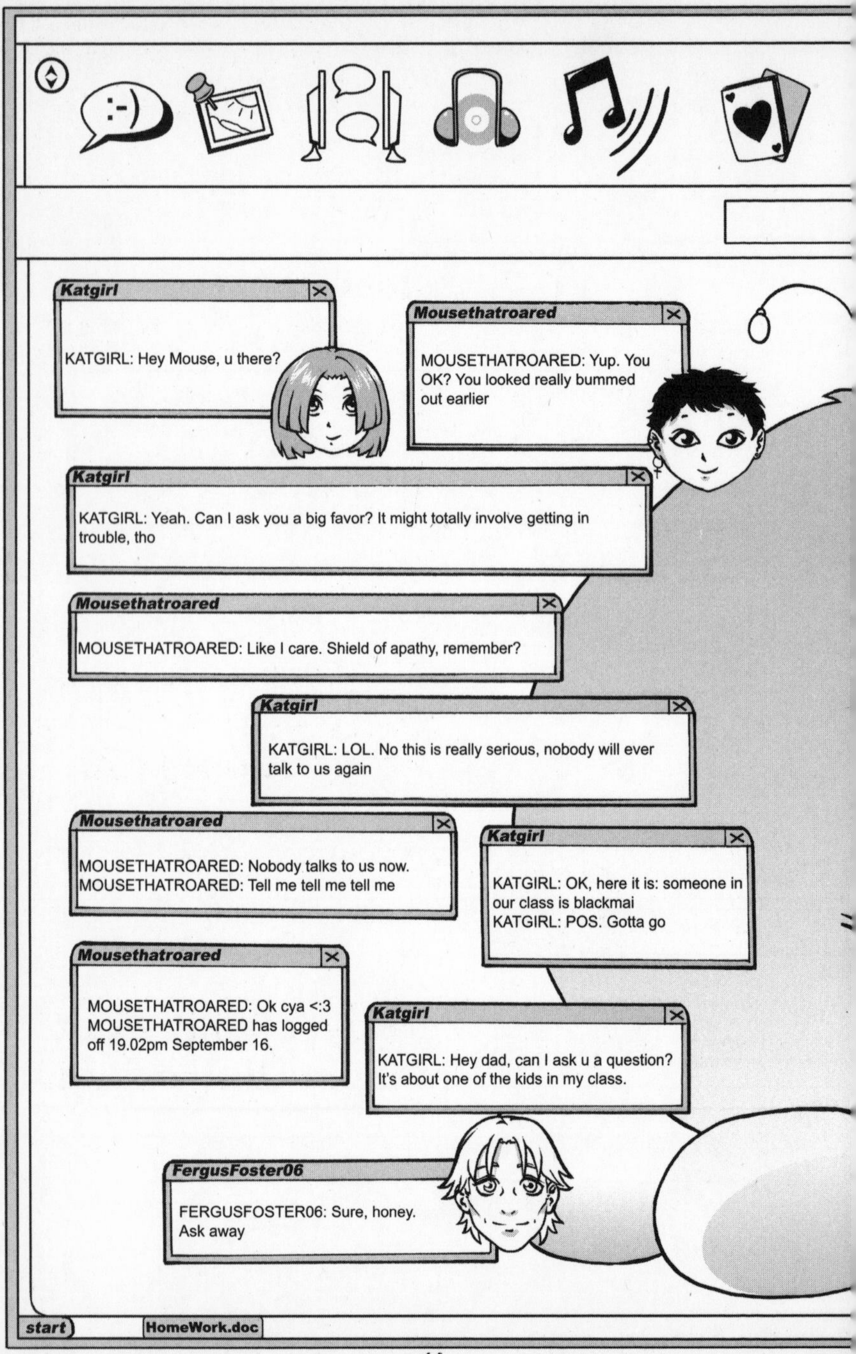

Katgirl

KATGIRL: Hey Mouse, u there?

Mousethatroared

MOUSETHATROARED: Yup. You OK? You looked really bummed out earlier

Katgirl

KATGIRL: Yeah. Can I ask you a big favor? It might totally involve getting in trouble, tho

Mousethatroared

MOUSETHATROARED: Like I care. Shield of apathy, remember?

Katgirl

KATGIRL: LOL. No this is really serious, nobody will ever talk to us again

Mousethatroared

MOUSETHATROARED: Nobody talks to us now.
MOUSETHATROARED: Tell me tell me tell me

Katgirl

KATGIRL: OK, here it is: someone in our class is blackmai
KATGIRL: POS. Gotta go

Mousethatroared

MOUSETHATROARED: Ok cya <:3
MOUSETHATROARED has logged off 19.02pm September 16.

Katgirl

KATGIRL: Hey dad, can I ask u a question? It's about one of the kids in my class.

FergusFoster06

FERGUSFOSTER06: Sure, honey. Ask away

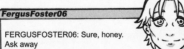

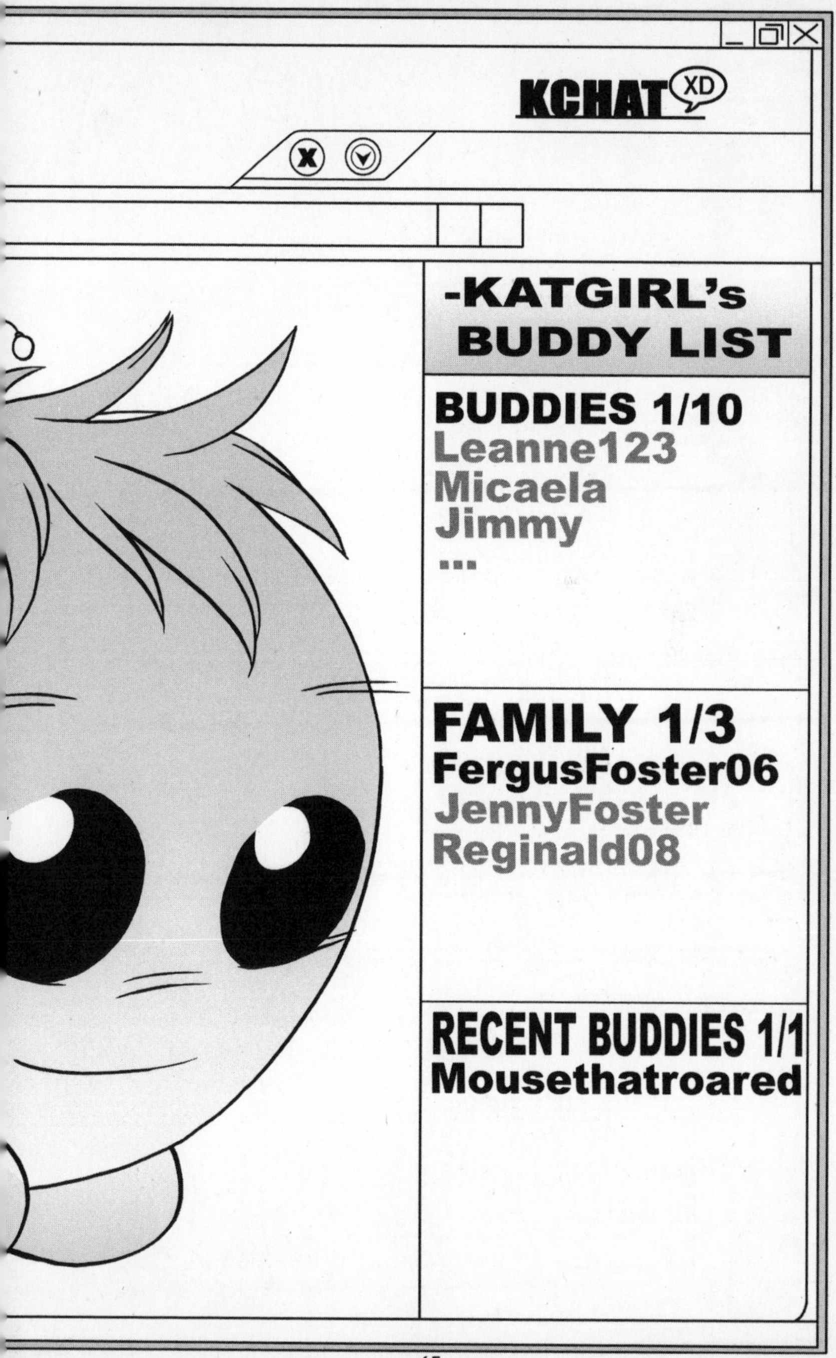
KCHAT XD
-KATGIRL's BUDDY LIST
BUDDIES 1/10
Leanne123
Micaela
Jimmy
...
FAMILY 1/3
FergusFoster06
JennyFoster
Reginald08
RECENT BUDDIES 1/1
Mousethatroared

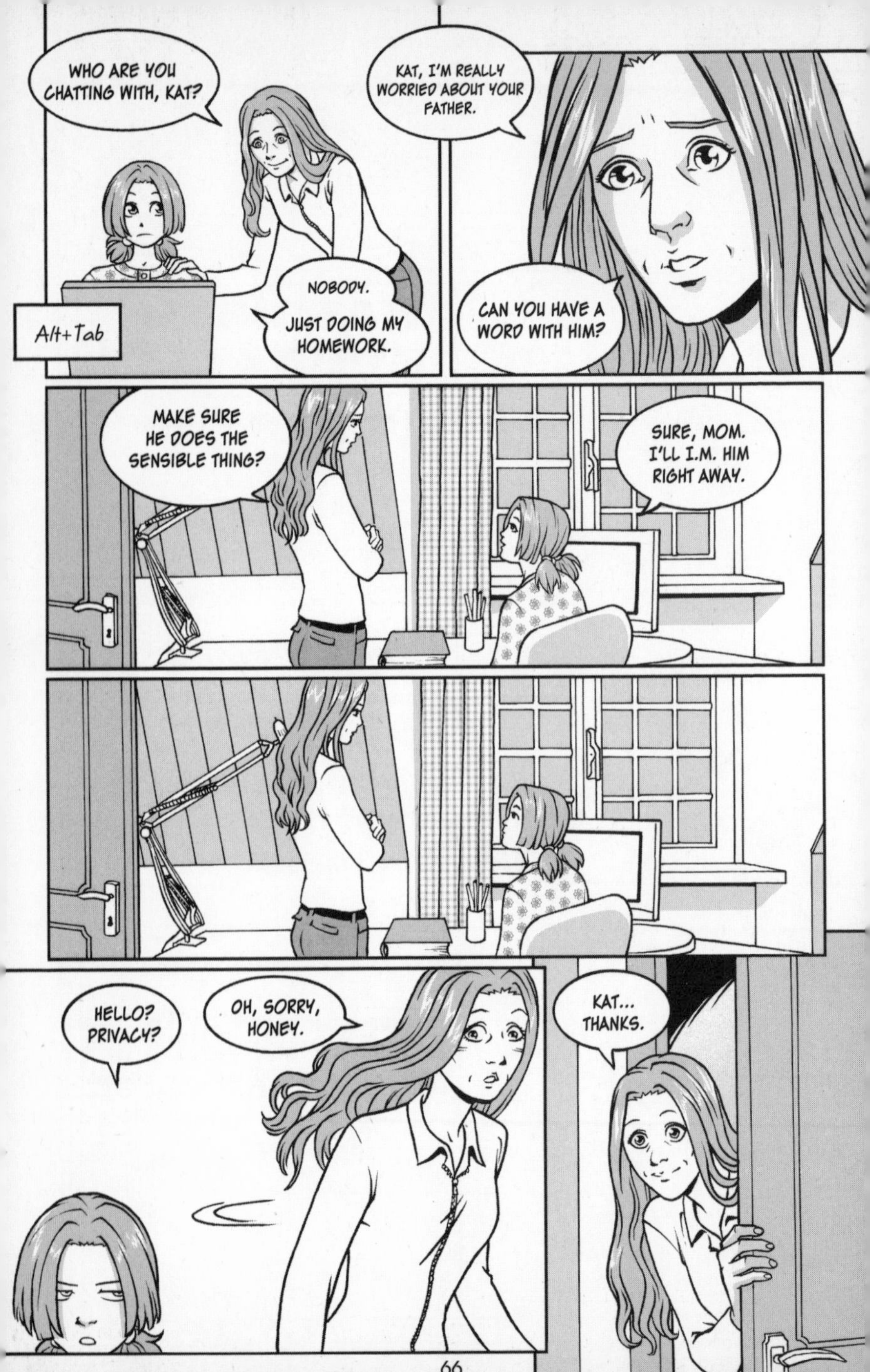
WHO ARE YOU CHATTING WITH, KAT?
Alt+Tab
NOBODY.
JUST DOING MY HOMEWORK.
KAT, I'M REALLY WORRIED ABOUT YOUR FATHER.
CAN YOU HAVE A WORD WITH HIM?
MAKE SURE HE DOES THE SENSIBLE THING?
SURE, MOM. I'LL I.M. HIM RIGHT AWAY.
HELLO? PRIVACY?
OH, SORRY, HONEY.
KAT... THANKS.

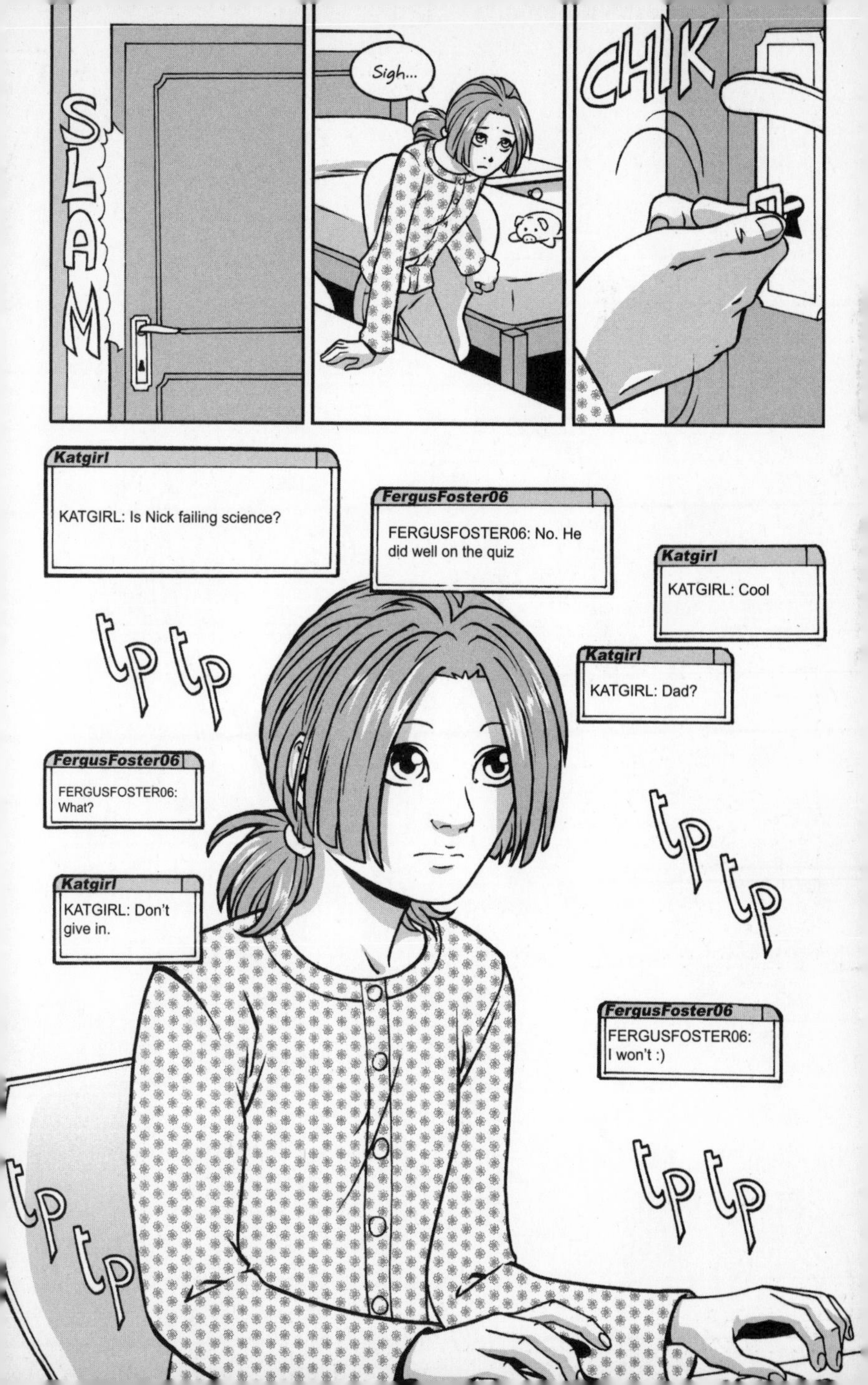
SLAM
Sigh...
CHIK
Katgirl
KATGIRL: Is Nick failing science?
FergusFoster06
FERGUSFOSTER06: No. He did well on the quiz
Katgirl
KATGIRL: Cool
tp tp
Katgirl
KATGIRL: Dad?
FergusFoster06
FERGUSFOSTER06: What?
tp tp
Katgirl
KATGIRL: Don't give in.
FergusFoster06
FERGUSFOSTER06: I won't :)
tp tp
tp tp

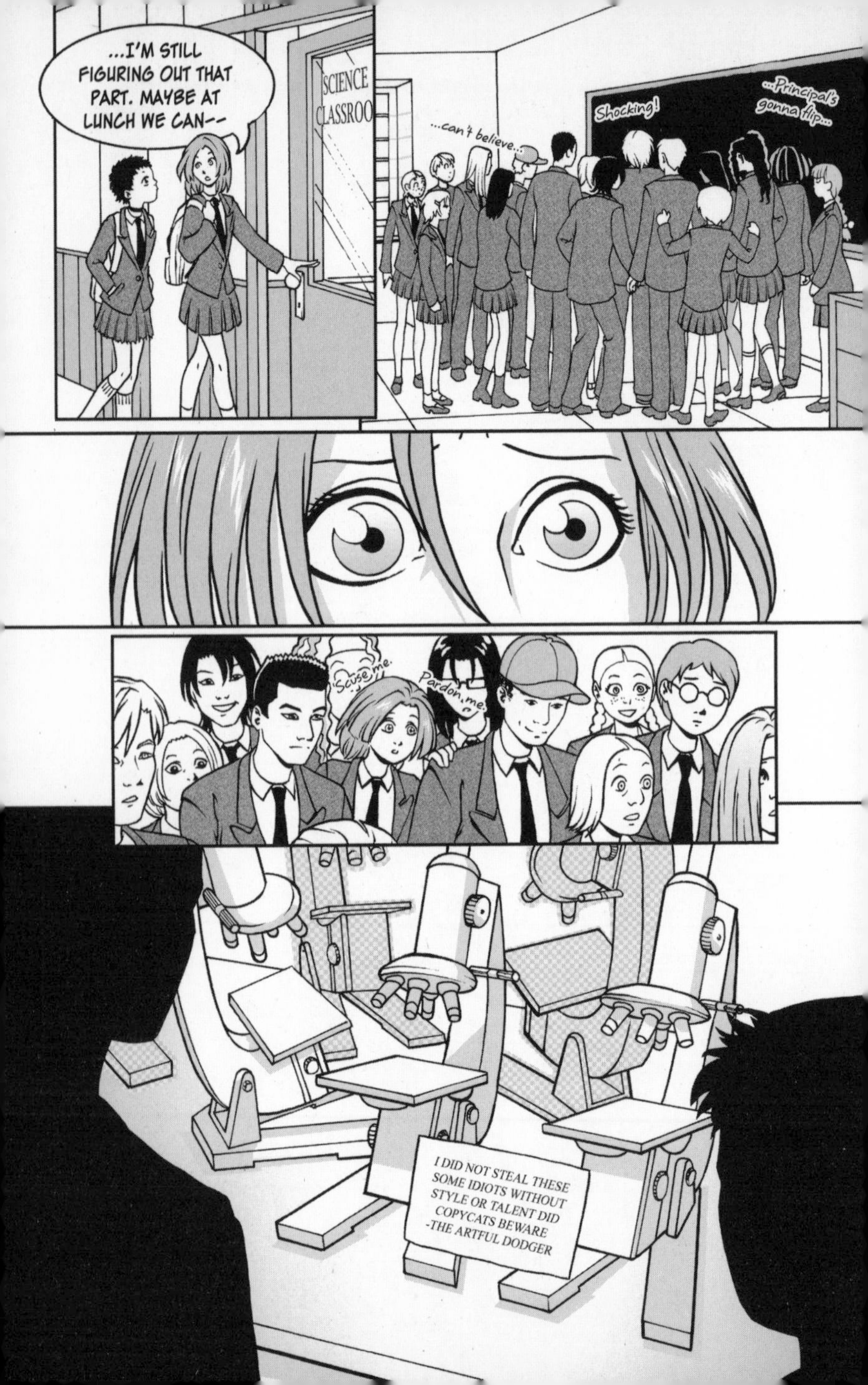
...I'M STILL FIGURING OUT THAT PART. MAYBE AT LUNCH WE CAN--
SCIENCE CLASSROO
...can't believe...
Shocking!
...Principal's gonna flip...
'Scuse me.
Pardon me.
I DID NOT STEAL THESE
SOME IDIOTS WITHOUT
STYLE OR TALENT DID
COPYCATS BEWARE
-THE ARTFUL DODGER

Chapter 4:
The Sting

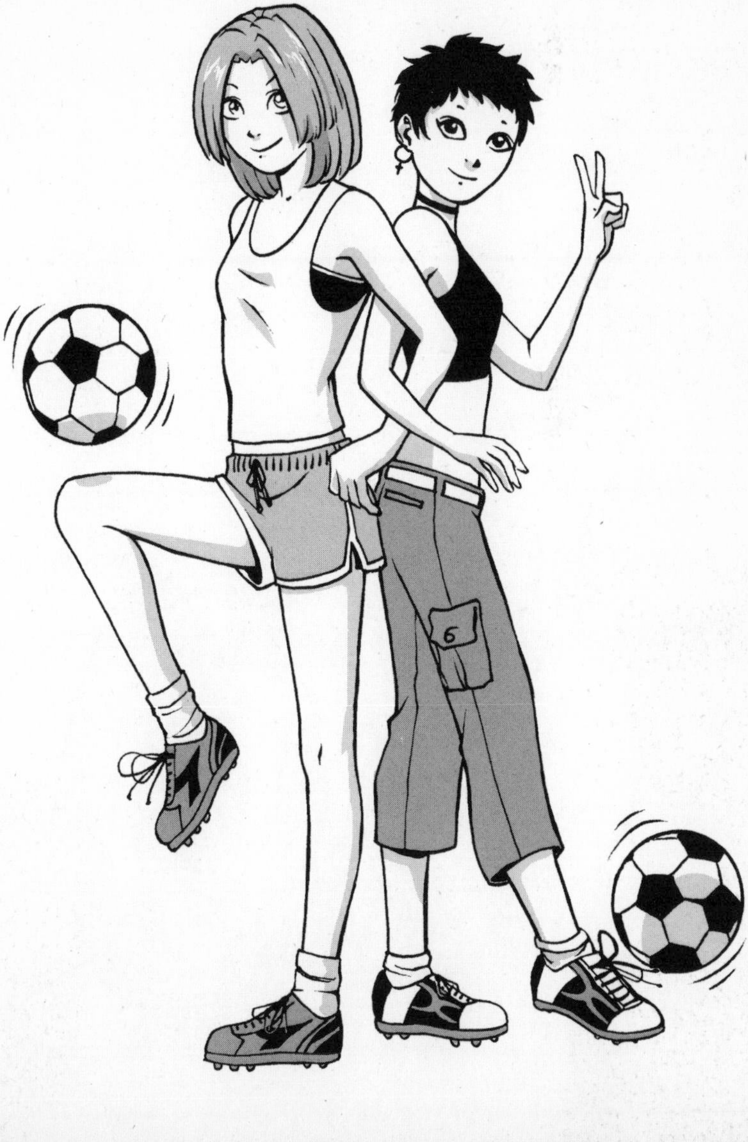

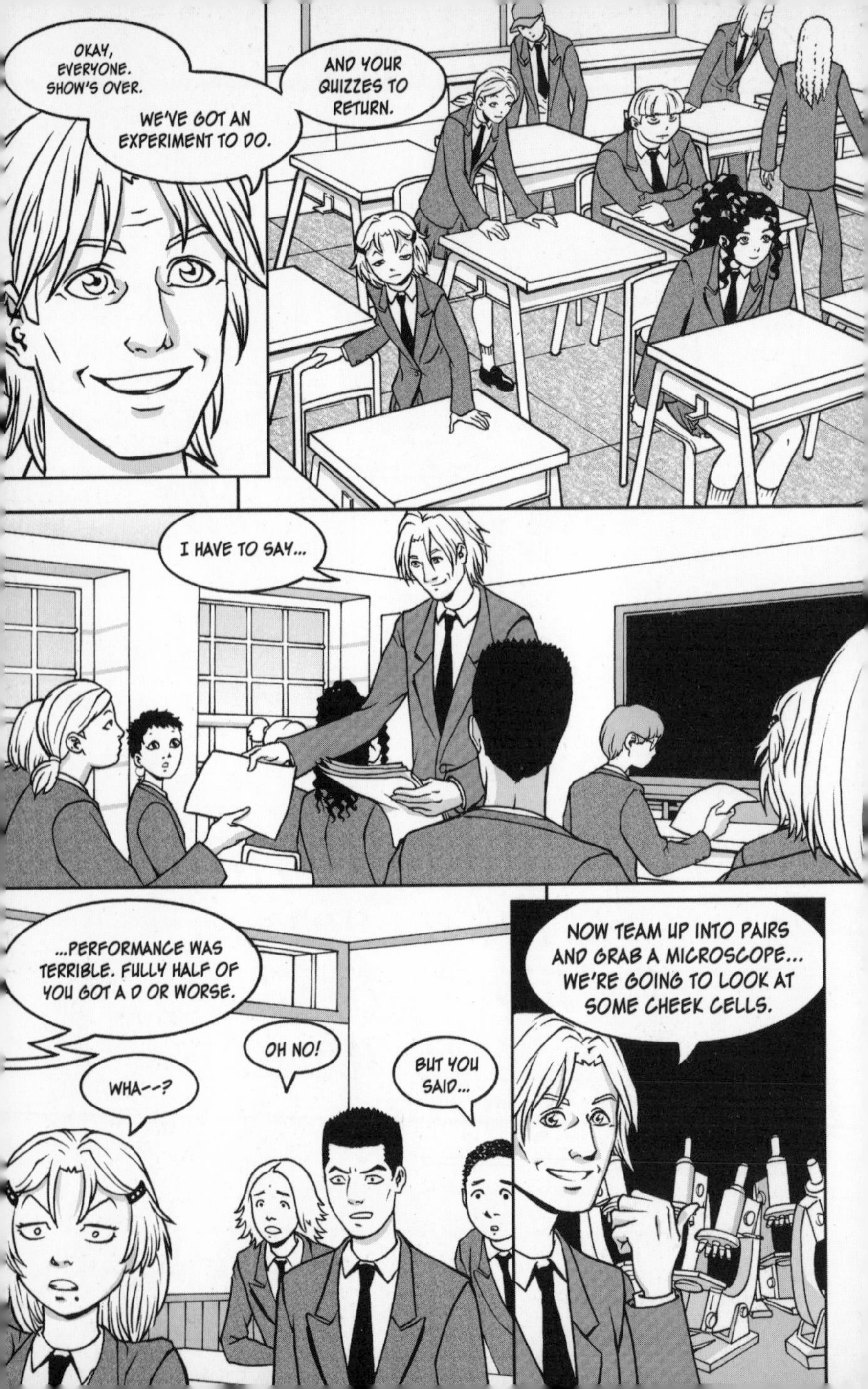
OKAY, EVERYONE. SHOW'S OVER.
WE'VE GOT AN EXPERIMENT TO DO.
AND YOUR QUIZZES TO RETURN.
I HAVE TO SAY...
...PERFORMANCE WAS TERRIBLE. FULLY HALF OF YOU GOT A D OR WORSE.
OH NO!
WHA--?
BUT YOU SAID...
NOW TEAM UP INTO PAIRS AND GRAB A MICROSCOPE... WE'RE GOING TO LOOK AT SOME CHEEK CELLS.

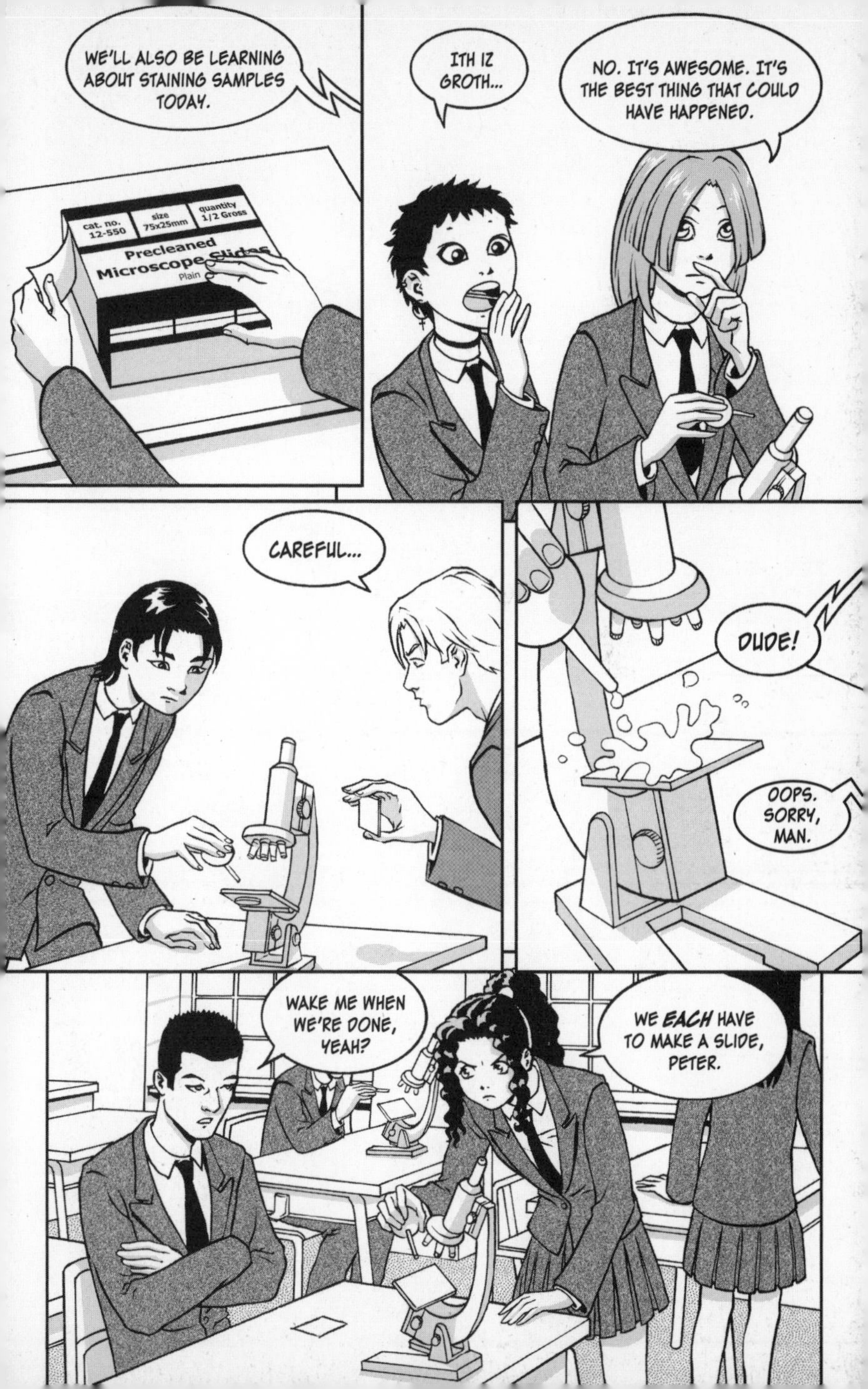
WE'LL ALSO BE LEARNING ABOUT STAINING SAMPLES TODAY.
cat. no. 12-550
size 75x25mm
quantity 1/2 Gross
Precleaned
Microscope Slides
Plain
ITH IZ GROTH...
NO. IT'S AWESOME. IT'S THE BEST THING THAT COULD HAVE HAPPENED.
CAREFUL...
DUDE!
OOPS. SORRY, MAN.
WAKE ME WHEN WE'RE DONE, YEAH?
WE *EACH* HAVE TO MAKE A SLIDE, PETER.

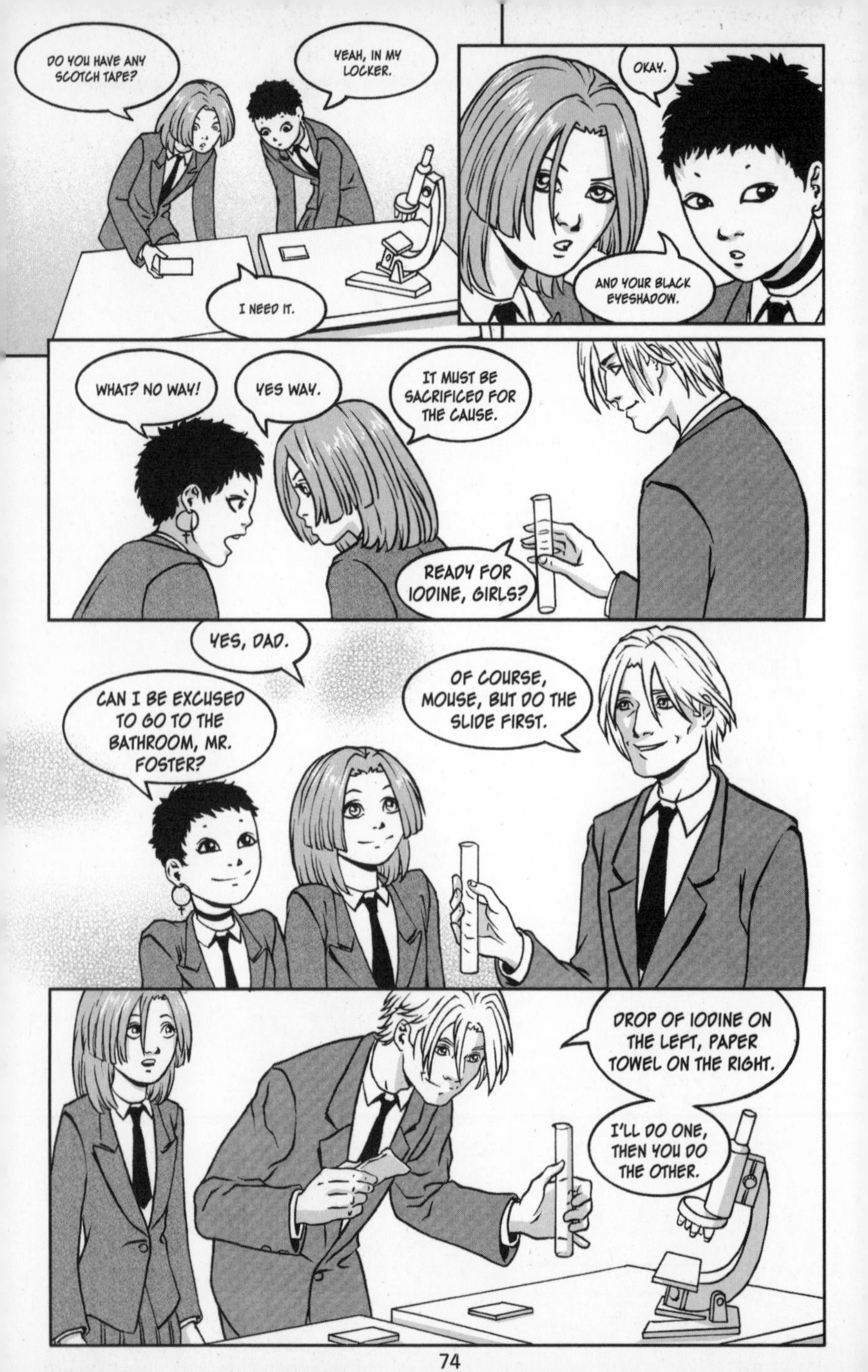

DO YOU HAVE ANY SCOTCH TAPE?
YEAH, IN MY LOCKER.
I NEED IT.
OKAY.
AND YOUR BLACK EYESHADOW.
WHAT? NO WAY!
YES WAY.
IT MUST BE SACRIFICED FOR THE CAUSE.
READY FOR IODINE, GIRLS?
YES, DAD.
CAN I BE EXCUSED TO GO TO THE BATHROOM, MR. FOSTER?
OF COURSE, MOUSE, BUT DO THE SLIDE FIRST.
DROP OF IODINE ON THE LEFT, PAPER TOWEL ON THE RIGHT.
I'LL DO ONE, THEN YOU DO THE OTHER.

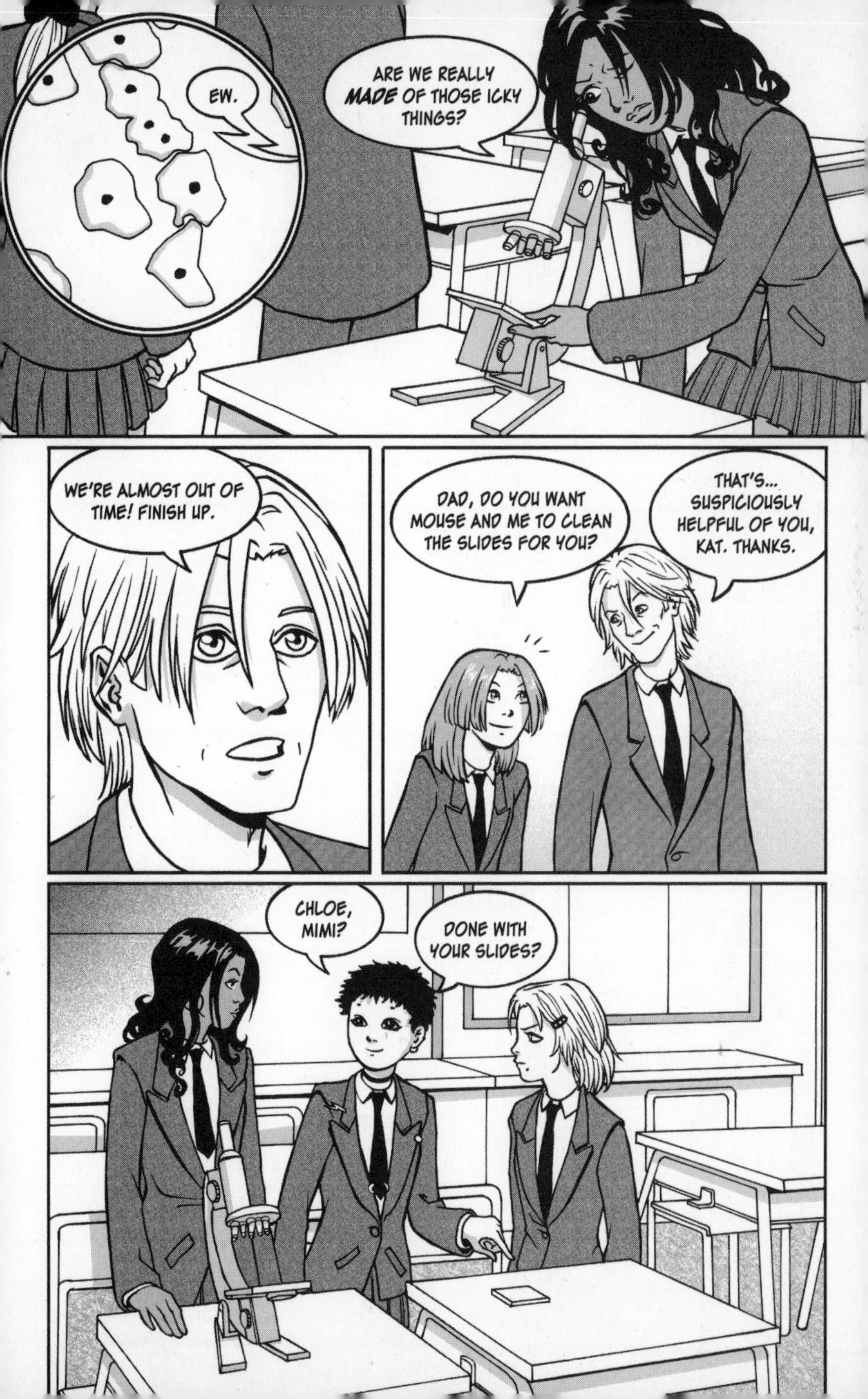
EW.
ARE WE REALLY ***MADE*** OF THOSE ICKY THINGS?
WE'RE ALMOST OUT OF TIME! FINISH UP.
DAD, DO YOU WANT MOUSE AND ME TO CLEAN THE SLIDES FOR YOU?
THAT'S... SUSPICIOUSLY HELPFUL OF YOU, KAT. THANKS.
CHLOE, MIMI?
DONE WITH YOUR SLIDES?

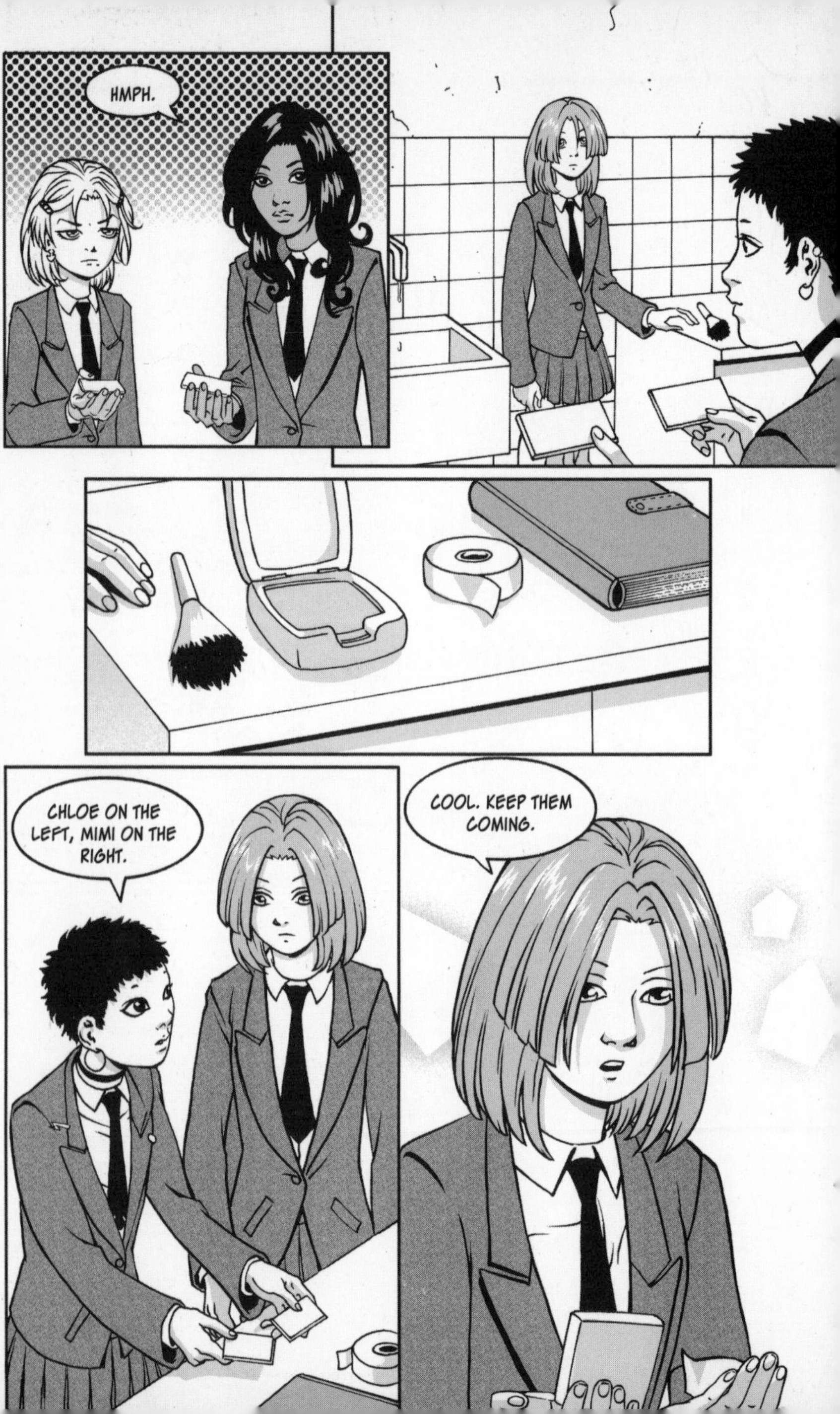
HMPH.
CHLOE ON THE LEFT, MIMI ON THE RIGHT.
COOL. KEEP THEM COMING.

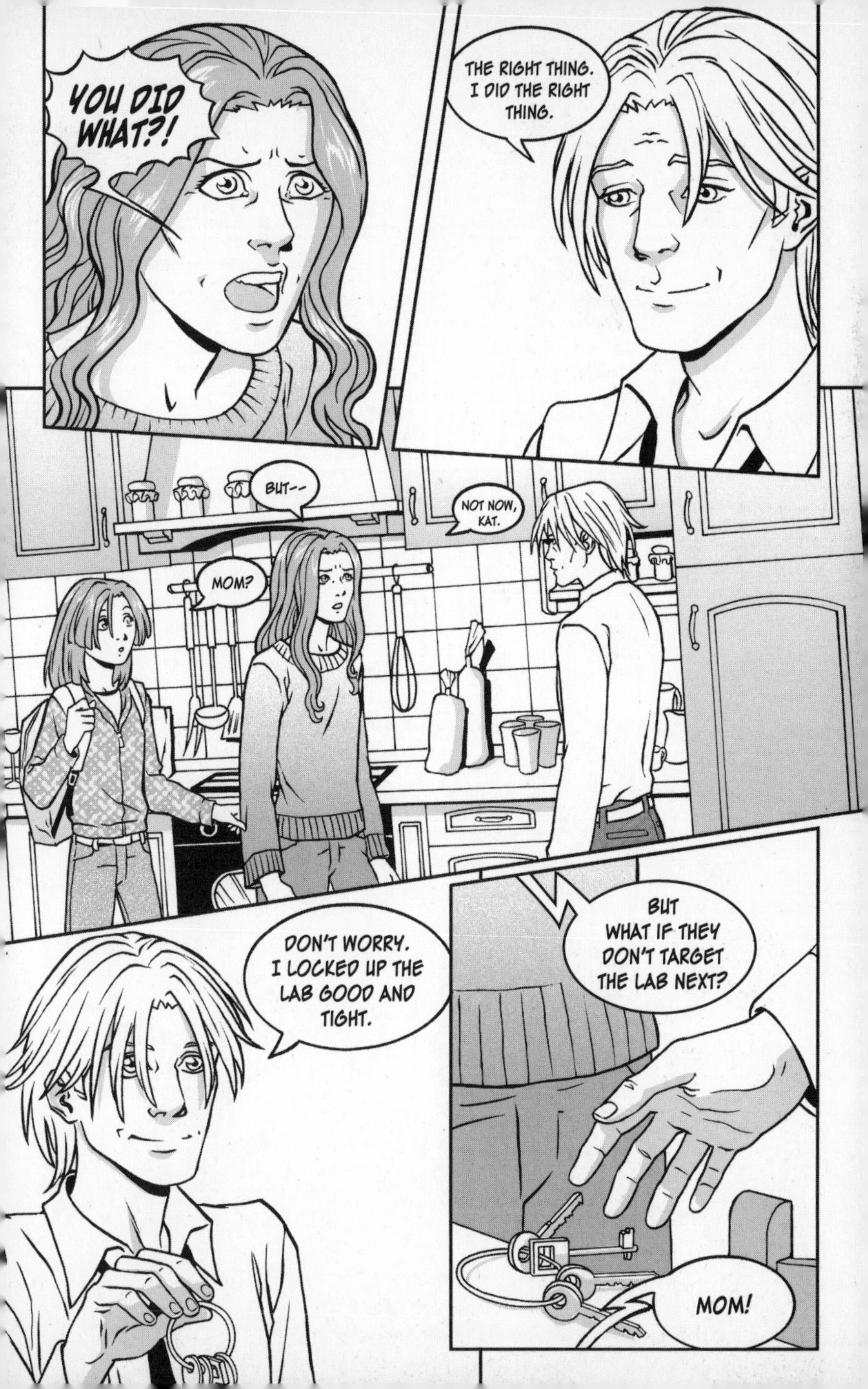
YOU DID WHAT?!
THE RIGHT THING. I DID THE RIGHT THING.
BUT--
NOT NOW, KAT.
MOM?
DON'T WORRY. I LOCKED UP THE LAB GOOD AND TIGHT.
BUT WHAT IF THEY DON'T TARGET THE LAB NEXT?
MOM!

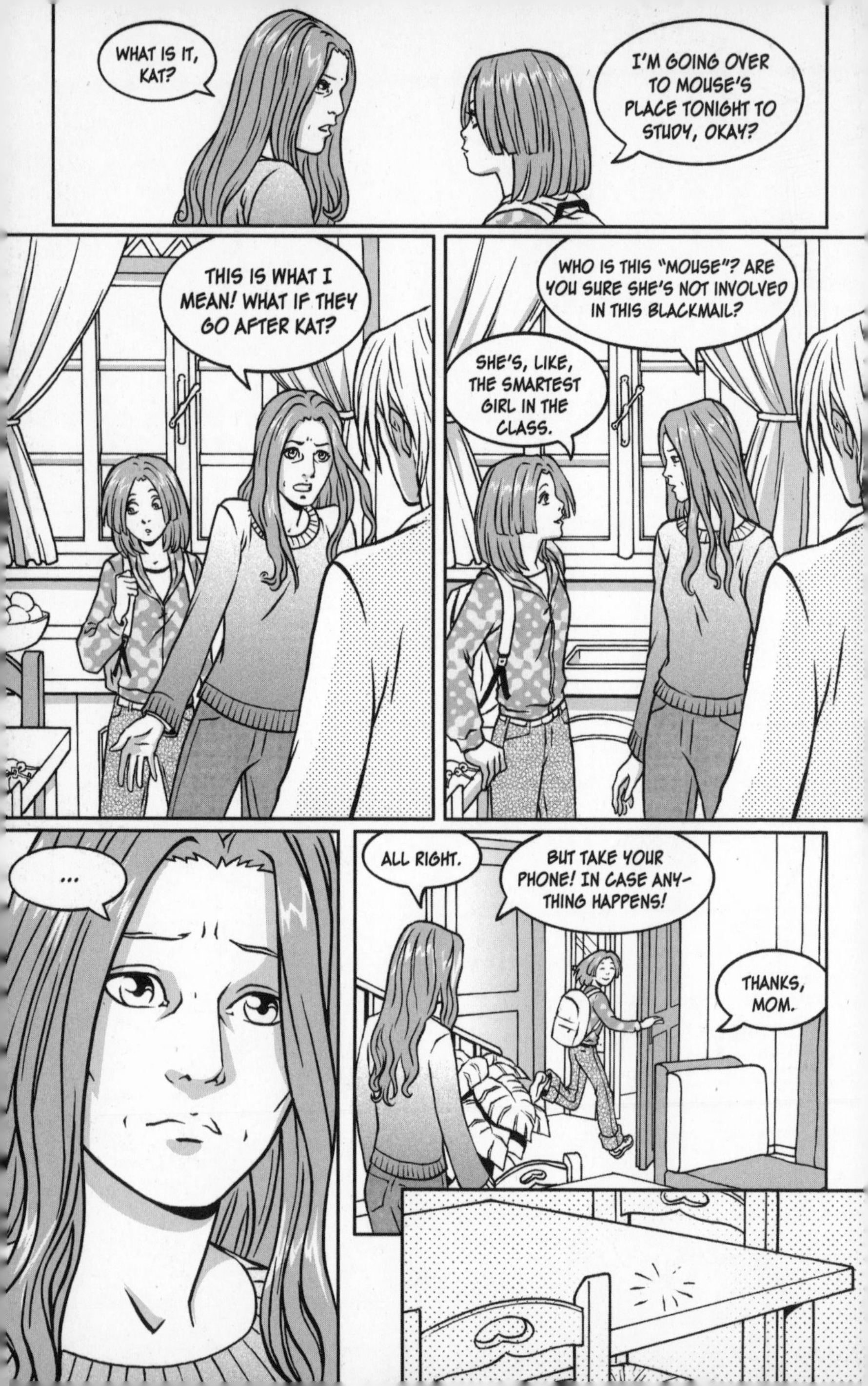
WHAT IS IT, KAT?
I'M GOING OVER TO MOUSE'S PLACE TONIGHT TO STUDY, OKAY?
THIS IS WHAT I MEAN! WHAT IF THEY GO AFTER KAT?
WHO IS THIS "MOUSE"? ARE YOU SURE SHE'S NOT INVOLVED IN THIS BLACKMAIL?
SHE'S, LIKE, THE SMARTEST GIRL IN THE CLASS.
...
ALL RIGHT.
BUT TAKE YOUR PHONE! IN CASE ANY-THING HAPPENS!
THANKS, MOM.

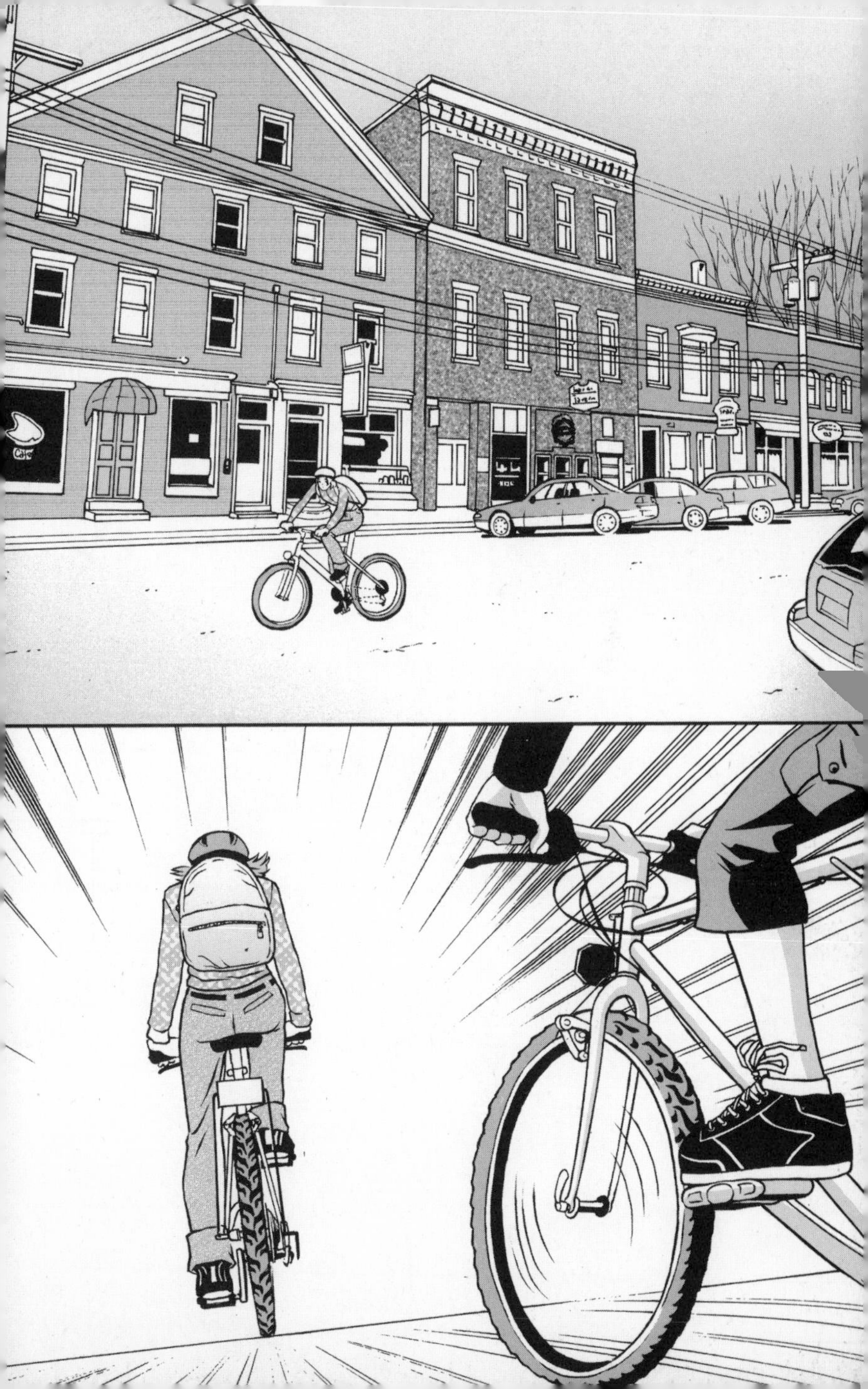

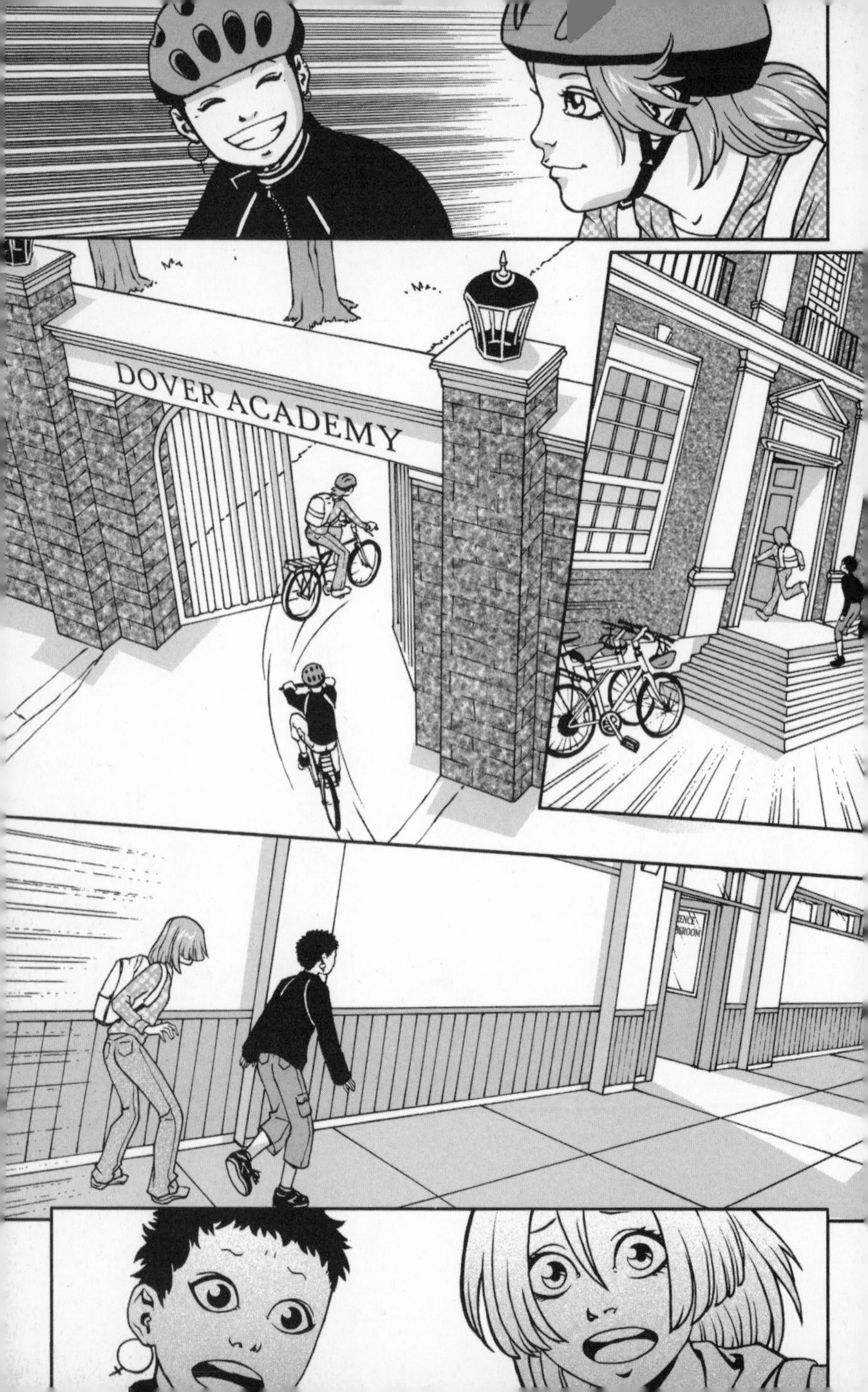
DOVER ACADEMY

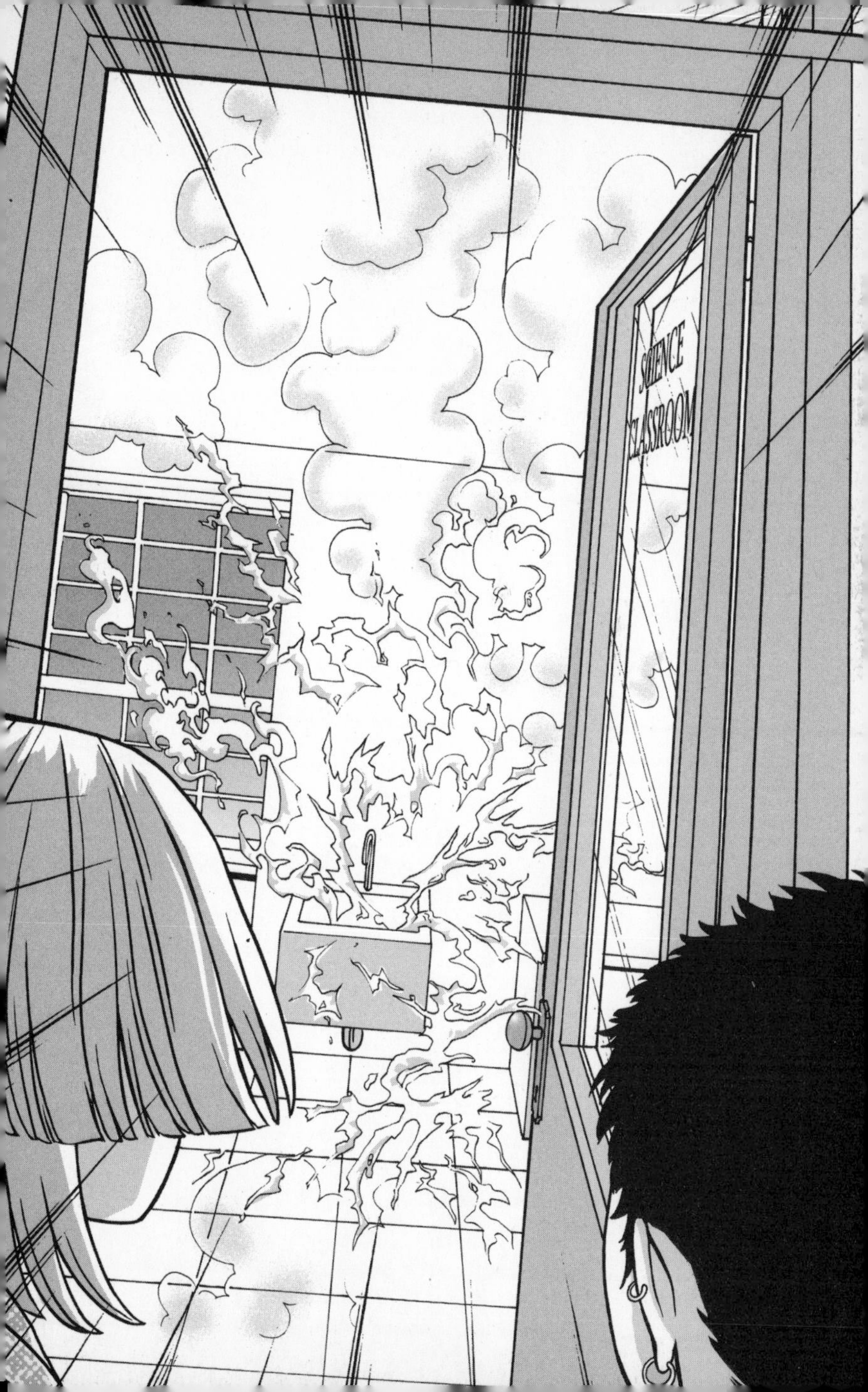
SCIENCE
CLASSROOM

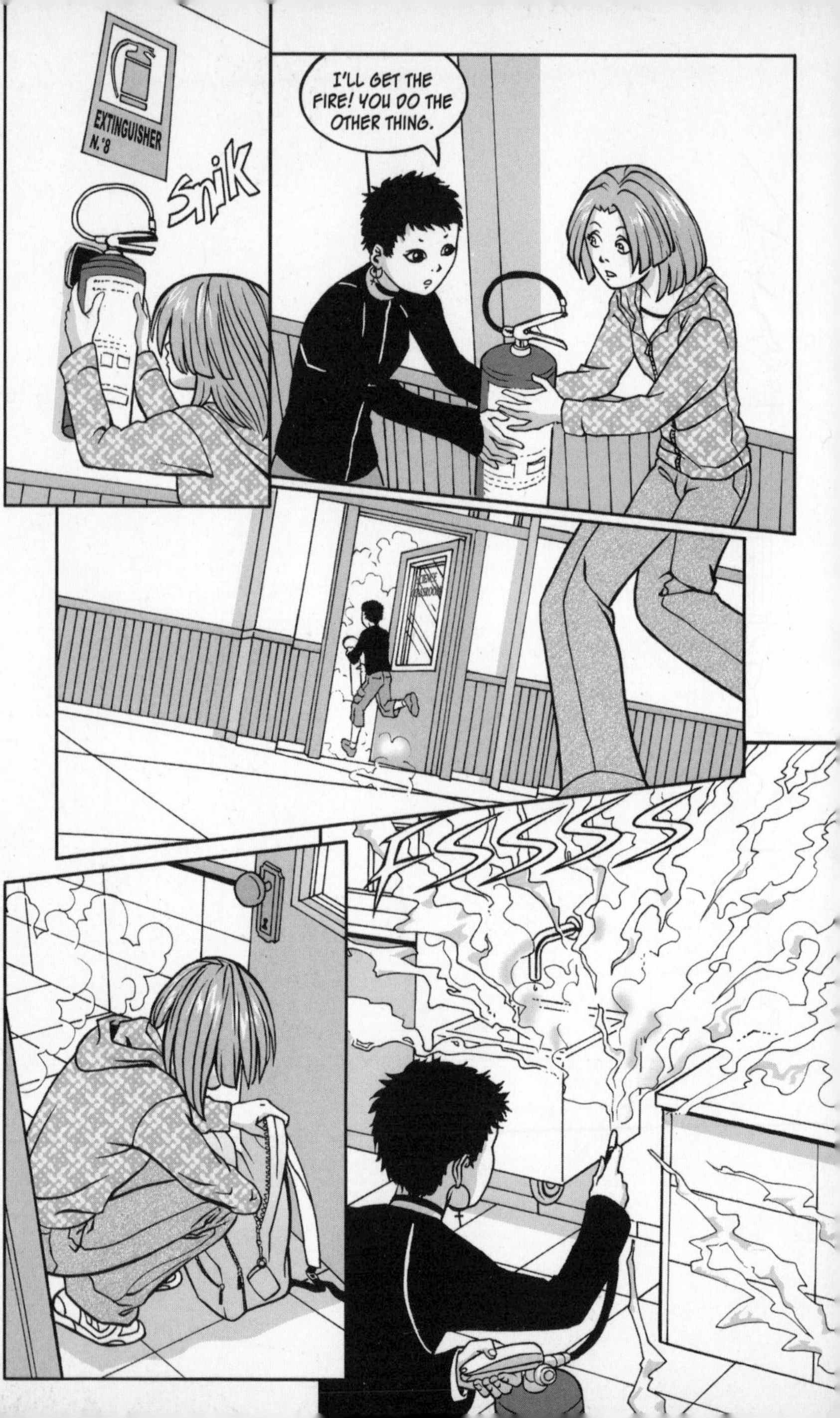
EXTINGUISHER N.°8
SNIK
I'LL GET THE FIRE! YOU DO THE OTHER THING.
FSSSSS

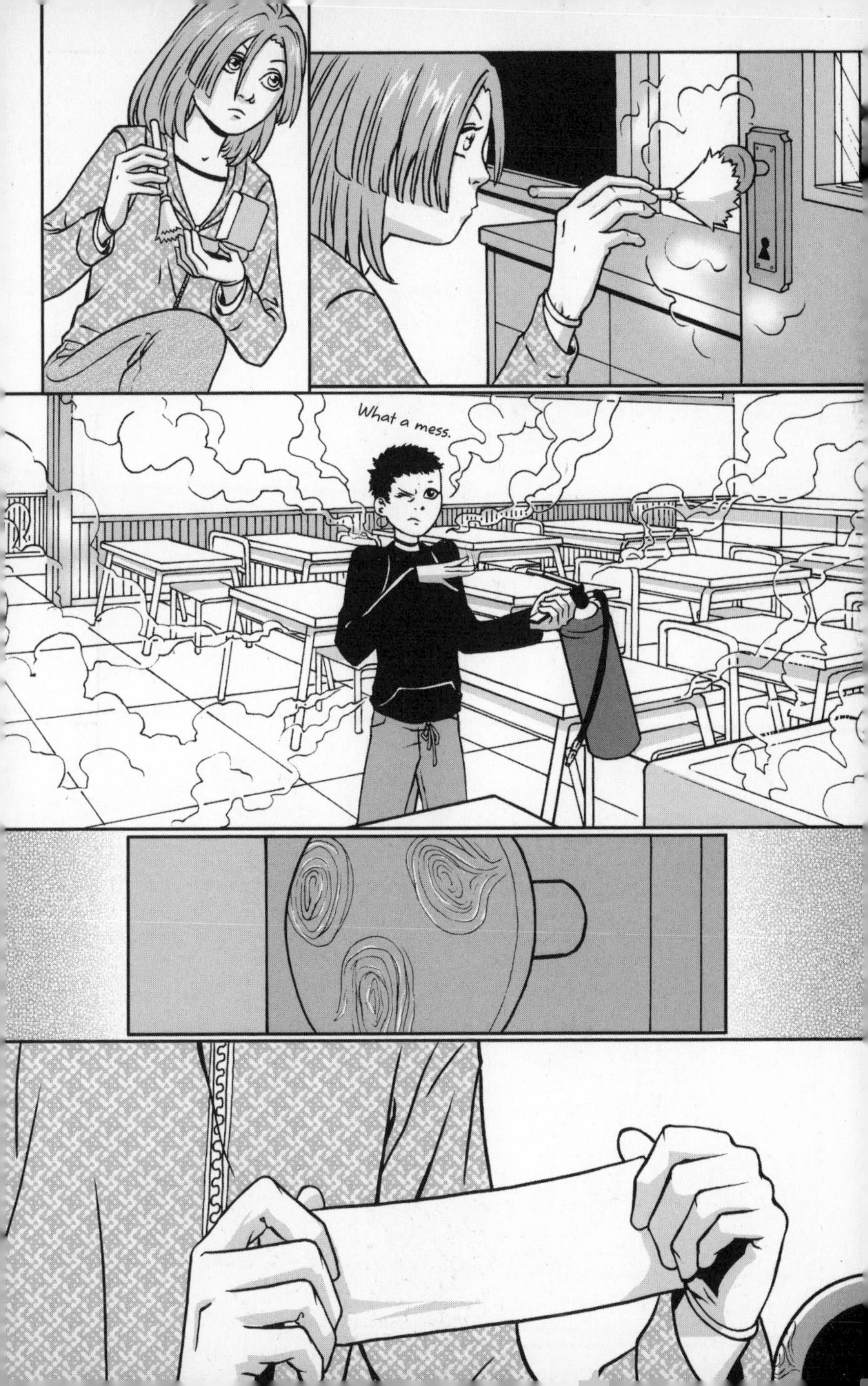
What a mess.

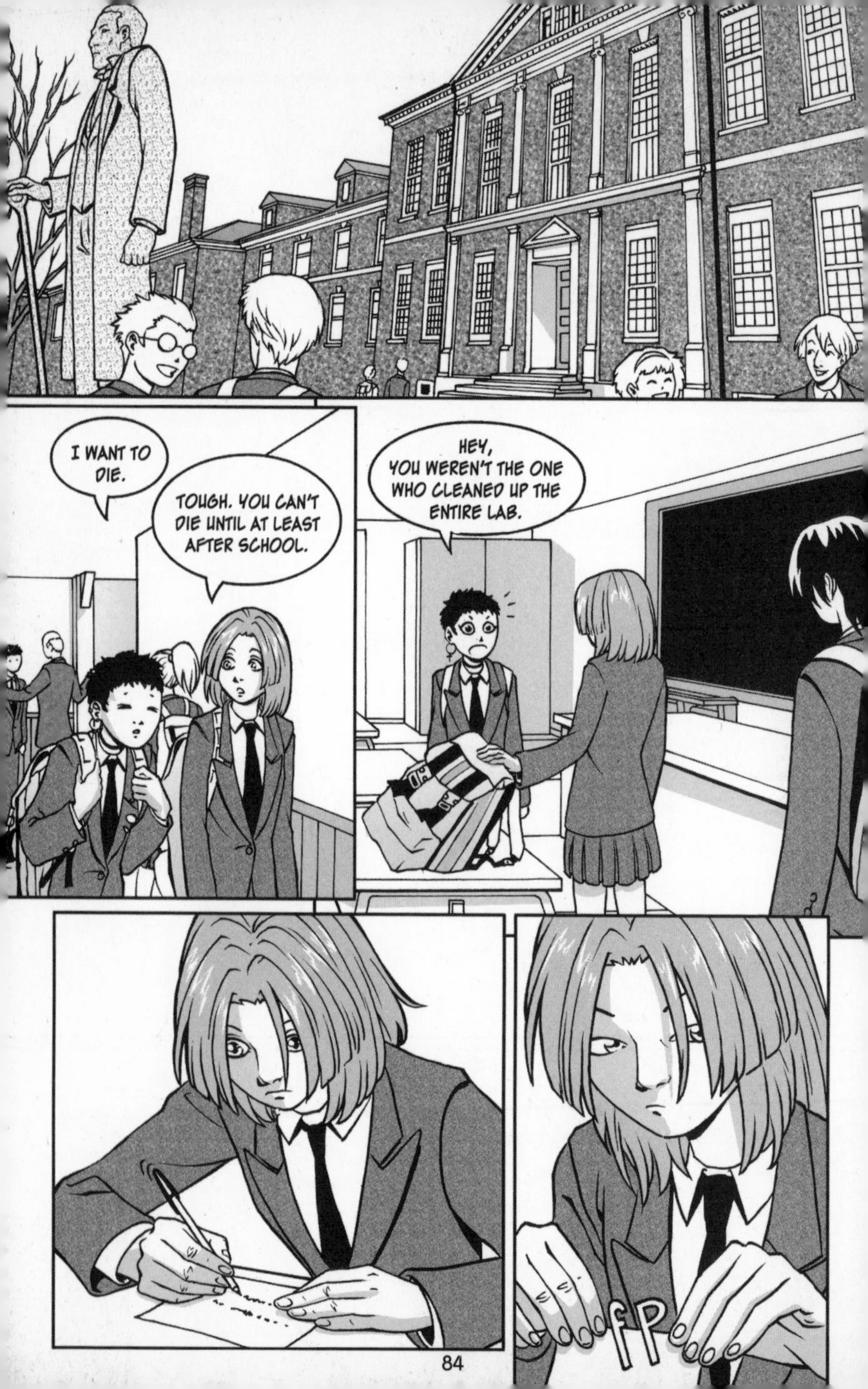
I WANT TO DIE.
TOUGH. YOU CAN'T DIE UNTIL AT LEAST AFTER SCHOOL.
HEY, YOU WEREN'T THE ONE WHO CLEANED UP THE ENTIRE LAB.
fP

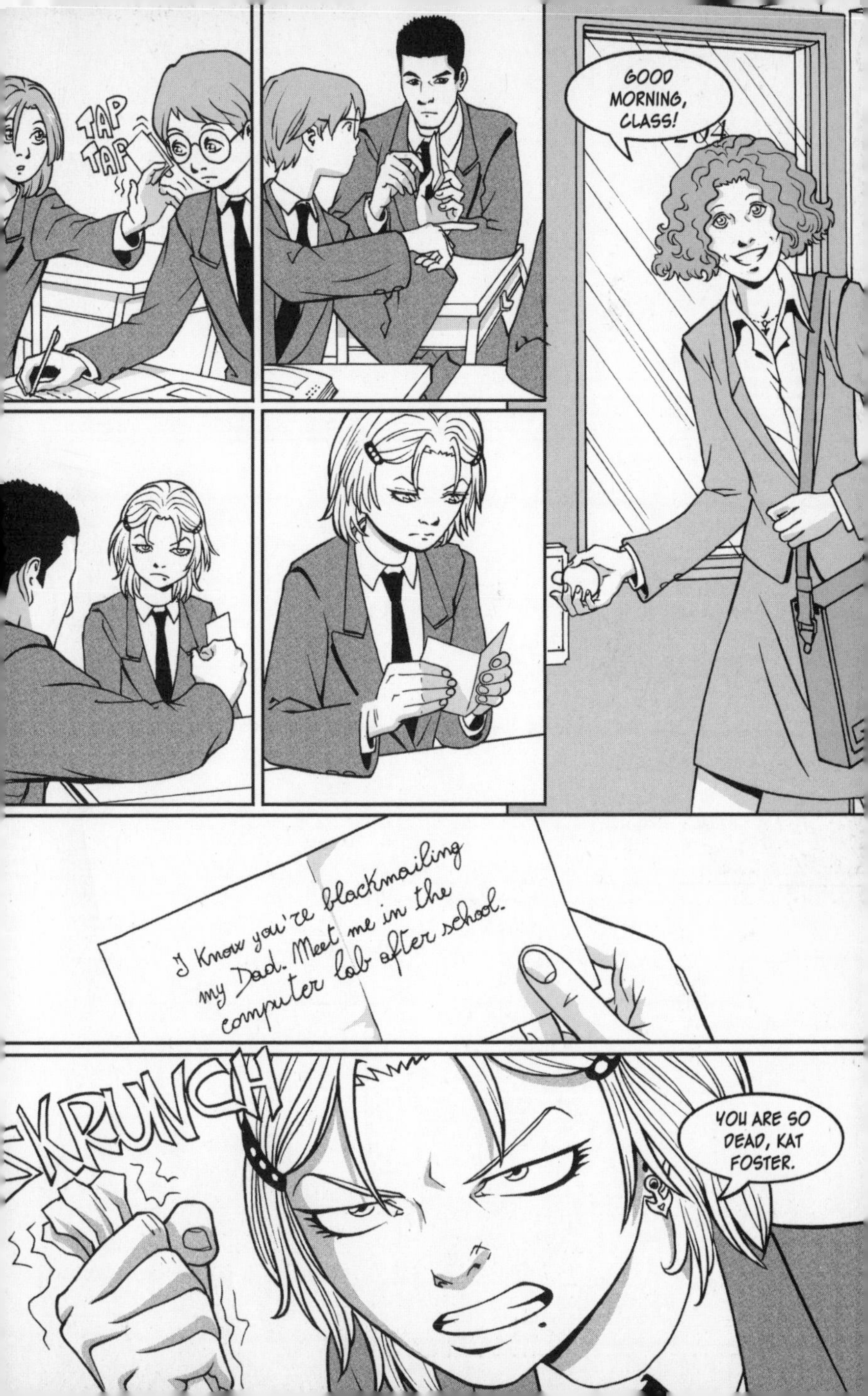
TAP TAP
GOOD MORNING, CLASS!
I know you're blackmailing my Dad. Meet me in the computer lab after school.
KRUNCH
YOU ARE SO DEAD, KAT FOSTER.

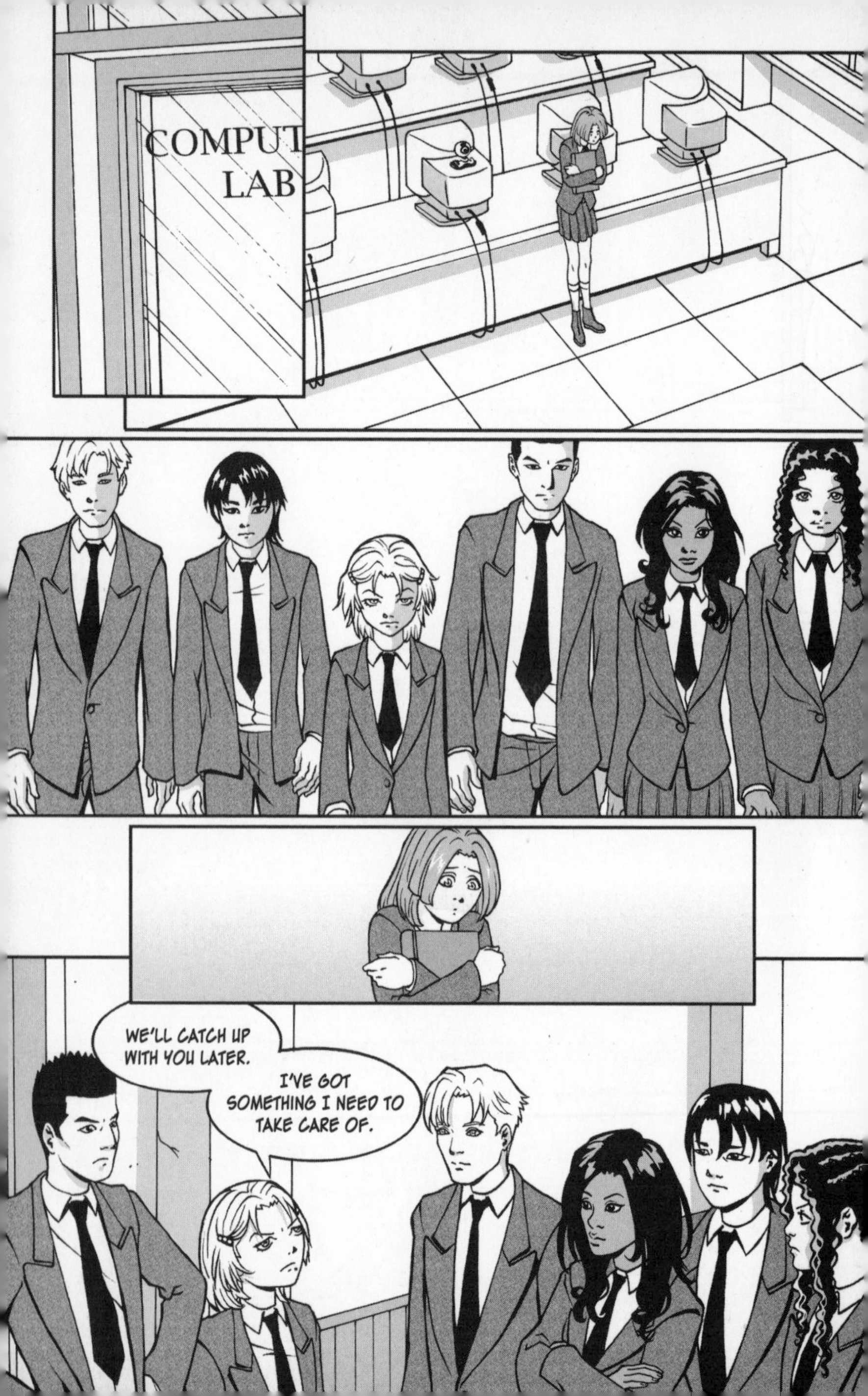
COMPUT
LAB
WE'LL CATCH UP
WITH YOU LATER.
I'VE GOT
SOMETHING I NEED TO
TAKE CARE OF.

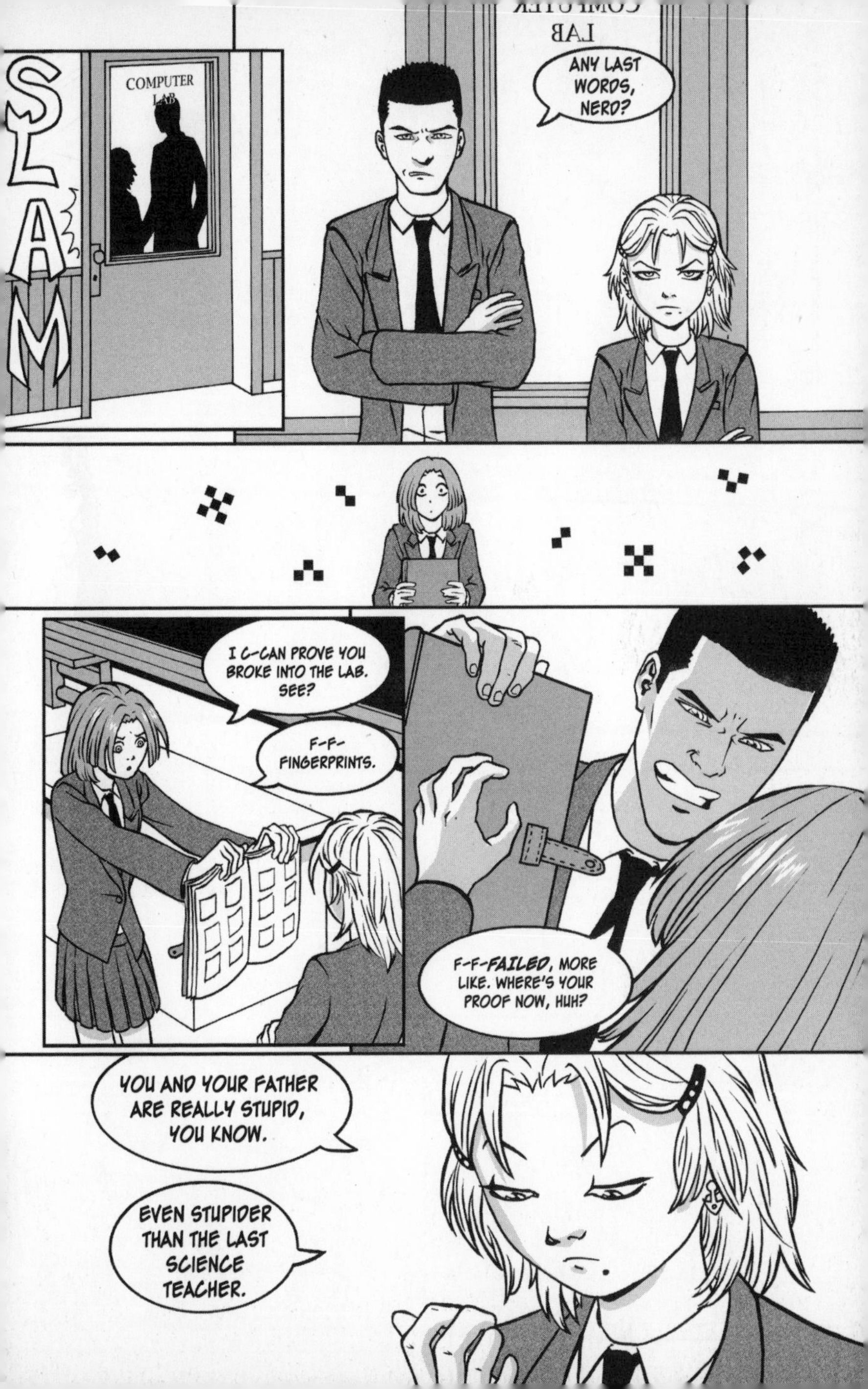
SLAM
COMPUTER LAB
ANY LAST WORDS, NERD?
I C-CAN PROVE YOU BROKE INTO THE LAB. SEE?
F-F- FINGERPRINTS.
F-F-*FAILED*, MORE LIKE. WHERE'S YOUR PROOF NOW, HUH?
YOU AND YOUR FATHER ARE REALLY STUPID, YOU KNOW.
EVEN STUPIDER THAN THE LAST SCIENCE TEACHER.

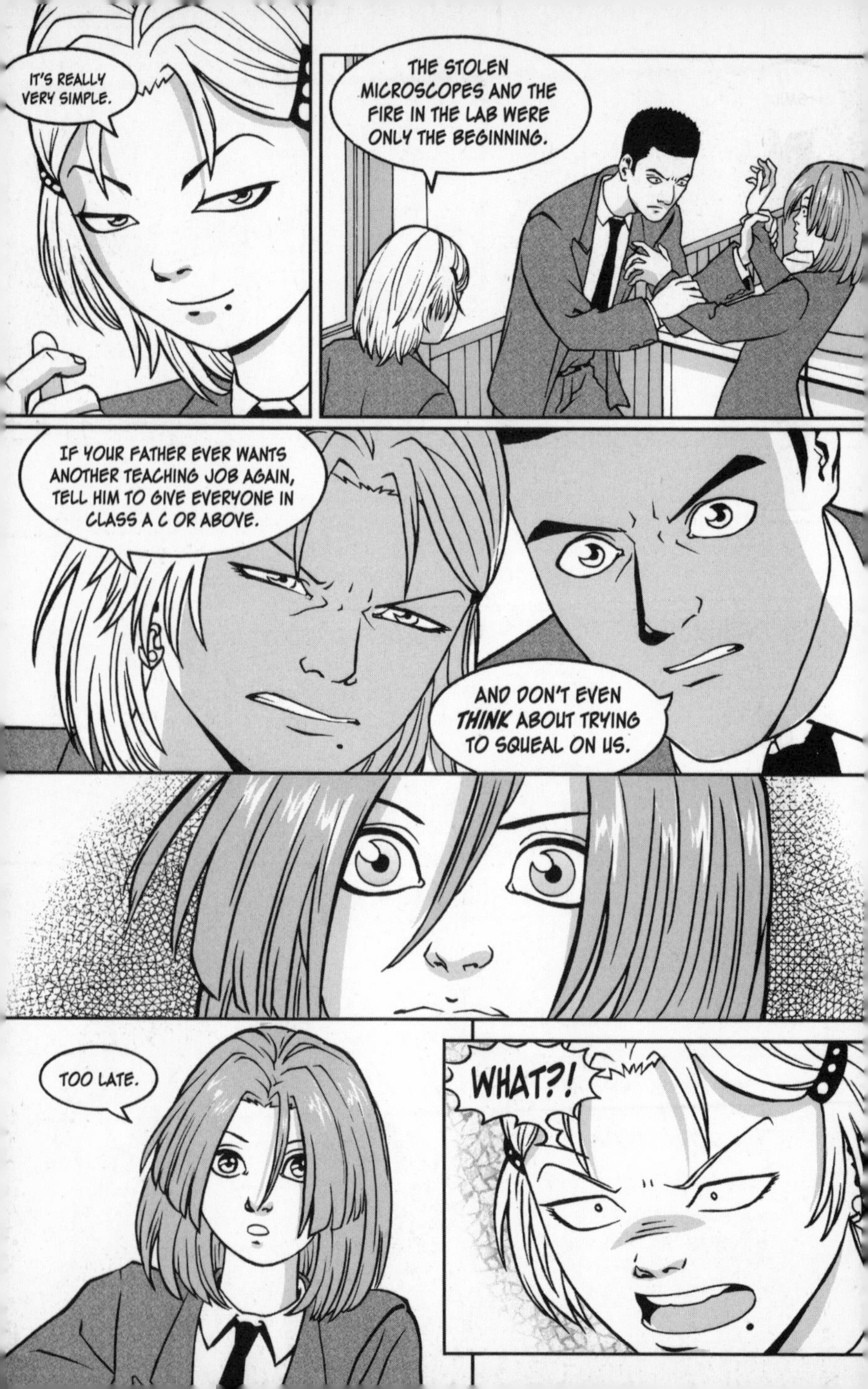
IT'S REALLY VERY SIMPLE.
THE STOLEN MICROSCOPES AND THE FIRE IN THE LAB WERE ONLY THE BEGINNING.
IF YOUR FATHER EVER WANTS ANOTHER TEACHING JOB AGAIN, TELL HIM TO GIVE EVERYONE IN CLASS A C OR ABOVE.
AND DON'T EVEN *THINK* ABOUT TRYING TO SQUEAL ON US.
TOO LATE.
WHAT?!

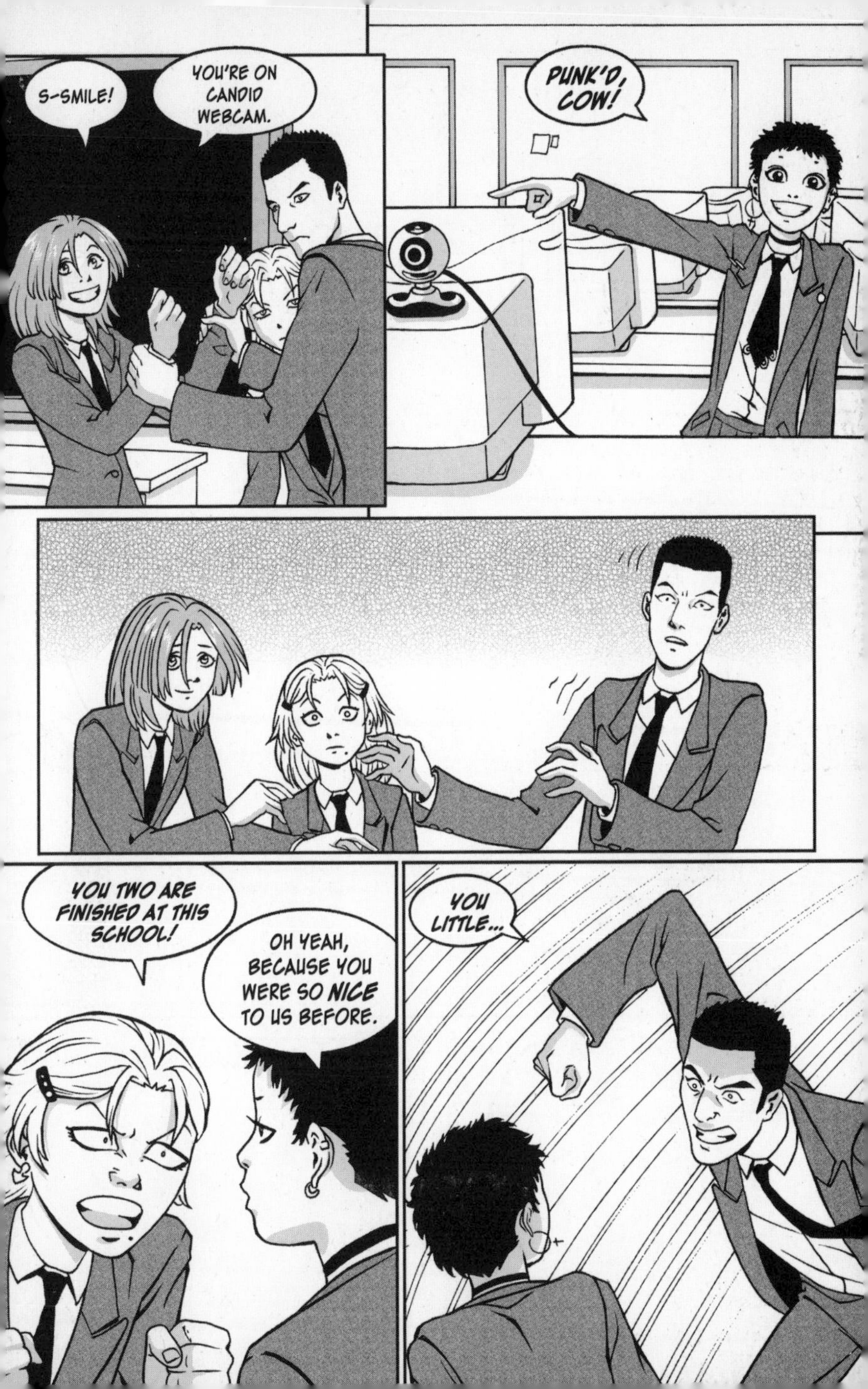
S-SMILE!
YOU'RE ON CANDID WEBCAM.
PUNK'D, COW!
YOU TWO ARE FINISHED AT THIS SCHOOL!
OH YEAH, BECAUSE YOU WERE SO NICE TO US BEFORE.
YOU LITTLE...

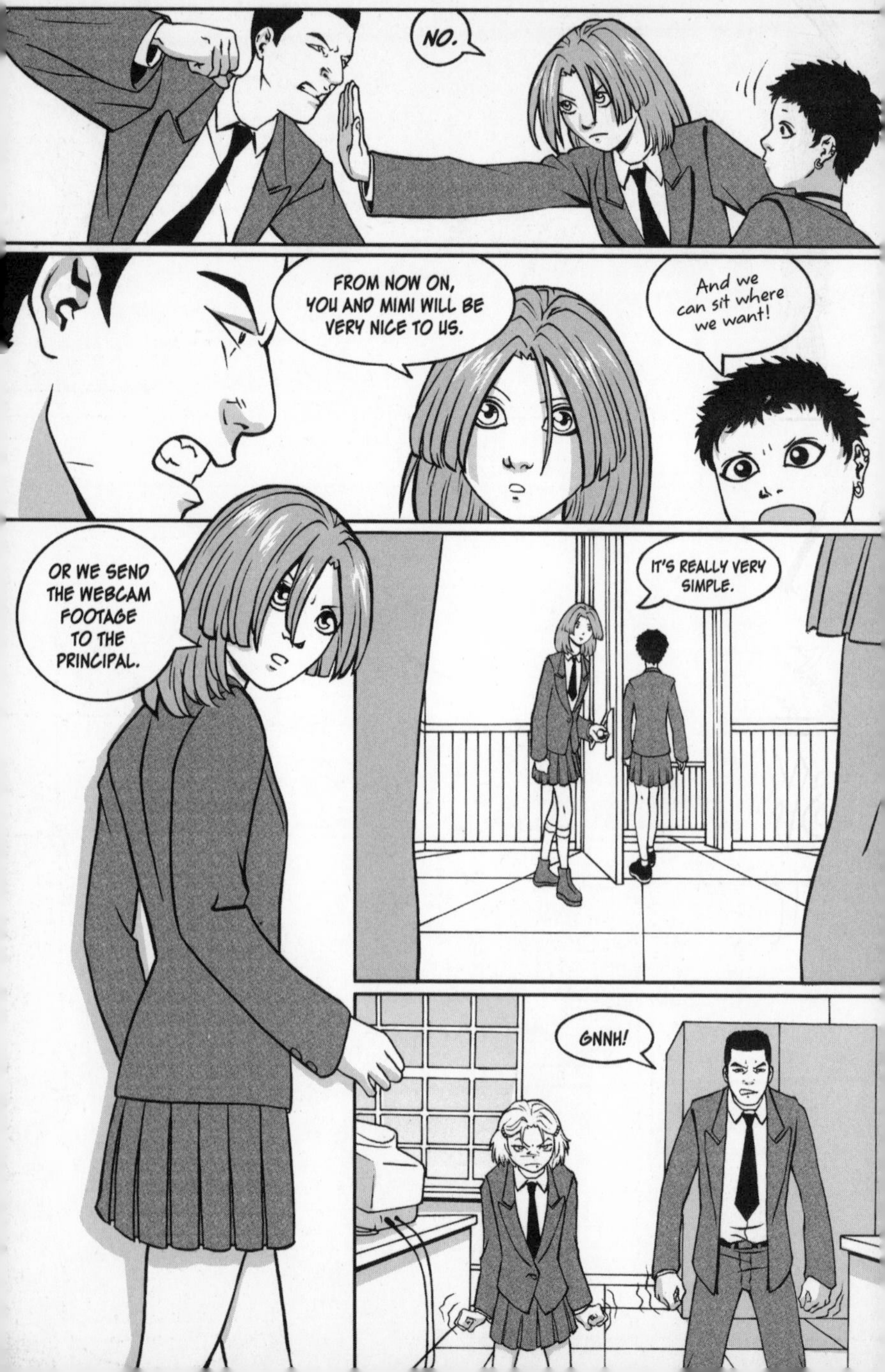
NO.
FROM NOW ON, YOU AND MIMI WILL BE VERY NICE TO US.
And we can sit where we want!
OR WE SEND THE WEBCAM FOOTAGE TO THE PRINCIPAL.
IT'S REALLY VERY SIMPLE.
GNNH!

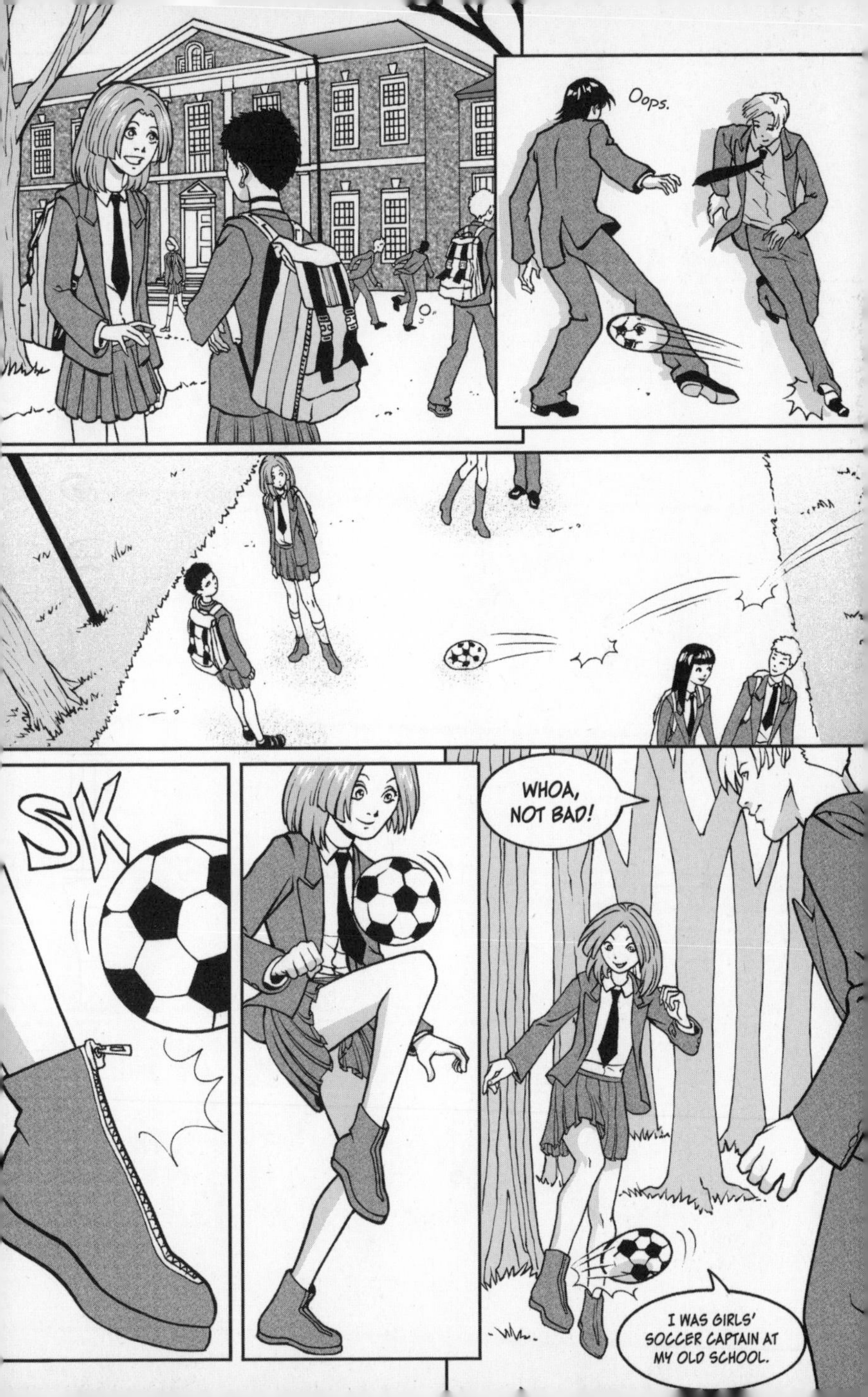
Oops.
SK
WHOA, NOT BAD!
I WAS GIRLS' SOCCER CAPTAIN AT MY OLD SCHOOL.

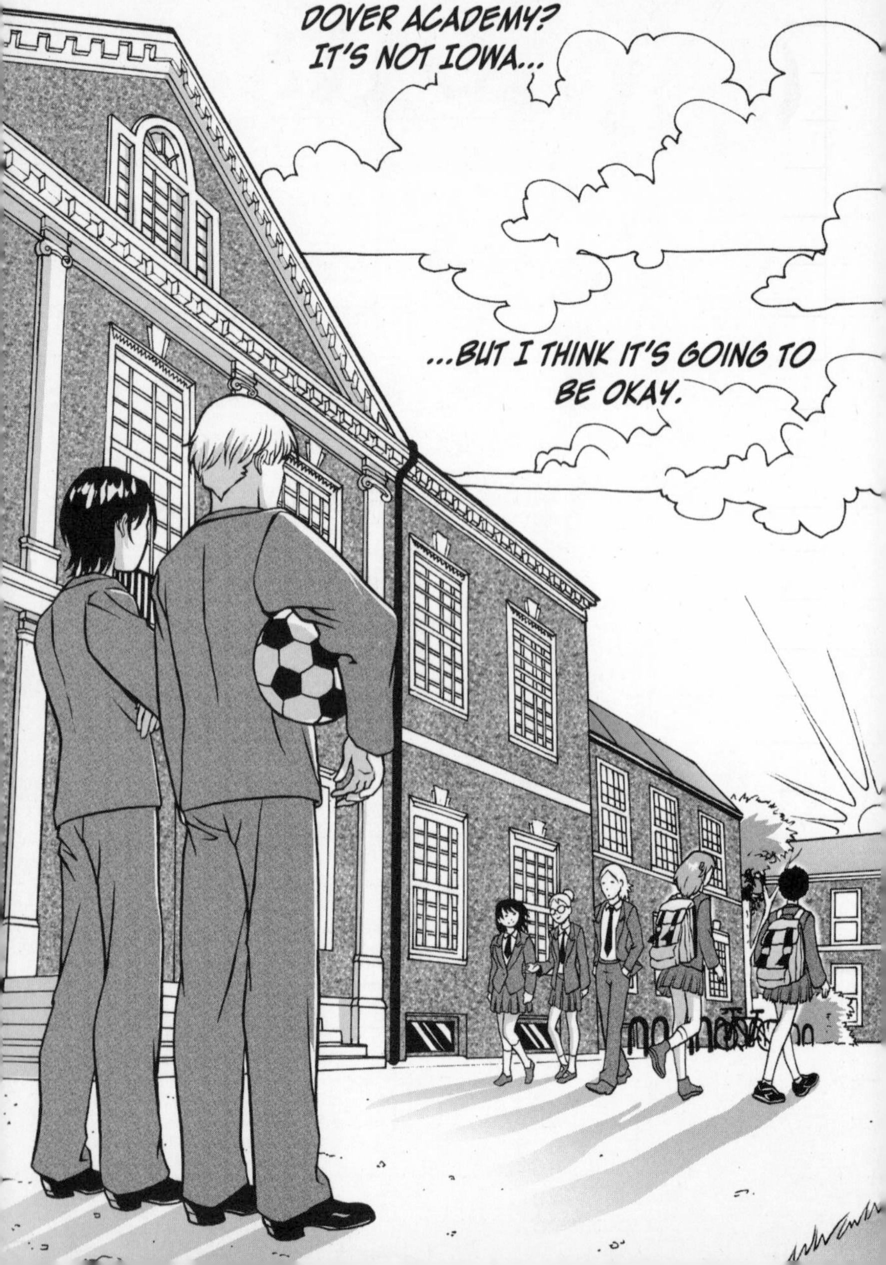
DOVER ACADEMY? IT'S NOT IOWA...
...BUT I THINK IT'S GOING TO BE OKAY.

Kat & mouse

2 tripped

When Kat and Mouse's class takes a trip to an art museum, a painting is stolen. Is it just a classmate's prank getting out of hand, or are they stuck in the museum with a real, dangerous criminal? Kat and Mouse are in the big city and on the case!

Try This at Home!

Want to dust for fingerprints the way Kat & Mouse do in Chapters 3 and 4? Here's how!

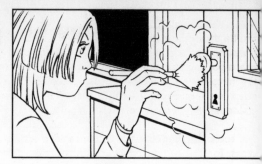

You'll need:

- A package of index cards
- A washable inkpad (make sure it's not dried out!)
- A clean, dry, fine paintbrush or makeup brush
- Clear adhesive tape
- Cocoa powder (unsweetened--the kind used for baking)
- Newspapers

First, get a record of your family's fingerprints. Have them lightly touch each of their fingers (both hands) on the inkpad, then press the fingers from each hand onto a separate index card--one card per hand, two per family member. Make sure you write names at the top of each card, so you won't forget who's who!

If you look hard at the fingerprints your family made, you'll notice that each falls under one of the seven types shown here. Can you match up each fingerprint with its type?

Sticky fingers make the best prints, so first try fingerprinting the drinking glasses your family uses during dinner (note: glass works a lot better than plastic for this).

Double Loop
Whorl
Loop
Plain Arch
Tented Arch
Accidental
Central Pocket Loop

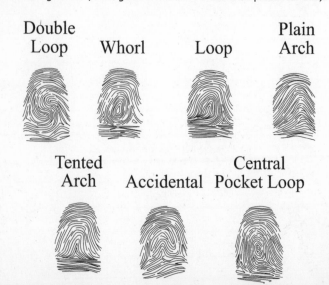

Shuffle the dirty glasses so you don't remember who was drinking out of which. Put newspapers under the place you'll do the dusting, then dip your dry brush into the cocoa powder and gently dust it over the area where hands would touch the glass. A light touch is important--if you brush too hard, you'll just smudge everything. Also, keep your face away from the dusting. Trust us, cocoa is not something you want in your eyes or up your nose.

The cocoa powder will stick to the residue left by the fingerprints, but not to the glass. To "lift" the print, cover it with the sticky side of the clear tape, then carefully peel the tape off and stick it down on a new index card--one card per glass.

Now, see if you can match the prints you lifted from the drinking glasses to the "index" prints your family did with the ink! Oh, and don't forget to wash the glasses and put everything away when you're done. Parents are much more forgiving about home experiments if they don't have to clean up after them.

This method works best on hard surfaces like drinking glasses, refrigerator doors, cabinets, and doorknobs. For darker surfaces, you can use talcum powder instead of cocoa. For softer surfaces, more advanced techniques are needed. Using chemicals, crime labs can get fingerprints off items like newspapers or leather jackets, and techniques like iodine fuming can be used for spy work, since it causes the prints to show up briefly, then disappear again.

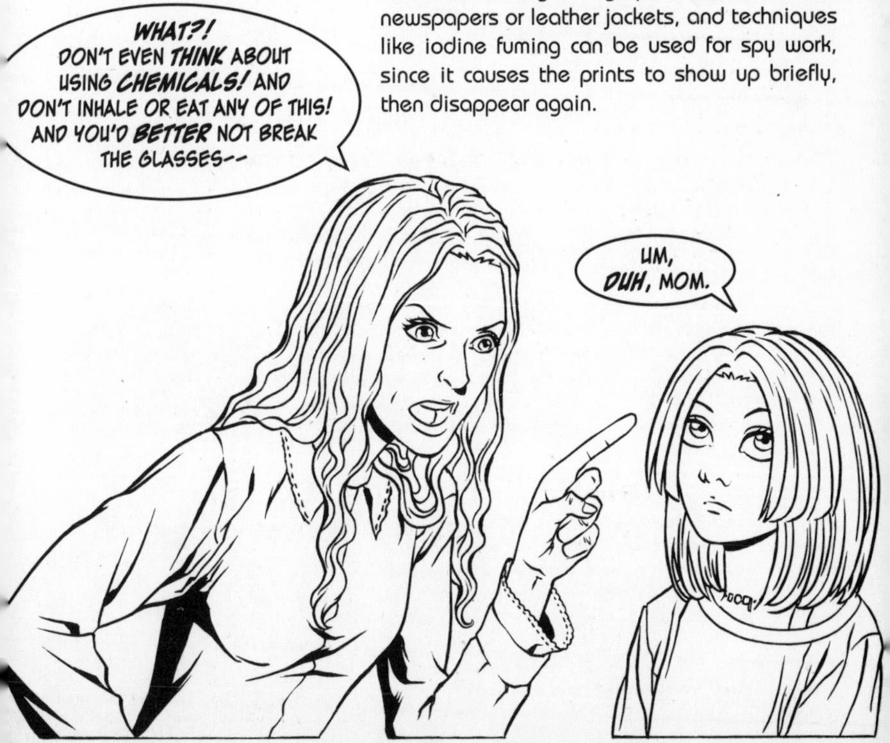
WHAT?! DON'T EVEN THINK ABOUT USING CHEMICALS! AND DON'T INHALE OR EAT ANY OF THIS! AND YOU'D BETTER NOT BREAK THE GLASSES--
UM, DUH, MOM.

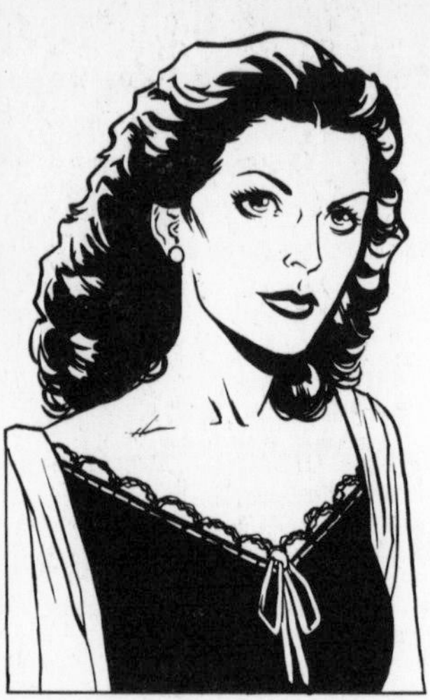

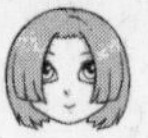

KAT'S HEROES 1: HEDY LAMARR

The "Most Beautiful Woman in Films," Hedy Kiesler--stage name Hedy Lamarr--starred in 25 films from 1938-1954. She also made five films in Germany in the '30s, and was a heartbreaker even then--reportedly, a German nobleman committed suicide after she broke off their engagement.

Hedy then married wealthy arms dealer Fritz Mandl. Hedy had lots of ideas for improving the engineering of Fritz' weapons systems, but Fritz refused to listen to a "little woman." Hedy soon fled him and Nazi Germany in 1938, by sneaking out dressed up as her maid.

On a cruise ship to the U.S., she negotiated an acting contract with Louis B. Mayer, the most important producer in Hollywood. She stepped off onto American soil as MGM's next film star--but while audiences only saw a beautiful face, Hedy was far more passionate about her inventions.

She and co-inventor George Antheil created a radio system for guiding torpedoes, and she gave the patent to the American government to support the war effort. Although the system wasn't used much in the war due to technology limitations at the time, it has since become the basis for Spread Spectrum, on which almost all wireless phone and Internet communication depends.

Hedy also invented a small cube that could be put into drinks to carbonate them, so American soldiers could have sodas at the front lines!

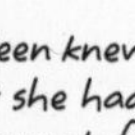

MOUSE'S HEROES 1: EILEEN COLLINS

Some of NASA space shuttle commander Eileen Collins' fondest childhood memories were of driving out with her dad to watch the planes take off and land at the airport near her home in upstate New York. But she didn't decide to become a pilot until high school, when she read stories about pilots in the Vietnam War who were shot down and captured as POWs, then escaped.

Eileen knew it would be difficult to qualify as an Air Force test pilot, but she had always been a hard worker: Her parents had made her work for her allowance, and she had cleaned classrooms in order to afford tuition at Catholic school. So she saved any extra money she had for flying lessons. Her dream came true with her first flying lesson, taught by an instructor who had been a Phantom F-4 pilot in Vietnam... and who treated her as an equal.

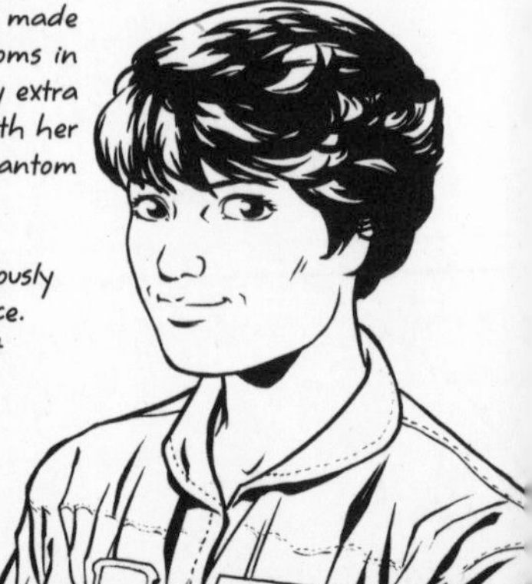

Eileen wasn't much for sports, but she was a tremendously talented pilot, flying solo after only eight hours of practice. After graduating from the Air Force Undergraduate Pilot Training Program at Vance Air Force Base in 1979, she was an instructor pilot and assistant mathematics professor--until 1990, when she passed NASA's extremely competitive selection program.

Eileen was the first woman pilot of the Space Shuttle, and has logged four space missions and over 872 hours in space.